Every Hill and Mountain

I have a dream that one day every valley shall be exalted, every hill and mountain shall be made low, the rough places will be made plain, and the crooked places will be made straight, and the glory of the Lord shall be revealed, and all flesh shall see it together.

—Dr. Martin Luther King, Jr.

Every Hill and Mountain

BOOK 3

DEBORAH HEAL

WRITE BRAIN BOOKS
www.deborahheal.com

Every Hill and Mountain

All Scripture quotations are taken from the Holy Bible, King James Version except Deuteronomy 7:9 which is from the NIV.

This is a work of fiction. Any references to real people, events, institutions, or locales are intended solely to give a sense of authenticity. While every effort was made to be historically accurate, it should be remembered that these references are used fictitiously.

This title is also available as an e-book.
Other novels by Deborah Heal

Time and Again (book 1)
Unclaimed Legacy (book 2)

Once Again: an inspirational novel of history, mystery & romance
(book 1 in the Rewinding Time Series)

ISBN: 1482609169
ISBN: 9781482609165

Fiction: Christian: HistoricalFiction
Fiction:Sci/fi: time travel

In Memory

For my dad Earl Woods,
who was born and raised in the
hills of Eagle Creek

CHAPTER 1

"Did Doug say how long this is going to take?" Abby said, blowing her bangs out of her eyes. "And remind me. Why exactly are we using this antique instead of an electric one?"

"He said using an electric ice cream maker meant it didn't count as homemade," John said, wiping his forehead with first his left T-shirt sleeve and then his right.

"Really?"

"Really. And I'm supposed to crank until I can't turn it anymore."

The day was typical for southern Illinois in late August: hot and humid. At least she was sitting on an icy, albeit uncomfortable, seat in the shady pavilion. Doug Buchanan had to be sweltering out in the sun where he manned the deep-fat fryer along with three of his cousins. Wearing a Cardinals cap to keep the sun off his balding head and an apron that said, "Kiss the Cook," Doug looked so friendly and benign that Abby wondered again how she had ever thought of him as The Hulk.

One of Doug's cousins gestured their way and said something that she couldn't make out. Whatever it was made the other men laugh.

A short distance away, under the shade of a maple tree, Jason and Jackson, Doug's twin teenage sons were practicing their washer-throwing skills in preparation for the tournament to be held tomorrow. The washers clinked and clacked, depending upon how, or whether, they hit the sand-filled wooden boxes. Those sounds, along with the rhythm of the turning crank and the hot afternoon, made Abby drowsy, and she surveyed the activities going on around her through a sleepy haze.

Next to them, Doug's wife Dora and a dozen other Buchanan women began unpacking coolers and setting out dish after dish onto the groaning picnic tables under Alton City Park Pavilion #1. Abby turned and smiled at the look on John's face as cakes, pies, bowls of watermelon chunks, and dozens of other goodies made their appearance.

"Hey, Dora, is that potato salad?" he asked.

"Yep," she said with a wide smile. "And I brought macaroni salad and deviled eggs."

John sighed blissfully.

"This is nothing. Wait'll tomorrow," Doug called to them. "That's when the ladies go all out. I heard Aunt Hil's making her chocolate chip cake."

Under the second pavilion reserved for the event, Eulah and Beulah played dominoes with several of the other elderly relatives. Fanning themselves with paper plates, they chattered happily while they waited their turns.

Abby smiled and a wave of contentment washed over her, knowing that she had been instrumental in getting the Old Dears in touch with their Buchanan relatives. And now the 85-year-old twins were at their first-ever family reunion.

Eleven-year-old Merri came over, panting and red-faced, but smiling. On each arm clung—as they had from the first half hour there—an adoring little girl. One little blonde looked about four, the other about six.

"What are you doing?" Abby asked.

"We're taking a break from the kiddie games," Merri said. "I'm hot."

Merri was a different girl from the one Abby had met when she had arrived at the beginning of summer to be her tutor. Naturally, she still had her moments of sadness and snarky attitude. After all, her mother was hardly ever around and her father was serving time in Joliet Prison. But Eulah and Beulah had made her their pretend granddaughter and invited her to come along to the Buchanan reunion.

Abby pushed Merri's hair away from her sweaty face and grinned. "It's hard work being an honorary cousin, isn't it?"

Merri frowned, but it was easy to see she loved the little girls' attention. "Yeah, tell me about it," she said. "Is the ice cream about done?"

"Not quite," John said. "I can still turn the crank. Slowly, but still."

"Come on, Mewwi," the smaller girl lisped. "Wet's go swing on the swings."

"Okay," Merri said good-naturedly. She turned to look back as she was being dragged away. "But don't forget, John. You're on my team in the water balloon war."

"I won't forget, squirt."

Abby lifted her hair and waited for a breeze to cool her own sweaty neck.

John blew gently and then leaned down to kiss it. "Watch out, girlie. That's what led to the ice incident before."

Earlier John had put a piece of ice down the back of her T-shirt, which had made her leap up from the ice cream churn with a squeal. He had chased her around the pavilion threatening her with more ice until she told him to behave or he'd have to get someone else to help.

John's breath on her neck did anything but cool her off. Abby leaned back and kissed his cheek. "Just stick to your job, ice cream boy."

Doug Buchanan brought a huge platter of fried fish over and handed it to his wife. "Is the ice cream about done, John?"

"I'm still cranking."

Doug laughed and glanced back at his grinning cousins. "You can stop now. Anyone else would have quit a half hour ago. Anyone with normal-sized muscles, anyway."

"Dang it, Doug!" John said. "I think my arm may fall off."

Abby rose from her bumpy perch and rubbed her sore rear. "Yes, and a certain part of my anatomy."

Doug packed the ice cream maker with more ice and covered it with thick blankets. Then, after conferring with the women about the readiness of the food, he put his fingers to his mouth and whistled for everyone to come and eat.

After Reverend Goodson, the Old Dears' pastor, prayed an uncharacteristically short prayer, Merri and a gaggle of other kids converged on the food table. Dora shooed them back and invited the oldest members of the family, including Eulah and Beulah, to fill their plates first. John held Eulah's plate while she made her selections, and Abby held Beulah's, and then they helped the ladies onto the awkward picnic benches near their friends.

Then she and John filled their plates and went to sit by Merri.

"What's that pinky fluffy stuff?" John said, pointing to Merri's plate.

"Dora said it's a salad, but it tastes good enough to be dessert."

"Sounds good to me," he said after he had swallowed

what looked to Abby like a mountain-sized bite of potato salad. "I'm going to get some on my next trip."

"This is going to take a while, isn't it?" Abby said.

"Yep," John said.

"Could you try to hurry?" Merri said. "Me and Abby have to—"

"Abby and I," Abby said.

"Whatever," Merri said. "Anyway, we have to get home and get ready for our girls' night with Kate. We're going to make snickerdoodles and—"

"You are?" he said. "Bless you, my child. You know how I love snickerdoodles."

"Well, you're not a girl, John," Merri explained earnestly. "So you know you can't come to our girls' night, right?"

"Yeah, John," Abby said, patting his bicep. "You're definitely not a girl."

"That's okay, Merri," he said. "I'll survive."

"Merri, you're going to love Kate," Abby said. "She's a riot."

"That doesn't sound good."

Abby laughed. "I mean, she's a lot of fun. She always thinks of something crazy to do."

After Abby's disastrous roommate her freshman year at Ambassador College, Kate had been a Godsend. After only a few weeks as sophomores, they had become best friends. They didn't share any classes together since Kate was majoring in art and Abby in elementary education. But together they had explored Chicago's art museums to Kate's delight, and bookstores and coffee shops to Abby's.

While it was true that Kate's personality was so different from her own, Abby knew they each brought balance to the friendship. As for herself, she needed to stop being so serious all the time, to lighten up and go with the flow once in a while. When Kate had decided to wear outdated and mismatched polyester clothes from the thrift store to the dining hall just to see people's faces, Abby had gone along with the joke. Seeing the reactions had been educational, like one of the experiments in her sociology class. And it had been amazingly freeing to do something spontaneous and random.

But sometimes Kate needed Abby to be the voice of reason. When Kate got the idea to paint their dorm room purple suddenly after chapel one day, Abby had reminded her that she had a test to study for, and that they'd have to pay a small fortune in primer and paint to convert the walls back to boring white for the next students to occupy 205b Whitaker Hall.

Kate's visit today was another example of her spontaneity. Abby had been trying to get Kate to come visit for weeks, but she had been caught up in a project with her mother and unable to get away. Then, just two hours ago, she'd texted to say she was coming. Now. But instead of spending their time together at Merri's house as they had planned all along, Kate had proposed a "friend-fest weekend" in Equality, which according to John was a tiny, Podunk town three hours southeast of Alton.

She would have to talk Kate down from that hare-brained idea when she got there.

"Look at the idiot," John said, gesturing with a thumb.

An electric blue PT Cruiser roared down the gravel road toward them, slowing only minimally before skidding to a stop alongside the pavilions.

White dust coated the windshield, and Abby couldn't see the car's occupants. But she recognized the ARTCRZY license plate and began to disentangle herself from the picnic table. "That idiot would be Kate," she said with a laugh.

"Oh. Sorry." John wiped his hands and rose from the picnic table.

"Come on, both of you," Abby said. "I want to introduce you."

Merri wiggled out of her space at the picnic table and went to stand expectantly at Abby's side. "I thought she wasn't supposed to be here until tonight."

"She wasn't," Abby said. "But that's Kate for you."

The car door opened, and Kate stepped out and rushed toward Abby. She was wearing a pristine white sundress and heeled sandals. Her hair was a shining mahogany mane that fell halfway down her back.

Abby threw her arms around her friend. "You look fabulous. How did you find us?"

"We went to the house first, and Merri's mom told us where you were."

"It seems like ages since the beginning of summer break. Wait a minute," Abby said, pulling back to look into Kate's face. "We? We who?" Then, over her shoulder she saw Kate's boyfriend unfolding his tall, lanky frame from the passenger seat. His polo shirt was the same brilliant white of Kate's dress, and he wore charcoal gray tailored slacks.

Abby felt a quick burst of disappointment and shot a look at Kate, but she was looking at Ryan as if he were the best thing since the invention of air conditioning. She must have gone spontaneous again and decided to bring him along. So much for their girls-only weekend.

Abby pasted on a smile and said, "Ryan. You came too. Good. I want you to meet Merri and John. Guys, this is my infamous roommate Kate Greenfield and her boyfriend Ryan Turner."

Ryan and John shook hands, but Kate thrust hers in Abby's face. "Not boyfriend anymore—fiancé! I told you he was going to ask. Isn't it gorgeous?"

The sun glinted off a huge diamond ring on Kate's left hand. "You're engaged? You didn't tell me." Abby shook her head to clear it. "I mean, yes, it's gorgeous."

"I wanted to surprise you. I've been dying to tell you ever since Ryan popped the question last weekend."

Abby hugged her again. "Have you set a date?"

Ryan smiled contentedly. "Next June after Kathryn graduates," he said with an indulgent smile. "One and a half carets of sparkle to hold her until then." He put an arm around Kate's neck and kissed her temple. "But don't worry, Kathryn. I promise to upsize it as soon as I get my law practice."

"Ryan just graduated from the pre-law program at the University of Illinois," Abby explained to John.

"Really? I've never seen you around."

"Chicago campus," Ryan said. "I think Kathryn said you're at Urbana?"

"That's right. Where will you go to law school?"

"Loyola," Ryan said. "It's really the only choice."

"Do you really think so?" John said. "I have my eye on Kent."

Ryan pushed a strand of silky dark brown hair back from his face. It was similar in color and texture to John's, only freakishly perfect in cut and style.

Kate pulled her to the side and said in what passed for her version of a whisper, "Why didn't you tell me how hot John is? Wow! No wonder you've been going crazy for him. We could have a double wedding, Abby."

Abby blinked in panic, but sneaking a look at the guys, she saw that they were still talking about law schools. Hopefully, John hadn't heard Kate's outrageous comment. "Kate! We've only known each other for a few weeks."

Kate just smiled knowingly and then turned and held

out a hand to Merri. "You must be Merri," she said. "Abby's told me so much about you."

Merri shook her hand, her expression changing to uncertainty. "Uh, really?"

"Really," Kate said. "About how smart you are, and nice."

Merri's face brightened. "Abby told me about you, too. We're going to my house after this."

"I'm looking forward to it."

"Come on, let's get you guys some food first," Abby said. "Wait until you see the selection."

"How about if John and I go get food so you two can get started gabbing?" Ryan said.

"You're so thoughtful." Kate patted his arm.

When the guys were lost in the crowd, Abby said, "Another imaginary star on Ryan's imaginary chart?"

Kate grinned. "He just keeps on racking them up."

"John, too," Abby said. "I've lost track of how many stars he's collected this week. But, hey, you're the one with stars—in your eyes." She put her arms around Kate and squeezed again. "I'm so glad you're here."

"Do you think I should tell Ryan about his chart—you know, since we're engaged now?"

"No way! Well, at least not here with John around." As far as Abby was concerned, the fact that they had been rating them as possible marriage material was something they never needed to know about.

Merri smiled slyly. "Hmmm. You'd better be nice to me."

"Come on, brat," Abby said, edging her way past a man carrying two heaping plates. "Let's show Kate where we're sitting."

Abby was glad that she'd worn shorts. Hiking first one leg and then the other over the picnic table bench, she managed to sit down halfway gracefully and then glanced doubtfully at Kate's skinny white dress.

Seeing her look, Kate said, "Don't worry. I'm the queen of picnic table sitting. I did a lot of contortions wearing fancy dresses when I ran for Miss Sangamon County. I didn't win the crown, but I did pick up this skill. Watch and learn."

Kate pulled it off gracefully, quickly, and without once flashing her underwear.

"Amazing," Abby said. "I can't imagine why they didn't pick you for queen. So quick, tell me all about it before the guys get back. Did Ryan get down on one knee when he proposed?"

"Yes, he did. Of course, he asked the waiter to bring an extra napkin to kneel on so he wouldn't mess up his pants. He took me to Sixteen in the Trump Tower. It looks out over the lights of downtown Chicago. It was so romantic. I wish you could have been there. Well, not really. But you know what I mean."

"Did they have waiters in tuxedos?" Merri asked. "I always thought that'd be cool."

"They did," Kate said, grinning at Merri. "And it was cool."

"Did he hide the ring in your dessert?" Merri asked.

"No, I don't think that's Ryan's style," Kate said, laughing. "But it was wrapped in beautiful paper and ribbons. I nearly fainted when I opened the box and saw the size of the diamond." She held her ring out for them to admire again.

"Kathryn, you're going to ruin your Manuela sitting on that picnic bench." Ryan was back with two plates. A small frown marred his handsome face for a moment and then was gone.

"It'll be fine," Kate said.

"Hey, Merri Christmas, move over," John said.

When she had scooted over, Merri looked up at Ryan. "What's a Manuela?"

John and Ryan set down the plates they carried and then squeezed in at the picnic table.

Kate smiled her thanks and answered the question for Ryan. "Manuela is a designer from New York," she explained. "I'm wearing one of her dresses."

"I bought that dress for Kathryn last weekend in Chicago. It set me back three hundred dollars." He smiled down at Kate. "But she's worth every penny."

Abby concentrated on keeping a pleasant expression on her face. People who dropped price tags into a conversation never impressed her. It was a pretty dress but not Kate's usual casual style. And she wasn't wearing the bright, funky jewelry she usually did—jewelry she had designed, created, and made a small business of selling on campus.

Kate looked from John's plate heaped high with fried fish and various side dishes to the plate of raw broccoli and carrot sticks Ryan had put in front of her. "Where's the food, Ryan?"

"Oh, drat. Is all the good stuff gone?" Abby asked.

"I assumed you wouldn't want any of it, Kathryn. It's all loaded with carbs and fat."

"Well, I do," Merri declared and headed back to the food table with her plate.

Ryan watched Merri leave and muttered something that Abby didn't quite catch. It sounded like, "I rest my case."

Abby blinked. She waited for her roomie to say she loved carbs and fat. That she lived for carbs and fat. That her favorite entertainment was carbs and fat.

But Kate merely smoothed the front of her dress and smiled. "You're right, Ryan."

"We'll get something later in the city." Ryan took a

meager bite of fruit salad from his plate. "I was reading online about St. Charles and the downtown St. Louis scene. Sounds like there are a few decent restaurants around."

"Yeah," John said drily, "they have a few."

"We want you to come celebrate with us," Kate said.

Ryan patted his lips with a napkin and took out his phone. "You, too, Roberts, of course. I'll make reservations. Is seven o'clock all right?"

"And then, after dinner," Kate said, "we can zip on down to Equality so that tomorrow we'll have all day to—"

"About that. What made you choose Equality for our little friend-fest weekend?" Abby said, using air quotes. "John says it's just a tiny town."

"Tiny town, but a big help with my project. At least I hope so."

"Kathryn says you have some kind of weird genealogy program." Ryan's voice rose at the end and Abby wasn't sure if he was making a statement or asking a question.

"That's not what *Beautiful Houses* is… not exactly."

"It's all your fault, Abby," Kate said. "I made the mistake of telling Mom about your adventures with the Old Dears' genealogy. Now she is obsessed with tracing our family tree. But we came to a dead end with the Greenfield side of the family. Since you got us hooked, it's only fair you lend us your expertise."

"Genealogy is kind of addictive," Abby said. "And Eulah and Beulah are so happy we found their Buchanan relatives for them."

"Mom wants me to paint a wall mural of our family tree in Dad's den as a surprise. Here, let me show you what I had in mind." Kate took a pen from her purse and began sketching a whimsical tree on a paper napkin. "I thought I'd draw faces on the leaves. And each person will have some sort of item symbolizing them. Like for me, I'll put a paint brush to show my love for art."

In mere seconds, Kate had drawn an amazingly detailed sketch, and as always Abby was astounded by her talent.

"That is so cool," Merri said, returning with a plate of mostly potato chips and pink fluffy salad.

Kate smiled. "Thanks, sweetie. But it won't look very cool if it's all lopsided. And I'm running out of time. The only opportunity I'd have to paint it is next month while Mom and Dad are gone to Colorado on vacation. So that's why I thought if you went with us and we used the program..."

Abby shot a meaningful look at Kate, willing her to stop talking. Fortunately, she seemed to get the message.

"Let's talk about it later," Abby said, tipping her head toward Merri. Whether or not she agreed to go along with them to Equality, it sounded like the girls-only night was off the agenda, and she needed time to figure out how to tell Merri.

Abby glanced at John for his take. He didn't look happy. It was flattering to think he was disappointed that she'd be gone for the weekend. But then he was probably only worried about losing control of the program.

Abby had been telling Kate about *Beautiful Houses* and all they'd uncovered with it for the past two and a half months. And for those two and a half months, Kate had steadfastly insisted Abby was joking about the program's abilities. Eventually, she had decided it was just as well Kate didn't believe her because they had begun to realize how dangerous it would be if the program fell into the wrong hands.

But now that Kate had finally come, she couldn't resist setting her straight. "Listen to me," she said, putting her face up to Kate's. "Look at my face. Read my lips. Notice that I'm not kidding around. This is not ordinary genealogy software. It—"

"It no longer works," John said, staring at Abby behind Kate's back. "Not right anyway, not since the Fourth of July."

"But it does still work a little?" Kate said hopefully.

"Yes, but—" John said.

"Great," Ryan said. "Let's go have a look at it."

"Okay," Abby said, shrugging her shoulders at the look John gave her. "But first I want you to meet the Old Dears. There they are at the far end of the pavilion."

The twins, in their identical lavender pants and sequined tops, stood one on either side of Doug Buchanan, as he struggled with a karaoke microphone.

"Aren't they cute," Kate said, laughing. "How do you ever tell them apart?"

"Beaulah's always cheerful and Eulah's…not so much."

The microphone squealed. "Test, test, test," Doug said into it. "Can you hear me in the back?"

A woman behind them called out, "Louder, Dougie."

A man two tables over called out, "Hey, if you're taking requests, I want Proud Mary."

The crowd laughed, and Ryan rolled his eyes. "If they're going to start singing, I'm leaving."

"No, wait," Abby said. "Doug's up to something."

"By now," Doug said, "you've all met these two sweet ladies. Now, it's time to welcome them officially into the Buchanan clan." One of Doug's sons handed each beaming lady a yellow T-shirt.

Grinning happily, the Old Dears held up the shirts so the audience could see that printed on the fronts were the words, I Survived My First Buchanan Reunion. The crowd erupted in applause and whistles.

"And we put their names on the back so you can tell them apart," Doug continued.

The cheers turned to laughter when the audience realized the twins had been handed the wrong shirts. After trading, Eulah and Beulah held the shirts up again for everyone to see their names in blue script. Doug went on to remind everyone to be back tomorrow for more great food, the water balloon war, the quilt auction, and the washer tournament.

"Can we leave now?" Kate asked. "I can't wait to try out your program."

"You sure you don't want to stick around?" Ryan said in a fake southern accent. "I have a hankerin' to play worshers. I bet you five dollars I can whup you, too."

"Okay. I guess we can leave now," Abby said. She had looked forward to Kate meeting the ladies, but Eulah and Beulah would have lots of questions that were bound to take more time than Kate—and especially Ryan—would want to spend.

On the way to their cars, John waited until Kate and Ryan were out of earshot. "I thought we agreed not to let anyone else in on this until we could figure out what to do with the program. You know how dangerous it could be if this gets out."

"Yeah," Merri said. "That's the first rule. Besides, we're the three musketeers. Whoever heard of the five musketeers?"

"I know, I know," Abby said. "I don't know what came over me. Kate's always been so…so…annoying about it, an agnostic, you might say. I don't know what made her change her mind, and I had no idea she had told Ryan about it."

"Speaking of which, how well do you know Turner?"

"I've only met him a few times when he came to campus to visit Kate. He seemed nice enough. Then."

"I think he's a jackass," Merri declared.

John snorted a laugh. "Yeah, you're right about that, squirt. But don't say that word, okay?"

"We just have to give it time," Abby said. "Maybe he'll grow on us."

"Well, until he does," John said, "I think we should stall on showing them the program."

"Why?" Merri said. "Now that it's not working right, all they'll see is a bunch of houses from around the world."

"It won't hurt for them to see that," Abby said, "We just won't mention that the way we helped Eulah and Beulah fill out their family tree was by time-surfing back to meet their ancestors."

CHAPTER 2

The late afternoon sun was making Abby squint and she wished she could remember where her sunglasses were. She sat between John and Merri on Merri's front porch in Miles Station, thinking about her first day as her tutor back in June. She had sat on the same steps and told Merri that Kate wanted to come meet her. Merri, sullen in her misery, had not believed anyone could like her. Merri's attitude had changed so much since then, and she had taken to Kate right away. She was bound to be hurt when she realized Kate wouldn't be staying for their planned girls' night.

Abby sent up a little prayer for Merri. She didn't need any more disappointments in her life.

"I thought they were right behind us. I hope they didn't get lost," Merri said.

John, looking movie-star quality in his own sunglasses, propped his forearms on his knees and gave a little grunt of disgust. "Maybe they decided to go to 'the city' to get tofu or sushi. Or whatever meets Turner's exacting culinary standards."

Abby laughed and swatted John's arm. "Oh, stop it."

"They're here," Merri said, jumping up from the step.

Kate's blue car pulled sedately up in front of the house and stopped. For once, she was driving below land speed records. Abby saw why when the driver's side door opened and Ryan got out. So Kate had actually let another human being drive her beloved PT Cruiser. It must be true love.

"We'll have to have your tires checked, Kathryn," Ryan said. "You're bound to have a flat from these wilderness trails that pass for roads."

"They are pretty rough," Abby said.

"Oh, don't mind Ryan," Kate said, studying the old house before her. "Wow. How old did you say this is? Let's have the tour, Abby. I want to see where you've spent the summer doing your Jane Eyre thing. Which reminds me, I've got to choose my service project soon. Ambassador College has been hounding me unmercifully. I got another letter yesterday."

"I hope you'll select something that isn't so far from civilization," Ryan said. "This is really…rustic."

Abby, too, had thought the ancient, sagging house was rustic at first, creepy even—that is, until she got to know it better. She put a protective arm around Merri.

"It's been the perfect service project. Merri's great and this house is really special. It was built in 1847 by Jonathan Miles. At one time there was a thriving little town here called Miles Station. It was really something back in the day."

"We've done some repairs," John said. "We'll get the house back the way it was."

John's generosity made Abby feel all warm and gooey inside, and she contemplated awarding him another imaginary star. The good thing about imaginary charts is that she could put as many stars on them as she wanted. John had spent most of his summer break renovating a house in Alton for Habitat for Humanity. As if that weren't enough, in his spare time he'd been doing repairs for Merri's mom. "Yeah," Merri said. "John put the trellises back up, and he told Mom he's going to help us paint the house before he leaves for college."

"Saint John, is he?" Ryan said, jingling the change in his pockets.

"And a girl named Charlotte used to sleep in my room," Merri said. "She was really nice and we—" Merri stopped and looked apologetically at Abby and John.

"Where is your mom, anyway?" Abby said.

"Right. Mom. She's showing a house. She won't be back until late. Come on, Kate. I'll show you the inside of the house."

Merri's brown cat Kit Kat greeted them at the door. Merri scooped her up and led them through the bare, shabby rooms, proudly explaining all the repairs and decorating her mother planned to do as soon as they had the money. She didn't appear to notice Kate's wide eyes and Ryan's curled lip as they took in the house's condition. Abby could appreciate their culture shock. It had been an adjustment for her, too. But being a "companion and tutor to an economically disadvantaged adolescent," as Ambassador College described it, was an experience she would never forget.

Merri opened the door to the spare bedroom they used as a schoolroom. A top-of-the-line computer looked incongruous on a scarred table in the dingy room. Merri's dad had sent the computer to her as a sop for his guilty conscience. It was his meth-making in their backyard that had caused Merri's Mom Pat to take her and flee to safety and him to end up in Joliet Prison. The irony of an educational gift bought with drug money was not lost on Abby.

"And here's where my heartless tutor has been torturing me with participles and long division all summer," Merri said, grinning at Kate.

"Hey, you had a break the week we got to stay at Lucy's house," Abby said. "Merri wrote an excellent report on Lewis and Clark. Didn't she, John?"

Ryan brushed past John before he could answer and went through the doorway and to the computer. "Not a bad model," he said. "Is the genealogy program on it?"

"It is," Abby said. "I mean, it's not really a genealogy program. But yes, the *Beautiful Houses* program we used is on this computer—and on John's laptop, too."

Merri edged around Ryan and sat down at the computer. When *Beautiful Houses* finished loading, images of all types of houses from around the world scrolled by on the computer screen. The title at the top invited users to *Take a Virtual Tour.*

"What does this have to do with genealogy?" Ryan asked.

"The way it is now? Nothing," John said. "But as we said, it's not working right."

"Sorry," Abby said, seeing Kate's disappointed expression.

Merri looked desperate to cheer up her new friend. "But even though we can't time-sur—" she broke off. "I mean the program won't let us…well, anyway, it's still fun. Here, Kate. I'll show you. Pick whatever house you want."

"My favorite is a thatched cottage in the Cotswolds in England," Abby said. "Merri's is a castle in Scotland."

Kate leaned over Merri's shoulder and pointed to a photo of a huge house that hugged a steep terraced hill covered in lush greenery and colorful tropical flowers. "Oh,

I like that one. Does it say where it is? It looks like Hawaii, maybe."

Merri clicked on the image, and the screen filled with an enlarged view of the hillside house.

"I wouldn't mind a house like that one day," Ryan said.

Even though it was undoubtedly worth tens of millions of dollars, he said it with a perfectly serious voice. Abby didn't risk looking at John, but she pictured his eyes rolling.

"You're right," she said to Kate. "It says Honolulu. You can look at all the rooms inside and see the back of the house, too."

"Here, Kate, you try it," Merri said, getting up from the computer.

"How do I make it work?"

Ryan took over the explanation. "It's simple, Kathryn," he said. "It is actually a fairly common software protocol—very much like typical architecture programs."

Merri turned a small snort into a cough.

Abby covered a smile and pointed to the buttons at the top of the screen. "Just click and you can go through all the rooms and see what everything looks like."

"What will we do after this?" Merri asked. "Can we have a beauty makeover, Abby, like we did before?"

"I don't know, Merri," Abby said, telegraphing a question to Kate. "Since the program's not working right, there's no reason to go to Equality, is there? You can stay the night after all, you know, for our girls' night."

Kate's face fell and she sighed. "I tried to call down there but never got anyone who seemed to know anything. That's why I thought if we went down there in person we could—"

Ryan put his arm around her and smiled. "Look on the bright side, Kathryn. At least we won't have to take your new car any farther out into the boonies."

"Mom said we can order pizza. You can get extra cheese if you want. Abby said the delivery boy is bound to find us this time," Merri said in a rush. "And me and Abby made Rice Krispy squares for dessert. But if you don't like Rice Krispy squares, we can make brownies. Or snickerdoodles. John loves those. I mean he's not a girl so he can't come to our girls' night, but we could save some for him. I have a really good recipe for snickerdoodles that Grandma Beulah taught me to make. Do you know how to crochet? 'Cause I know how and maybe, if you want, I could teach you too. Or maybe we could watch movies. I have one called—"

"Sorry, Marilyn," Ryan inserted into the barrage of words. "I made reservations for seven at a tapas restaurant called Mosaic. For the four of us."

Kate put an arm around his waist. "That was thoughtful of you, Ryan," she said, smiling adoringly up at him, as if she were imagining more stars for his chart.

Abby tried sending another silent message, but Kate's radar was still down. She patted Merri's cheek and said, "Maybe some other time, kiddo. And, Ryan? Her name is Merri, not Marilyn."

Kate looked up suddenly as if Abby's telegraph had finally arrived. She left Ryan's side and went to Merri's. "No, you're right," she said. "Of course, we have to have our girls' night. We can go to Equality tomorrow. And you guys will just have to find something else fun to do."

Ryan smiled tightly and jingled the change in his pocket. It sounded to Abby as if he had at least ten dollars' worth. He turned toward the doorway, and Kate went to him and took his hand. "Please, Ryan?"

"Oh, sure. I'll just hang out at the motel. Maybe I can get a cardboard meal from room service. It will be thrilling."

"You could watch a movie," Merri suggested.

"Good idea. I bet they have just the kind I like."

"I hate to ask, but where are you planning to stay?" John said. "The closest decent motel is about twenty-five miles away."

"It figures."

"Maybe you could stay here, Ryan," Abby said. "What do you think, Merri?"

"Well, I guess he could," Merri said, frowning in thought. "If he stayed in the living room, we wouldn't even notice a boy was here. We could take him some pizza and he could watch TV while we're doing our stuff."

Ryan hooked his arm around Kate's neck and pulled her close. "Yes," he said softly into her hair, "I could stay in the living room. All night."

Her eyes going large, Kate turned scarlet and pulled away from him. Abby wondered at her sudden embarrassment. Even though Ambassador College had fairly strict rules about what they labeled public displays of affection, a kiss on the head seemed a mild enough P.D.A.

"I've got an idea." John's smile was evil. "How about if I stay, too, and keep Ryan company? You probably have a few extra blankets, don't you, Merri? Ryan and I could have a sleepover too."

"I guess," Merri said. "But you've got to promise to stay in the living room."

"I wouldn't have it any other way," John said, staring at Ryan.

Ryan didn't look happy.

Abby paused in the doorway to the living room, studying the marked difference between the solemn atmosphere there and the happy one in the kitchen she had just left.

John and Ryan sat on the couch, watching a baseball

game. The game explained their intense concentration on the TV screen. That the Cardinals were beating the Cubs six to one explained the pained look on Ryan's face and the smug one on John's. To give him credit, John wasn't rubbing it in. Occasionally, he looked down at the laptop he held, as if to say the game was no big deal.

A clanking sound and then a burst of laughter from the kitchen made the two guys look up.

"As promised," Abby said, stepping into the room. "Merri's wondrous snickerdoodles. She told me to remind you to share, John."

John laughed. "Love the new hairdo," he said, taking the plate of cookies from her. "One of Merri's designs, I presume?"

"She believes it is her destiny to be a famous hair stylist. She pronounced this her greatest masterpiece to date." Abby batted her eyes and patted the braids that covered her head. "And just look at the manicure she gave me." She waggled her fingers with their multi-colored nail polish.

"Nice," John said, grinning. He took a cookie and offered the plate to Ryan, who wordlessly frowned and waved it away.

"Come on, don't look so wry, Ryan," he said. "Take a chance. A few carbs won't kill you."

"No thanks. I care about my health."

"Suit yourself," John said, setting the plate next to the empty pizza box on the coffee table.

Abby figured it would be safe to bet John had polished off the whole pizza. Cheers from the Cardinals' stadium rose to a crescendo. Ryan looked at his watch and sighed.

"Well, I'll leave you guys to your…fun," Abby said. "We'll be in the kitchen. Kate's going to give us drawing lessons."

CHAPTER 3

Abby realized she was awake. For no apparent reason. She started to turn over and then remembered Kate was sleeping next to her. She managed to complete the maneuver without flailing about as much she usually did and then concentrated on getting back to sleep.

The house was completely silent. Except for the rumbling in her stomach. If only she hadn't eaten that last piece of pizza. And that pile of cookies. And the Rice Krispy Treats. The three cans of soda weren't helping either. Her head was hurting, too, and she vowed she would never eat junk food again. Ever. Then she was relieved to find that the headache was only from the braids grinding into her scalp. She slipped off the elastic bands, unbraided her hair, and massaged the sore spots on her head.

Counting sheep never helped anyone fall asleep. The secret was to concentrate on sleepy thoughts. Take deep breaths. After a moment, she recognized with relief that she was drifting back to sleep. But as soon as that thought registered, it made her wake up all over again. Then John sneaked into her head and wouldn't leave. Finally Abby opened her eyes.

A blue light was streaming under the door into the dark room. Her eyes opened even wider.

She slipped out from under the sheet that covered her, and, remembering at the last second not to step on Merri who slept on a twin mattress beside the bed, she put her feet carefully on the floor and stood. Even knowing it was there, she managed to trip over the mattress. Merri mumbled incoherently.

Abby knelt beside her. "Merri," she whispered, shaking her shoulder. "Wake up."

"Whaa?"

"It's the blue light again. Come on. Let's go see."

Merri, instantly awake, scrambled awkwardly to her feet and followed Abby. The door creaked a little when she cracked it, and Abby looked back at the dim lump on the bed that was Kate. She didn't stir, and so Abby opened the door and they went out into the hall. She shut the door carefully. Even so, the click sounded loud in the quiet house.

The blue light came, as she knew it would, from Merri's computer in the room across the hall. And it meant, she hoped, that *Beautiful Houses* had decided to work again.

Merri rushed eagerly ahead of her and sat down at the computer. As soon as she put her hand on the mouse, the glowing blue screen morphed to a familiar scene.

It was the kitchen downstairs, only without electric appliances and running water. And the young woman wearing a calico dress who came into view was definitely not Merri's mom, Pat.

"It's Charlotte!" Merri said. "Oh, Abby, she's back."

Abby sat down next to Merri and squeezed her arm. "I

have to admit, I thought we'd never see her again."

Colonel Miles' daughter, Charlotte, bustled about the kitchen, her calico skirts swishing as she hurried back and forth between the chopping block work table in the center of the room and the cast iron cookstove where steam rose from a pot bubbling there.

"She looks stressed out," Merri said.

"Look at the clock on the shelf. It's almost six o'clock. About time for the train to come into the station. I wonder how many people she'll serve today. Well, not today. That day."

Abby checked the date on the menu bar at the top of the computer screen. It told her they were visiting September 23, 1861.

"Let's go virtual," Merri said. "I want to find out what's happening."

"Wait here. I'm going to go get John."

"In that?" Merri said dubiously.

Abby looked down at the skimpy knit shorts and T-shirt she wore. "Right. First, I'm going to have to sneak back into the room for some clothes. Without waking Kate."

"Hurry."

"I'll try."

They had left the kitchen light on in case John or Ryan needed anything in the night, and that helped as Abby padded barefoot downstairs. However, when she got to the living room she realized that it was a long way from the kitchen, and there was not enough light for her to distinguish the furniture from the room's occupants.

Ryan, she knew, had claimed the couch. It was light-colored and she saw it and the blurred shape on it easily enough in the gloom. The tricky part would be finding John. Pat had brought a sleeping bag from the hall closet for him, but Abby had no idea where he had put it. Other than the soft snores coming from the vicinity of the couch, the room was completely quiet.

She discovered the answer to her question when a hand came out of the darkness and grabbed her ankle. She stumbled and landed on a warm chest. A bare warm chest, from which came a soft whoosh of air. Right after the whoosh, a large hand covered her mouth. The precaution was unnecessary. She had recognized John's cologne and knew in an instant that it was no nightmare monster attacking her.

He put his mouth to her ear and whispered, "What are you doing here? I thought Turner was the one planning on nighttime shenanigans."

Abby pulled his hand away from her mouth and tried for indignant, which was difficult when whispering. "Don't be ridiculous, Mr. Roberts. If I was inclined to get into your bed, and I'm not, it wouldn't be with Ryan in the room."

"Well, you are in fact in my bed, and you'd better get out of it quick. I know the Bible says God will never give us any temptation stronger than what we can handle, but…"

"Just to be clear, you are the one who dragged me into your bed, and—"

"Abby. Please. Have pity. What is it you want?"

If felt wonderful being in John's arms, but she had promised him and God that she wouldn't intentionally tempt him to break his commitment—their commitment—to abstinence.

"Come up to the computer room," she whispered. "There's something you have to see." And then she rose less than gracefully and stood looking down at him. "And don't wake Ryan."

"Trust me. I have no intention of doing that."

"So I finally get to meet the elusive Charlotte Miles," John said a few minutes later.

Abby was relieved to see he was wearing a shirt. She tried not to think about what was beneath it. "Yes, although I have no idea why *Beautiful Houses* would suddenly start working again after all this time."

Merri's eyes were glued to the screen where Charlotte was stirring the steaming pot on her cookstove, and her cousin Joshua was bolting down a bowl of stew.

"This is the part where we found out about the gourd on the front door," Merri said.

"What do you mean?" John asked.

"This house was a stop on the Underground Railroad," Abby said. "The gourd indicated that to runaway slaves. Watch for how cool and collected Charlotte is when she's serving the train passengers—the whole time she's sheltering slaves in her attic."

"*Beautiful House*s must want us to see something," Merri said. "That's why it started working again."

"I know your theory, kiddo," Abby said, "but I'm having a hard time believing a computer program has an opinion one way or the other."

"Who knows," John said. "We've come to believe other strange things about it. Why not artificial intelligence?"

"I don't mean that—what you said, John," Merri said impatiently. "I think it's like God wants us to know certain things. Important things that could help people. You know. Like with the Old Dears and Reuben."

"Well, anyway," Abby said, "pull up a chair, John, and let's go virtual

CHAPTER 4

Charlotte wiped the perspiration from her face and hurried to pile the fresh rolls she had baked that morning into two baskets.

"You want me to take some of those upstairs?" Joshua asked.

"Not yet. We can't risk the noise."

When she got back to the dining room, she saw that her guests had wasted no time eating their stew and were happy for the rolls, some of which they ate and some of which they tucked into pockets for their journey.

Unfortunately, the soldiers were in no hurry to leave. Their hunger had been assuaged, but they seemed starved for conversation and peppered her with questions about her family. When had her father founded Miles Station? Where were her husband and father fighting? What was it like running a train stop kitchen all alone? Charlotte knew their questions were friendly. Perhaps they saw in her the sister or cousin they had left behind. But she wished them gone, the sooner the better.

"You should have more than a boy here with you, dear," Reverend Robbins said.

Charlotte heard a snort from the kitchen. "We're fine," she answered. "And I have my sisters-in-law and neighbors."

"Well, you be on the lookout for runaway Negroes," he said. "A Negro will rob you as soon as look at you. And a pretty white woman like you…"

Charlotte opened her eyes wide. "Surely, they're not stupid enough to run, what with a bounty on their heads?"

"And then there's the prison sentence and a thousand dollar fine for those aiding and abetting them," Lieutenant Hollis said with a grim glance toward her.

"I apologize. I'm sure the citizens of Miles Station are law-abiding Christians," Reverend Robbins said.

"I'm sure they are," Lieutenant Hollis said. He seemed eager to change the subject. "Do you and Mr. McGuire have children?"

"No, we haven't been so blessed," Charlotte answered. No sooner were the words out of her mouth than a child's faint cry, abruptly shut off, drifted down from above.

"What was that?" one of the soldiers asked.

Before she could come up with an answer, Joshua stumbled into the dining room carrying the cat she had just seen in the kitchen sleeping by the stove.

"I got her, Charlotte. Pesky thing was upstairs crying to be fed."

"The cat," Charlotte said. "That's good you brought her down then."

Lieutenant Hollis stood and gave her a small bow. "Thank you for the meal, ma'am." He took out his wallet, as did the other men, and paid Charlotte. "My men and I will stretch our legs in the garden before we leave, if that's acceptable."

Charlotte sent up a prayer of thanks. "Of course, Lieutenant."

She followed as the men filed out. Lieutenant Hollis paused on the porch. He glanced at the gourd dipper hanging beside the front door and then back at her. "You'd better hurry to feed your cat then." After putting on his hat he followed the others out.

Hand at her throat, Charlotte went back inside and locked the door behind them.

Joshua, white-faced, stared at her. "What do we do?"

"We feed the cat."

Abby paused it and turned to look at John's reaction.

"You're right about Charlotte," he said. "Man, she was brave."

"I'll fast forward so we can get to the attic."

"Oh, a movie. What're you watching?" Kate said from the doorway, yawning loudly. "I thought the party was over."

Abby nearly fell out of her chair trying to turn off the monitor before Kate got a good look at it.

"It's a western," John said quickly. "You wouldn't like it." Then expelling a huge breath, he said, "That's not exactly true, Kate."

"I think she should see it," Merri said. "Maybe that's why it started working again."

"*Beautiful Houses*? It's working?" Kate said. "Oh, good. Show me."

Abby shot a look at John and then Merri. "Maybe there's room for one more musketeer." She turned to Kate. "But you've got to promise you won't tell anyone, anyone, what we're going to show you. If this gets out…well, it wouldn't be good."

John went to the door and looked out into the hall. "He's still asleep. Go ahead."

"Remember how I kept trying to convince you we had met Charlotte, the girl who used to live in this house? Well, we found her again."

"Watch this." Merri turned the monitor back on. "See? That's Charlotte and her cousin Joshua."

"Don't go virtual yet," Abby said. "Give Kate a chance to figure out how it works."

Kate watched transfixed as Charlotte and Joshua moved around the kitchen gathering food. "You're saying that's your kitchen, Merri?"

"Yep. See? Same windows and doors. Same size and shape. It's our kitchen all right. Only in 1861."

"Oh," Kate said, "they're leaving."

"Don't worry," Abby said. "We can follow them."

Joshua, carrying the stew pot, followed Charlotte out of the kitchen into the dim pantry. She looked around cautiously and then opened a small door there.

"We can follow Charlotte in real time or speed up," John explained. "We can even go backward in time."

"Awesome," Kate said.

"You ain't seen nothin' yet, girlfriend," Abby said, grinning. "When we lock onto Charlotte and go virtual, you'll be inside her head."

"It's like reading a really good book," John said.

"Way better than movies," Merri said.

"What are they doing?" Kate asked.

"Let's find out," Abby said.

Charlotte and Joshua climbed the pantry steps to her bedroom and then went to unlatch the attic door. She opened it and called out softly to reassure those above. Joshua went up first, carrying the stew pot, and she carried the basket of rolls behind him.

When she reached the top, she saw the whites of three pairs of frightened eyes where Sally huddled on the cornhusk pallet with her two little boys.

"I be sorry, Miz McGuire," Sally said. "Little Frank hungry. I tole him to shut his mouth afore the man catchers git us."

"I'm sorry, Little Frank," Charlotte said. "It took much longer than I thought to bring you your supper."

Joshua set the stew pot on the floor in front of them and then reached into his pocket for the spoons he had brought. But the boys had already begun to dip their hands into the stew.

Sally looked on sadly. "Just like little fattenin' pigs. Ate cornmeal mush out of a wood trough at Master's yard." She shyly took the spoons from Joshua and gave one to each boy. "Little Frank, Solomon, these be spoons. You eat like real boys now we in Illinois."

Joshua turned to Charlotte looking like he'd been poleaxed. She set the basket of rolls down and looked away so Sally and the boys wouldn't see that her eyes had started leaking.

She took the lantern down from the post where it hung on a nail and lit it with a match from her pocket. After adjusting the wick, she went to the other cornhusk pallet in the far corner, where a huge man lay with his face to the wall.

"Ned?" Charlotte whispered. "Are you all right?" She put a hand on his shoulder and he jerked and turned onto his back. "I've brought food."

Rising up onto his elbows, he looked dazedly around the attic.

Charlotte brought the lantern closer, and he grimaced and shut his eyes. The rusty slave collar he wore had caused sores on his neck, and they looked even worse than when he had arrived. No telling what festering infections the collar hid.

"I'll go get Louie," Joshua said. "He'll know how to get that cussed thing off." Joshua had tried that morning to remove the iron collar but none of her father's tools could cut through it or break the latch.

"Louie's a good blacksmith, but he's also a raging bigot. He'd turn us all in and pat himself on the back for doing it. Mr. Bartlett will have something that will get it off. You go on and do your chores, Joshua. And keep your eyes open for him."

"All right," he said and went back downstairs.

Taking a small tin of salve from her pocket, Charlotte knelt beside the big man's pallet. "I got this from the Mercantile for your neck. Let me—" He jerked when she extended her hand toward his ravaged flesh. She pulled her hand back. "I'm not going to hurt you."

Even as she said it, she realized that the look on his feverish face, before he lowered his eyes, was one of confusion and horror, not fear. "The sores are infected," she said. "I need to put—"

"I can do it," he said. His voice was raspy and low. Charlotte wondered if these were his first words for the day. He had spoken no more than a dozen the night before when Jemmy had brought him and the others in.

Charlotte offered him the tin. When he didn't take it, she put it on the pallet next to him. He picked it up, opened it, and cautiously sniffed the contents. Seeming satisfied, he dipped a finger into the salve and rubbed some of it on his neck.

Sally brought the stew pot over and set it near him. Then she backed away as if she were afraid of getting bitten by a chained dog. "You better let that nigger man eat afore my childrens lick the pan clean."

Charlotte looked up at the woman in shock. "Why do you call him that?"

"I knows what he is," she said, settling back onto her own pallet next to the boys.

He didn't answer, didn't pay any mind to her, but hauled himself up enough to lean against the wall. He took the stew pot onto his lap and, using one of the spoons still in it, took a bite.

Charlotte moved the lantern so she could see his swollen and lacerated feet. They, too, were worse than before and so huge she hadn't a hope of finding shoes that would fit him. How far had he run barefoot through the woods?

"Your feet," she said. "Put salve on them too."

Charlotte went to the wooden trunk against the wall and set her lantern down so she could open it. After taking out the journal, pen, and ink she kept there, she closed the lid, sat on it, and settled her skirt around her.

"I have stories in this book," she said, looking in turn to each of her guests. "Stories the people who pass through tell me. Would you like to tell me your story so I can write it down?" Her gaze landed finally on the man in the corner.

He studied the stew pot in his lap. "It ain't fittin', ma'am," he said softly.

"I have all sorts of stories in here. There's a man in Boston who'll publish them so people—white people—will understand what—"

"No thank you, ma'am."

"Well, if you change your mind…"

"I know a story," Little Frank piped up from across the room. "'Bout Uncle Remus."

"Hush," Solomon whispered fiercely to his brother. "Ma'am don't mean that kind of story."

"I like that story," Charlotte said, hiding a grin. "But I want you to tell me about you."

"You write it in that book?" Sally said with wonder.

"Yes, indeed. Let's start with your surname."

Nervously eying the man in the corner, Sally pulled her pallet closer to Charlotte and settled the boys on her lap. "I be Sally," she said, "and this be Little Frank and Solomon."

"Yes, but I mean your last name?"

"They named Brooks, ma'am." Sally turned her face away. "They be Master's own boys."

Charlotte swallowed and dropped her eyes to the book in her lap. "Oh. Well, then. How about your last name, Sally?"

"Don't have no other name but Sally, Miz McGuire. Don't know who my pappy be neither. But I 'member my mammy. Came five, six times to see me. Had to walk four mile at night after her work done. She settle down all nice next to me and sing sorrow songs whilst I fall to sleep. Be gone when I wake up on account she had to be in the field by sunup or Master whup her. Don't know what happened to her. She didn't ever come no more."

Charlotte wrote it all in the book as fast as she could, pausing only once, when a tear landed on the page, to take a handkerchief out of her pocket and wipe her eyes.

"Can I see what you done writ in the book?" Sally said shyly.

Charlotte turned the book toward her. "This is your name, Sally. Right here. S-A-L-L-Y. And here's Solomon's and Little Frank's."

Sally and the boys' eyes were wide with wonder, and Charlotte wished she could teach them to read. She was perfectly willing to add that crime to her growing list, if only she had enough time. Maybe she could find her old school slate and bring it up to the attic.

"Sally, I don't understand. Why was your mother four miles away?"

"Master took all the childrens from they mammies and give to Granny Peg. She raise them so the mammies can work in the fields."

Charlotte focused her mind on getting the story down. There'd be time enough to weep over it later. "Where was this?" she said.

"Clarksville, Tennessee, Miz McGuire. When I was growed then I sold to Master Brooks, and he take me to Sikeston, Missouri. But we can't stay with Master Brooks no more. Miz Brooks hates Master's colored childrens. She always tells the whupping man to whup Master's childrens extra. I hear her say Master gots to sell all his colored childrens or she don't love him no more.

When Charlotte had written it down, she looked up to find Little Frank staring at her, eyes wide. Sally jerked him face down into her bosom and said. "He don't mean no disrespect, Miz McGuire. Just he just ain't never seen a white lady what smiled at him."

"That's quite all right, Sally," she said, wiping a tear away. "Thank you for telling me your story."

CHAPTER 5

Wiping a tear from her own cheek, Abby paused the program and then turned to find the others staring in shock at the now blank computer monitor. It was a full minute before anyone spoke.

"Sometimes you find out more than you want to know when you go rummaging around in the past," Abby whispered at last.

"When we were investigating Eulah and Beulah's ancestor," John said, "we saw a house burn down with a woman in it."

"I can't stand to hear them tell their stories," Merri said, putting her head on the table.

"Keep your voice down, kiddo," Abby said. "Don't wake Ryan."

There was no need to caution Kate, because she still sat, eyes wide but mouth shut, staring at the computer. Finally, she said, "So this is what you've been trying to tell me about all this time? Oh, Abby, I am so sorry for not believing you."

"That's all right, roomie. Who could, without seeing it in person?"

"It's really not a genealogy program, is it?"

"Nope."

"So, the way you found the Old Dears' ancestors for their family tree was by going back in time?"

"Only virtually." Merri lifted her head and wiped at her eyes with her T-shirt sleeve.

"So why don't we want to wake Ryan?"

"Because until we know what to do with this, we're not telling anyone else about it. Even Merri's mom doesn't know."

"The media would blast the story all over the world," John said. "And what if someone really evil got a hold of it? For that matter, what if our own government got a hold of it?"

"Why not?" Kate said. "Just think how this could revolutionize history classes. At last we could finally know what it was really like way back when. And…and…think of it! Police detectives could easily follow up on leads. They'd never prosecute the wrong person. And schools and daycare centers could check out applicants so they wouldn't hire some child molester. And…and—"

"I know, Kate. We've thought of all that," Abby said. "But what about privacy? You'd never know if someone was snooping around in your most private moments, watching you in your home—in your bedroom or bathroom."

"But they couldn't. The Constitution guarantees our privacy."

"Actually, there's some question about that," John said. "But even if you're right, once people see all the good applications for this, with this kind of power—well, it would only be a matter of time before Big Brother began using it to keep us all in line."

Kate was quiet for a moment and then said, "So what are you going to do with it?"

"We don't know," Abby said, looking at John. "But we'd better start thinking about it, now that it's working again."

"Maybe the safest thing is to turn it over to the government. At least they'd have the resources to keep our enemies from getting their hands on it. My dad works for the state. Actually, one of his friends knows the governor."

John's face registered alarm. "No offense to your dad, Kate, but letting Illinois politicians get their hands on it is almost as scary. You know the state motto. Illinois: where the governors make the license plates."

"So are you saying you won't use it to help me?"

"I know we used it to help Eulah and Beulah, but—"

"I promise not to tell anyone. Even Ryan, if you insist, although I hate keeping things from him."

"Anyway, I can't just leave Merri here alone and go off to Equality with you."

John laughed softly. "Look at her."

Merri was conked out, snoring softly, her head on the computer table next to the keyboard.

"She's got the right idea," Abby said, rising from her chair. "Let's sleep on it." She yawned and then shook Merri's arm to wake her.

By the time they had settled back into their beds it was three-thirty. Merri went back to sleep instantly. Actually, Abby wasn't sure she'd even been awake when they walked her back to the bedroom.

And Abby had no difficulty falling back asleep this time. Midway during her prayer for God to help her know what to do, she too conked out.

Pat was making pancakes while patiently listening to Merri's steady stream of chatter about their girls' night. Grinning, Abby set the table and then poured orange juice into six blue glasses.

"Thanks," Kate said when she got to her place at the table. "I wish you'd let me help."

"Don't be silly," Abby said. "You're our guest. Right, Merri?"

"If you want, me and Abby will let you help us wash the dishes," Merri offered graciously.

"And," Pat said from the stove, "I'll let you come get your own pancakes. I've got three hot ones here with your name on them."

"Gladly." She took the plate Pat handed her and stood for a moment looking at her outdated, avocado green stove.

"Do you need more?" Pat asked.

"Oh, heavens no. This is plenty. I was just thinking how lucky we are to have modern conveniences like electric stoves."

Abby saw that Merri was grinning at the expression her mother wore. Pat had no idea how different her kitchen was from when Charlotte had cooked in it so many years before.

"I don't mind at all that we don't have a dishwasher," Merri said. "At least we have running water."

Pat smiled at her. "You're right, honey. We all should count our blessings more often."

John came in sniffing the air. "Do I smell coffee?"

"You sure do," Pat said. "Help yourself."

John assigned himself the job of pouring cups for everyone except Merri.

"Hey, how come I don't get any?"

"Because you're just a pipsqueak, that's why," John said, ruffling her hair.

"Oh, there you are, Ryan." Pat smiled a welcome.

He stood uncertainly in the doorway. He was probably starving. As far as Abby knew he hadn't had anything to eat since fruit salad at the reunion the day before.

"Do you want bacon with yours?" Pat asked.

"Sure," he said, eagerly taking the plate. "Thanks."

Abby smothered a smile. It just went to show that if a person got hungry enough they'd eat anything.

After they had their fill of pancakes, Pat went to dress for work. Abby, Merri and Kate cleaned up the kitchen, Abby washing while they dried the dishes. With two to one, Abby had to work fast to keep them busy.

Merri took a plate from the drainer and began wiping it dry. "Abby, I think you should go with Kate."

"We, my dear student, have work to do." After a moment, she added, "And besides, I can't just leave you here alone."

"Don't worry. I already called the Grandmas. They said I can stay with them."

"Why would you do that, kiddo?"

"Like I keep saying, *Beautiful Houses* wouldn't be working after all this time for no reason. I think it wants you to help Kate. So you better go with her to Equality and see what's going on."

"Really?" Kate said. "You wouldn't mind, Merri?"

"Mom said she'd drop me off on her way to work."

"Kathryn, I got the bedding folded and the sleeping bag put away," Ryan said from the doorway where he stood with John.

"I see you don't need any help here," John said.

"You'll come back though, right, Abby?" Merri said, ignoring John's attempt at humor.

"Of course I will." Abby hung up her dishtowel and gave Merri a hug. "But we probably won't get back until tomorrow or maybe Monday. It'll take almost three hours to get there, and I doubt we'll find out much today with it being Saturday."

"Where are you going?" John asked.

"Equality," Abby answered. "I'm going with Kate and Ryan."

"But I thought we'd given up on that idea," Ryan said. "If the program's not working properly—"

Kate darted a glance at Abby. "But it might work in Equality," she said. "And Abby's an expert with genealogy. She can—"

"No, I'm not," Abby said, "and there's no guarantee we'll find anything." Then seeing the look of desperation on Kate's face she added, "But I'm going to try." Although she didn't know how on earth she was going to get the chance to time-surf without Ryan seeing it.

"That is if John will let us borrow his laptop." At the confused look on Ryan's face Abby added, "John's friend Timmy Tech copied the program onto it."

"Sure," John said. "I'll just run home and shower and pack a few things."

Abby felt like doing a happy dance but managed with effort not to. "You're coming too?"

John smiled at her, his eyes bluer than ever. "You bet. I wouldn't miss the fun for anything."

She caught a frown that appeared briefly on Ryan's face. Either he didn't want to make the trip to Equality, or he was annoyed that John had invited himself along. Probably both. No doubt he regretted he hadn't driven Kate down in his own car.

CHAPTER 6

The first hour of the trip was spent listening to Ryan talking on his phone as he tried to find the perfect motel for the night. If any of them attempted to say anything, no matter how softly, he glared and shushed them, saying it was hard enough to understand foreigners without the added background noise. He quizzed each proprietor about amenities and price as if they were on a luxury vacation instead of a one-night fact-finding trip. Complaining that they all sounded like dumps, he finally made reservations at a place called the Shawnee Chief, saying it was the dump closest to Equality.

They stopped at a McDonald's in Mt. Vernon for burgers; or rather, three of them had burgers. Ryan ate a salad.

As soon as they got on the highway again, rain started to fall. It was only a drizzle, but enough that Ryan reached over to turn Kate's windshield wipers on.

The clouded windows made the PT Cruiser's backseat

feel like a cozy cocoon, and Abby snuggled as close to John as her seatbelt would allow.

"Are you sure we should go on, Kathryn?" Ryan said. "With this rain?"

"A little rain never hurt anyone," Kate said.

"Yes, Kathryn, it did. You'd better slow down."

John must have felt the same way, because he seemed a little tense until Kate slowed the car. It always took people a little time to get used to her driving.

"So anyway," Kate said. "I guess it wouldn't have been so frustrating to come to a dead end if Mom and I hadn't gotten spoiled. She joined three online genealogy sites, and it was easy—at first—to find plenty of information. We were able to fill in a lot of blank spots on the Greenfield family tree. Of course, I knew Dad's family came from Chicago. And when I went last weekend to visit my grandparents—"

"And me," Ryan added, smiling complacently.

"And you," Kate agreed, patting his cheek. She raised her left hand to admire her engagement ring.

"Hey, keep your eyes on the road," Ryan said quickly.

"Oh. Right," she said, putting her hand back on the wheel. "Anyway, as I was saying, Gramps told me more stuff—which just made it all the more annoying when the trail ended with Ned Greenfield, born in Equality in 1834."

"Your three times great grandfather, right?" Abby said. "Shouldn't you be grateful you went that far back?"

"I am. Really. It's just that I have information for Mom's side all the way back to 1689. I want the mural to be balanced."

"Sounds like the same problem the Old Dears had," John said.

"Exactly," Kate said. "So can't we just, you know, go back—"

"Maybe," Abby said, willing Kate to stop before she said too much. "It's really difficult to…you know…."

"Equality is the seat for Gallatin County, so we should be able to get some information at their courthouse," Kate said. "And then hopefully, their library will have a genealogy department."

"Good," Abby said. "We'll start there."

"And I have a clue that might help," Kate said. "The records say he was born at Hickory Hill, Equality. When they name their houses they must be pretty important, right? More like an estate."

"Ned Greenfield of Hickory Hill," Abby said. "I like the sound of that."

"That's a lot cooler than mine—John Roberts of State Route 67. So if we can find this Hickory Hill, we can…" he stopped, obviously remembering Ryan was in the car.

Abby nudged his knee with her own in warning. "Of course," she said drily, "there is the possibility that Hickory Hill is just, you know, the name of a hill. We'll just have to see what we can find."

"I still don't know why we couldn't have used the program at the kid's house," Ryan muttered.

"It doesn't work that way, right, Abby?" Kate asked.

"Right."

Abby changed the subject before Ryan could dwell on that line of thought but then wished she had come up with something more interesting than their wedding plans. Kate and Ryan spent the next forty-five minutes discussing every facet in excruciating detail.

Abby faked interest for Kate's sake but wondered if there was something wrong with her X chromosomes. She would never be able to drum up the same level of concern that Kate had for matching her bridesmaids' dresses to the precise shade of green as the leaves in their silk flower arrangements. She'd probably be expelled from the Universal Girls Club when her time came to plan a wedding.

She smiled and made what she hoped sounded like enthusiastic comments, and when Ryan dropped several price tags into the discussion, she kept her annoyance to herself.

John's eyes were closed and his head rested against the doorframe, but she had a sneaky suspicion he was faking sleep so he wouldn't have to be a part of the tedious conversation.

The rain had stopped somewhere along the line, but it had left behind bruised clouds above and a hazy atmosphere below. They passed a town called Eldorado, which according to the map in her lap meant they were on the last leg of their trip. When she had come from Chicago to Merri's house at the beginning of the summer, that had seemed like southern Illinois. But now they were entering the last county before Kentucky. Now they were really in southern Illinois.

The flat terrain planted in corn and soybeans at the beginning of the trip had given way to gentle green hills and then increasingly higher ones. And the map showed they would be entering the Shawnee National Forest soon. Trees were visible on the horizon, but in the near distance, men in huge earth-moving equipment worked the red clay. A sign on the right side of the highway said "Sherman Coal Company, Big Boy Mine." They were in coal country, all right. Sherman's sign nearly eclipsed Equality's welcome sign, which read "Village of Equality, Population 823."

Route 142 ended suddenly, morphing into Lane Street. But then orange sawhorses blocked their way, and a uniformed officer leaned against his squad car, its flashing red and blue lights doing little to add cheer to the afternoon.

"There must be an accident," Kate said.

"I don't see anything." John sat up suddenly and looked out the window, proving he hadn't really been asleep during the interminable conversation about the wedding.

"Faker," Abby whispered.

He turned and grinned at her.

Kate, curious as always, and not afraid to ask questions, stopped the car and lowered her window. A blast of super-charged, humidity-laden heat rushed into the car.

"What is it, officer?" she asked. "I hope no one is hurt."

The officer chuckled and stooped to look inside the car. His slow, easy grin and friendly, unworried demeanor was a little like Andy Griffith on the Classic TV Channel. "No one hurt so far," he said, his slow drawl rich with irony. "But we'll be on the lookout for sun stroke. Maybe heart burn or sugar-induced hyperactivity with the kiddies."

The others looked as confused as Abby felt until he added, "You must not be from around here. It's our annual Salt Festival."

She sat forward in her seat to see better. A little way beyond the roadblock people stood in the street, and a bright yellow banner, reading Salt Days Village of Equality, Illinois, established 1735, fluttered overhead.

"We're visiting," Kate said.

"Then welcome to Equality and have a good time, folks. You can park over that way."

"Thanks." Kate rolled the window up and turned left where he had pointed.

"I don't know what a salt festival is, but I don't care as long as they have funnel cakes," John said.

Kate turned to grin at John, looking as excited at the prospect as he did. "As soon as I find a parking spot we'll check it out."

Ryan mumbled something that sounded like,

"Disgusting."

Kate parked the car, and as they walked toward the festival she asked, "So where do we start, Abby? You're the expert."

"Well," Abby said, "we should start by just asking people if they've ever heard of the Greenfields. And then we'll find the courthouse and library."

"Shouldn't we see if your genealogy program is working?" Ryan asked.

"Not yet," Abby said. "We'll need to narrow our search first."

Ryan seemed to be satisfied with her answer and took the lead with Kate. John put his backpack on his shoulder and took Abby's hand. "Then all we have to do is look for the oldest buildings around," he said softly. "And then get in them without getting arrested for trespassing. And then time-surf in them without Rye noticing what we're doing. Easy- peasy. It'll be a snap."

"I know, I know," Abby said. "But I have to try. We'll just have to be ready to take any opportunities we find."

As they caught up with Ryan and Kate, a microphone squealed and then the sound of lively fiddle and banjo music came to them from somewhere down Lane Street.

Ryan called upon God's name, but not in devout petition. "What is that awful noise?"

Kate just smiled adoringly at him, apparently not noticing his blasphemy.

"Hey, watch it," John said. "And besides, that's not noise. It's bluegrass."

"I've never heard bluegrass before," Abby said. "But it's beautiful. Let's go see."

Lane Street was clogged with a small crowd of people who were milling around the stands that had been set up in the middle of the street. Various individuals and groups were selling refreshments and handmade crafts. Squealing kids were crawling over and into an inflated Disney castle, which seemed to be the biggest attraction on the street. And the smallest Ferris wheel Abby had ever seen peeked over the buildings from one street away. The scene was quaint, and Kate immediately pulled out her pad and began sketching.

The first stand they came to was labeled Gallatin County Tourism. The man behind the table wore a brass nametag that identified him as Mayor Windham. Abby wanted to ask him about the Greenfields, but he was explaining about tourist attractions in the area to a group of six or seven men who stood politely listening.

"Where y'all from?" Mayor Windham asked.

"Quincy," one man answered. His pale skin was sunburned as if he were seldom outdoors.

"We're camping over at Jones Lake," his friend said, picking up a brochure from the table. "Heard the fishing is good and came on down."

"Well, that's great, just great," the mayor said. "Welcome to Egypt." The mayor noticed Abby and her friends standing behind the fishermen and beckoned them forward. "Y'all may be wondering how we got that nickname," he continued with a wide smile. "Back in the 1830s when a drought sent many of our northern friends down to our area looking for grain, someone coined the phrase *Going Down to Egypt.* Just like the Hebrews did in the Bible—although we didn't require them to stay and make any pyramids." Mayor Windham laughed loudly at his joke.

"I noticed on the map that there are several towns in the region with Egyptian names," a fisherman said. "Like Karnac and Thebes and Cairo."

The mayor smiled proudly. "Right you are. Except we pronounce that last one like the syrup—Kay-ro."

"Really?" Ryan said, wearing a superior expression that Abby was coming to hate.

"And some claim the Ohio River Valley looks a bit like the Nile. Anyway, I'm so glad you came on down to visit. Equality was settled by the French in 1735, and the name comes from their motto, Liberté, égalité, fraternité. Egalité—that means equality."

The mayor's French was thickly overlaid with his southern Illinois accent, and it took Abby a moment to realize what he was saying. Ryan and Kate started to move away, but it didn't seem polite to leave during such an enthusiastic history lesson. Abby held onto John's arm to keep him there.

"The French remained in control of the area until the British won it in 1763. Then, during the Revolutionary War, George Rogers Clark and his band of Long Knives captured the region for the Americans in 1779."

Turning to the fishermen the mayor said, "The General Lawler Bed and Breakfast will be opening soon. Perhaps you gentlemen will bring your lovely wives next time you visit."

The fishermen seemed to be tired of the mayor's promotional spiel, and mumbling their thanks, they began to move away. It didn't stop the spiel.

"The Lawler family has provided the music today—The Eagle Creek Boys—and the rides. Not that you gentlemen are here for that, of course," he called after them, laughing again. "How about you young fellas?" Mayor Windham asked, holding up a roll of blue tickets to John. "You want to take your girlfriends for a spin on the Ferris wheel?"

Ryan and Kate had already followed the fishermen, and after gauging Abby's reaction, John said, "No thanks," and started to move away too.

"Wait a minute, John," Abby said and slipped her hand out of his. "Mr. Mayor, could you please direct us to the courthouse? We need to do some research."

The mayor smiled sadly. "I'm sorry, missy. We don't have a courthouse anymore."

"Isn't Equality the county seat?"

"We used to be," the mayor said. "But you see, back in 1850, Shawneetown stole all our court documents. Came in the night, they did, and plum stole 'em, and thus our position as the county seat. We're still mad about it. You can see where our courthouse once stood on the town square. It's right by our new water tower. We're very proud of it. And be sure to see the memorial for General Michael Kelly Lawler too. He was a hero for the Union in the Civil War. He was commander of the 18th Illinois Volunteer Infantry Regiment."

John tugged discreetly on her arm, and so Abby smiled at the mayor and said as she was being led away, "Thanks. We'll look for it."

"Even though he was wounded in the battle of Fort Donelson, General Lawler went on to fight with distinction at the Battle of Vicksburg, Port Gibson, and Big Black River Bridge."

Abby hurried to keep up with John.

"Later he secured the Atchafalaya River, used by the Confederacy to transport ammunition and men, and then he…"

Mayor Windham was still talking when they got to the next stand, sponsored by the Shawnee Telephone Company. A vinyl banner announced that high-speed DSL internet service had arrived in Equality and that Shawnee Telephone Company was at the leading edge of communications. Several people were discussing the new options.

John ducked around them and picked up a free telephone directory from the stack at the end of the table. Abby looked over his shoulder as he quickly flipped to the Gs. No Greenfields were listed. He put the directory back on the table and they moved on.

The group of fishermen was now being accosted at the next stand by a lanky, bearded young man, who begged them to sign his petition. But the fishermen walked on past. A sign was taped to the table that read, "Stop the Destruction! Don't Let Sherman Blow Up Any more Mountains."

The young man looked out of place among the other citizens of Equality. His longish hair, gold wire-rims, and beaded bracelet gave him a sort of neo-hippy look. He thrust a brochure into Abby's hand. "Please sign the petition," he implored. "And mark your calendars for our town hall meeting on the 27th."

Abby wanted to explain that they didn't live in the area and wouldn't be around for the meeting. But Ryan had already led Kate away, and so she and John hurried to catch up. Abby turned to smile apologetically over her shoulder at the worried young man.

The next stand they came to advertised "home-made goat soap," which sounded rather disgusting. But the bars of soap were prettily wrapped in colorful calico and tied with pink string. The proprietor was a dark-haired young woman whose beautifully smooth face was a good advertisement for her product. "Goat milk is really good for your skin," she said, smiling shyly at Abby. "I don't put any chemicals in any of my soaps."

Abby picked up a bar labeled "vanilla" and held it to her nose. "Come smell this, Kate. Wouldn't they make great Christmas gifts?"

Kate was busily sketching the soap maker. "Christmas? Someone remind Abby it's only August."

"Well, I can't help it." Abby grinned and then lowered her voice. "You know why I've been thinking of Christmas so much lately."

Kate looked up from her pad and grinned at Abby. Glancing slyly at John, who stood nearby patiently waiting to leave, she whispered, "Yeah, well, it's a pretty lame strategy to keep your mind off jumping him."

"What?" John said.

"Never mind." Abby glared at Kate and turned quickly back to the soap.

The young woman held out another bar. "A lot of folks are partial to my lavender mint."

"Oh, yes," Abby said. "I can see why. It's wonderful."

She went to John and held it to his nose. He inhaled appreciatively and said, "Get this one."

"I'll take one of the lavender mint and one vanilla," Abby said, taking out her wallet.

The woman's face lit up with a smile. "Y'all are not from around here." Her voice had a soft southern lilt and rose at the end, making the statement a question.

"No, we're here to do genealogy research," Abby said.

"We're hoping to find information about an ancestor of mine named Ned Greenfield," Kate added.

"So where's the library?" Ryan asked, adding "Miss" after a slight pause.

"Sorry, I can't help with your relative, but the library's on Lincoln Boulevard," the young woman said. "Right beside the Dollar Store. You can't miss it. It's—"

"Thanks," John said and pulled Abby away.

It took more time than she expected to work their way through the gauntlet of vendors and happy festival-goers. On the lookout for either the Dollar Store or the source of the music, they passed His and Hers Beauty Shop, the post office, and Anderson's, which appeared to be a combination grocery, household, and hardware store. A sign advertising Bunny Bread was painted on the side of the building. In front of it, a pretty blond teenage girl stood on the sidewalk smiling and waving to passersby. She wore a tiara and a blue sash over her dress that read Salt Queen.

Several area churches had set up food stands. The Catholic church sold brats along with raffle tickets for a quilt that was displayed behind the volunteers manning the stand. The Church of Christ had fried catfish, the proceeds of which were to go to a missionary in India. And the Social Brethren Church handed out free cotton candy along with gospel tracts.

The Methodist Church capitalized on its location right on Lane Street by conducting a cakewalk in front of the church. The glassed-in sign indicated their pastor was the Reverend Dwight Henderson and that they were celebrating their 200th anniversary.

Abby and John looked at each other at the same time. "Surely the building can't be that old," he said. "They must mean the entity is 200 years old."

"Right. The brick is too new. But if they built this building over the original church then we might be able to pick up enough vibes from it to time-surf."

John studied the church. "Maybe. It worked at the Lewis and Clark museum."

Ryan and Kate appeared to be giving no thought to any of the sights or sounds of the festival or anyone but themselves as they walked on ahead, holding hands and smiling.

"Quick, this may be our only chance," Abby said.

If they were lucky, Kate and Ryan would stay occupied, the church would be unlocked, and the sign would be right about Shawnee Telephone Company being on the cutting edge of technology—the kind that would allow John, with the help of the app Timmy Tech had given him, to borrow a little band width for time-surfing.

It was a lot to ask, but if Merri was right about God wanting them to use the program to help Kate…well, after all, nothing was impossible with God. Abby sent up a little prayer and followed John.

Spectators in front of the church were laughing at one of the cakewalk contestants who was blatantly cheating so he could win his wife's German chocolate cake. No one appeared to notice when Abby and John walked past them and up to the church's double front doors.

They opened easily, and Abby said a prayer of thanks as they stepped into a dim foyer. A bulletin board with photos of missionaries and children's drawings of Noah's ark hung on the wall. Under it was a table laden with bulletins, pamphlets, and stacks of hymnbooks. Taking his backpack off his shoulder, John hurried past it all and went through the inner doors that led into the sanctuary.

Abby liked the simple, spare décor. The walls were a creamy white and the floor a dark oak. Light streamed in from three plain windows on each side. A small round stained glass window glowed high on the back wall behind the pulpit.

A large painting of Jesus as the Good Shepherd hung on one wall. Another famous painting, one Abby disliked because it made Jesus look like a wimpy whiner, hung on the opposite wall.

They sat down in the last row on a pew padded in deep burgundy. John took his laptop out and began loading *Beautiful Houses*. "Do you think this could be the original building after all?" he said. "Maybe they just bricked over it."

"I was wondering the same thing."

"Don't get your hopes up, Abby. Even if the church is old enough for Ned Greenfield's era…"

"If he wasn't a member, time-surfing here won't do us any good. I know. But let's see what happens. I have a feeling this is right."

The program sprang to life.

CHAPTER 7

Reverend Farris held his hands up and smiled out upon the congregation. "Receive now the Lord's benediction."

In the third row, John Granger reverently bowed his head and hoped he could get down the aisle in time to catch Lawler before he left the church.

"'Now may the God of peace, our Lord Jesus, that great shepherd of the sheep, through the blood of the everlasting covenant, make you perfect in every good work to do his will, working in you that which is well pleasing in his sight, through Jesus Christ, to whom be glory forever and ever. Amen.'"

Reverend Farris descended from his pulpit and, straightening his black robe, hurried down the center aisle toward the church door where he would greet each departing parishioner.

Granger stood and offered his wife his arm. She took it and rose decorously from the pew. "Hurry along, Martha," he said. "I need to talk to Michael before they leave."

Fellow worshipers crowded into the aisle to leave, but nevertheless he managed to steer his wife on a course that took them to where their son-in-law stood with their daughter Elizabeth and the two children.

Michael Lawler bent his head and said something to Elizabeth and then stepped away from her side. Martha dutifully went to join Elizabeth and the children.

"What do you want?" Lawler asked. "If it's about that scheme of yours to—"

"Keep your voice down," Granger said.

Elizabeth and Martha looked up. Granger frowned at them and they turned away. "Not that. Come out to Hickory Hill this afternoon while the women are napping. I need your legal expertise. I have a little problem that—"

"Is there something I can help you with?"

Abby jolted back to the present. A middle-aged man dressed in black stood in the aisle looking at them and their computer. John shut it and they rose awkwardly.

"Oh, I was checking—"

Abby jabbed her elbow into John's side because it sounded like he was about to break the eighth commandment. In church, no less.

"E-mail? I check mine a dozen times a day," the man said, chuckling.

"The church is beautiful," Abby said. "Are you the pastor here?"

"Yes," he said, extending his hand. "Dwight Henderson. Glad to meet you."

They rose and John introduced Abby and himself. "Not e-mail," he said with a smile for Reverend Henderson and a small discreet jab of his elbow into her side. "I have this program that keeps going on the fritz. Thought I'd see if it was working."

"We try to leave the door open as much as we can for folks to come in when they need to." Reverend Henderson grinned. "Mostly had in mind praying, but still."

"Don't you worry about thieves?" Abby asked.

"It used to be we didn't need to worry too much about that. Of course, we're too young to remember those days. Most every church had an open door policy at one time. But now that crooks have sunk so low as to rob offering plates and loot sanctuaries—so low as to bomb a church in Alabama during Sunday School. Well, anyway, we take precautions nowadays. But that's a dreary subject. Why don't you come on by tomorrow? We'd love to have you worship with us."

They thanked him for the invitation, saying they weren't sure what their plans were for Sunday. Reverend Henderson sent them on their way with a smile and God's blessing.

"Sorry for the jab," Abby said when they stepped out onto the sidewalk.

"I wasn't going to lie. Give me a little credit, okay?"

"I said I was sorry."

John put an arm around her and pulled her close to his side as they started down Lane Street. "Guess I should thank you for watching out for my immortal soul." Abby turned her face up hoping for a kiss, but he just grinned and kissed her hair. "That's the only P.D.A. you're getting from me in the middle of the street."

"If only we'd had a little more time, maybe we'd have found Ned Greenfield."

"Yeah," he said. "Too bad. Just when Hickory Hill came up."

"I'm confused," she said. "That Granger guy owned

Hickory Hill."

"At least in 1853," he said. "Maybe he bought it from Greenfield."

"Mayor Windham would be so proud to know we met his hero, the famous General Lawler—well, soon-to-be hero, anyway."

Kate and Ryan were no longer in sight, and so they hurried past the rest of the craft and food stands on Lane Street, which turned out to be only two blocks long. It ended at the intersection with Calhoun Avenue with a muddy, rock-studded ravine. Abby wasn't thrilled about going near the edge, but John coaxed her over to see.

"It looks like storms washed out the street," he said. "I wonder why no one ever repaired it."

Across the ravine, the road resumed, and Abby saw what looked like a school along with more houses. No doubt there was access via another road, but she couldn't see it from where they stood.

"The street must have been very steep. It's no wonder it gave way."

A voice behind them called out, "Be careful there!"

Abby spun around so fast she nearly stumbled, but John put out a steadying hand and she grabbed it. The police officer they had met coming into town was walking toward them, a cigarette hanging from the corner of his mouth.

"You'd better step back," he said.

"Sorry, officer," John said, taking a step away from the edge.

Abby read his brass name badge and added, "That is, Chief Logan."

"Lane Street used to go on down the hill and out to the Half Moon. Equality was a booming little town back in the day when salt was king." Chief Logan drew on his cigarette and contemplated the washout. "Now, the mines closed down, and there aren't enough funds to rebuild the street. Ironic, huh? The Red Onion used to be down that way in the old days. It was sort of a—" He stopped suddenly and looked apologetic. "But you don't want to hear about that. Are you having a good time today?"

"We are," Abby answered. "But actually we didn't come for the salt festival. We're trying to help a friend trace her roots. Do you know of any Greenfields living around here?"

"I do," he answered.

Abby waited for him to go on. When he didn't, she said, "Can you tell us where they live?"

"I could." Chief Logan turned away to blow out a stream of cigarette smoke. "But if your friend's the young lady with you in the car, I don't reckon the Greenfields I know are the Greenfields you're looking for."

Abby frowned, but before she could ask more, John changed the subject. "Kate's ancestor apparently lived at a place called Hickory Hill. Do you know where that is?"

Chief Logan dropped his cigarette on the pavement and ground it out with the toe of his shoe. "Can't help you there." He started to walk away.

"Who could we ask?" Abby said. "Surely someone around here would know."

He turned to study them. "There's nothing there to see. Why don't you go on over to the square and learn about General Lawler. Listen to Eagle Creek play. They're just a local band, but we're proud of them." Giving them a little salute, he walked a short way down Calhoun Street, then crossed over and went into the municipal building.

"What was that all about?" John asked.

"I don't know, but it was weird." Abby took his arm. "Come on. Let's go find Kate and Ryan."

Up ahead they saw the shiny, new water tower that the mayor had bragged about and the band playing bluegrass music in its shade. Most listeners sat on lawn chairs. Others stood in back, including Ryan and Kate, who was busily sketching the scene on her pad.

Abby started toward them, but John held her back. "Wait," he said, pointing to the right. "Look at that. It's got to be old. Really old."

The huge two-story building John had spotted was nearly hidden by tall trees. It was made of brick, time-weathered to a beautiful rosy shade, and had seven sets of tall windows across its front. Someone had used black spray paint on a piece of plywood to make a sign that said, "General Lawler Bed and Breakfast Opening Soon." A wheelbarrow full of remodeling debris stood next to the front door, which was propped open with a length of two-by-four.

It was surely too large to be an ordinary home and too plain to be a rich man's mansion. It looked more like a hotel, but whatever it had been, a building that old was sure to have a history.

"Looks like the perfect place for a little time-surfing," she said.

"Not so fast," he said grabbing her arm. "Obviously, someone's there."

She slithered out of his grasp and went up to the door. "I don't think so. Look."

A yellow post-it note was stuck on the doorframe advising someone named Zeke to put the drywall in the kitchen and that he'd be back at four o'clock. She grinned at John. "This seems to be our lucky day for time-surfing."

John stuck his head in the door and then went in, already taking out his laptop.

"Opening Soon" seemed a little optimistic. Paint cans

still sat on drop cloths, and an over-sized ladder stood against one wall where someone was trying either to remove the wallpaper or to re-glue the loose strips of it that hung from the wall.

They decided the best place to sit was on the stairs. *Beautiful Houses* took its time to load, and when it did, nothing happened—that is, nothing other than that the houses began scrolling by as usual. The old house they sat in wasn't one of them.

"We may be too far from an internet connection," John said.

Abby pointed to the indicator at the bottom right of the screen. "No, that's not it. You're online. Do you think the program's broken again?"

"I hope not," John said.

After a minute she said, "If Merri's theory is right about the program only working when it wants us to learn something it wants us to know…"

"As crazy as that sounds, I'm beginning to believe it." John put the laptop back in his backpack and pulled Abby to her feet. "Come on. We might as well go."

"Yes, I don't want to be here when the three bears come home."

The crowd was still enjoying the music on the town square, but Kate and Ryan had moved on. In reality, what Mayor Windham had referred to as the town square was no more than a grassy area with Calhoun and Jackson Streets forming a roundabout. There were no buildings there, nothing to indicate Equality's business district had once extended that far. But Abby could picture a time when it had, when the square was lively with people shopping and horse-drawn buggies and wagons clattering by.

They found the memorial for Equality's favorite son at the edge of the square. The brass bas-relief sculpture of

Michael Kelly Lawler didn't do him justice, but then how could an image in stone or metal capture the real living, breathing man? A brass plaque below the sculpture said pretty much what Mayor Windham had already told them.

Steps led up to a stone platform where visitors could sit on benches flanked by flower-filled urns to contemplate the general and his military exploits. Kate and Ryan were sitting on one of the benches, Kate bent over her sketchpad and Ryan sourly watching the audience. He didn't seem to be enjoying the music any more than he had earlier.

"There you are," Kate said, looking up from her drawing. "Where have you two been?"

Ryan, arms folded across his chest, turned from scanning the audience to glance at them.

Abby angled her body away from him. "I'll tell you later," she said softly.

When she turned back to watch the band, she saw that Ryan wore a sneering smile, and she realized that he had overheard her and obviously come to the wrong conclusion about their delay.

"We struck out with the courthouse," Abby said. She explained to Kate and Ryan what the mayor had told them. "Also, there are no Greenfields listed in the phone directory, and the police chief was disinclined to tell us where to find the ones he knew."

"Or where to find Hickory Hill," John added.

"Why on earth not?" Ryan asked. "He seemed like the helpful sort."

"He went from nice to weird just like that," Abby said, snapping her fingers.

"Makes you wonder what he's covering up," John said. "Did you guys find the library?"

"Not so far," Kate said. "We kind of got sidetracked here."

They had a clear view of the Eagle Creek band from their elevated position. One bald guy played an upright bass in back. A man wearing a black suit and a huge white hat played a banjo. Two guys played guitars. And a young woman stood with a violin at her side. They all sang into microphones, harmonizing in a way that was unlike anything Abby had ever heard.

"I love it," she said. "Different, but I love it."

"They're playing Uncle Penn," John said over the music. "It's an old Bill Monroe tune straight out of Appalachia. They're pretty darn good, too."

"Why is that one guy playing his guitar sideways?" Kate asked, pointing with her sketchbook.

"It's a dobro," John said. "Not a guitar."

Violin in hand, the young woman stepped forward, and Abby realized it was the Salt Queen they'd seen earlier, still wearing her tiara and sash. She put the violin under her chin and began to play an intricate counterpoint to the other instruments. The guy playing the guitar, a bearded man wearing a plaid shirt, smiled up at her.

"She's really good on that violin," Abby said.

John put an arm around her shoulders and laughed. "Yes, but don't let her hear you calling her fiddle a violin."

When the song was finished Abby joined in the applause and waited eagerly to hear what they'd play next. But then the musicians began putting their instruments in cases at their feet on the grass.

She sighed. "I guess we got here just in time for it to end."

"Maybe it's just as well," Kate said. "If we're ever going to find the library—"

"And the funnel cakes," John added.

Beyond the square, more vendors' stands beckoned, and Ryan, with Kate in tow, started toward them.

At one stand, Abby bought a jar of homemade raspberry jam from a man with nothing much to say and at another a necklace made of tiny woven ribbons from a woman who had plenty to say. Tragically for John, there were no funnel cake stands.

The little Ferris wheel marked the end of the festival, and John suggested they go up in it, that maybe they'd be high enough to spot the library. But there was a long line of people waiting to ride. To get tickets they'd have to walk all the way back to the mayor's stand and listen to another spiel, not something any of them cared to be subjected to again. Abby wished they'd asked the mayor for directions right off, but none of them had expected it to be so difficult to find the library in such a tiny village.

As they stood there discussing what to do next, the Salt Queen came bouncing down the crumbling sidewalk toward them. As she got closer, Abby estimated her age at fifteen or sixteen.

Abby smiled at her. "I loved your music. I'm sorry I didn't get to hear more."

"Thanks," the girl said. "But if y'all are going to be around, we'll be playing 'til dark. We're just taking a break."

"Pardon us, Your Highness," John said with a courtly bow, "We are from a distant land and know not of this salt festival. Can you tell us about it?"

She laughed and curtsied to him. "I guess I'd better be able to," she answered, winking at them. "It's part of my job description, after all. But can y'all walk with me as I tell you? I need to check on my grandma up yonder before I go back to fiddling on the square."

Just ahead on the right, a small house covered in gray asphalt shingles stood in the shade of a mulberry tree. A small wooden table sat crookedly on the sloping sidewalk in front. Abby couldn't tell what was on the table, but she and the others followed as the girl continued on down the sidewalk toward it.

"You see," the girl began, "salt was really important around here—since way back—because of the salt springs. You can see buffalo trails all over the place, if you know where to look. The Half Moon Salt Mine just outside of town is named for the crescent-shaped indentation where for thousands of years mastodons, buffalo, and other animals came to lick the salty soil. The Piankashaw and later the Shawnee Indian tribes made salt at the springs using clay evaporation bowls. They traded the salt to other Native American tribes in the area and as far away as Cahokia and Peoria. You can see evidence of their presence by the pottery shards, arrowheads, and other cool artifacts they left behind. Thomas Jefferson considered our salt springs national treasures. And in the early years after Illinois became a state in 1818, as much as one-seventh of the state's revenues came from the sale of salt. Unfortunately for us, the saline content of the spring eventually declined until it became unprofitable to manufacture salt here."

When the girl paused for a breath, Abby said, "Wow, you're an excellent salt queen."

"You could say," John said, "she's worth her salt."

"Why thank you," she said, smiling again at John. "I'm glad you know that saying. Which, as you probably already know, comes from the fact that it was such a valuable commodity that people were often paid in salt. We get the word salary from the word salt. Our Saline River flows into the Ohio, and Saline County is just next door." She stopped suddenly and grinned sheepishly. "I'm sorry. I tend to get carried away. That was probably more than you ever wanted to know about salt."

"No, that was great," Abby said. "I love learning about stuff like that."

When they got to the table in front of the little gray house, Abby saw that jars of some amber-colored substance stood in rows on it. Beside them, colorful handmade potholders were fanned out, each cleverly designed and expertly stitched. "They're like little quilts," she said, picking up one fashioned from coordinating blue and white fabrics. "Look at the workmanship."

"Aren't they darling?" Kate said. A hand-lettered sign made from a brown paper grocery bag taped to the side of the table indicated the potholders were two dollars each.

"Thank you, ma'am," the Salt Queen said.

"You made these?" Abby asked.

"Yep. My grandma taught me to sew. She's minding the stand while I fiddle."

John picked up one of the jars and studied it. "Maybe I'll get some of this honey for my dad." He looked around. "Do I pay you or your grandma?"

Abby heard a creaking sound coming from the porch. An elderly woman she had not noticed before was rising from a porch swing. "Sold three while you were gone, Patty Ann," she said as she trudged slowly down the front walk toward them.

"Hey, Grandma," the girl said, walking forward to put an arm around the old woman's waist. "I thought you'd gone on in to look at TV. This is my Grandma Ethel Frailey."

After Abby introduced herself and the others, Patty Ann said to John, "That's sorghum, not honey. My dad makes it."

"I've never heard of it." Ryan said it as if he doubted her since he hadn't been aware of sorghum before. "What is it for?"

Patty Ann looked shocked at his ignorance. "For putting on your biscuits," she said kindly as if she were dealing with a particularly slow child. "I like it on leftover cornbread too."

"Do you live nearby, Patty Ann?" Abby asked.

"No. We live out in the hills. Least ways for now."

"Do you ladies mind if I draw you?" Kate asked, turning to a fresh page in her sketchpad.

"I don't mind," Patty Ann said. "Do you, Grandma?"

Nodding her permission, the old woman looked solemnly at Kate.

"Smile," Kate said, already starting to draw.

"She's not wearing her teeth today," Patty Ann explained.

"You're an artist, too," Abby said, turning back to the potholders on the table. "These are all so great. I don't know which ones to choose."

"Why, thank you." Patty Ann said it from the corner of her mouth as she stood beside her grandma trying not to move.

Finally, John decided on two jars of sorghum, and Abby picked out several of the potholders. They laid their money on the table, but Abby felt a bit like a bandit for paying such a small sum for the little works of art.

"Kathryn, you'd better hurry," Ryan said. "if we're ever going to find that library." He turned to Patty Ann. "Are we close?"

"I wouldn't plan on walking if I were you," she said with a twinkle in her eyes.

"Well, we've walked this far."

"It's your business, of course. But the nearest library is ten miles away in Shawneetown."

"But the goat woman said it was by the Dollar Store."

Patty Ann, obviously forgetting about posing for Kate, drew herself up to her full height and turned to glare at him. "That's Mrs. Barnett. She must have assumed you'd realize that a village the size of Equality couldn't possibly support a public library—or a Dollar Store—and that Equality citizens use the library—and Dollar Store—in Shawneetown, which is the nearest real town." She looked at her watch. "But it's closed now, so you'll have to wait until Monday." There was a hint of satisfaction in her voice.

Ethel cackled behind her hand. "Now, Patty Ann, you be nice to our visitors."

Abby held back a laugh herself when she saw that Ryan had received Patty Ann's message loud and clear and was looking a little chastened.

"Why can't we go to the library tomorrow?" Ryan asked.

"It's Sunday, Rye," John said. "Libraries are closed on Sundays."

"How should I know that? I buy all my books."

"What about restaurants?" John asked hopefully. "I don't suppose...." He put the sorghum and Abby's potholders in his backpack and zipped it closed.

No doubt John sincerely wanted to know, but he was also obviously trying to change the subject. She'd have to give him a star for diplomacy.

"Sure, we've got a restaurant," Patty Ann answered with a small sniff. "The Red Onion on Lane Street."

"How do we get across the ravine?" John asked.

A loud boom sounded and then a series of smaller ones followed. They all automatically ducked at the sudden noise, John drawing Abby close to his side. A dog started barking from inside the gray house. It sounded like the small yapping type.

Ryan swore, but had the grace to look apologetically toward Patty Ann and Ethel. "What on earth was that?"

"Just Sherman doing some more blasting," Patty Ann said. Her expression was one of deep sadness as she looked at her grandmother.

"Don't you worry so, Patty Ann." The old woman pulled her granddaughter into a hug. "Remember, God's going to make all things new again one day."

"I know, Grandma." Patty Ann drew away from her and said, "Well, you'd better go in and calm Brownie down. I've got to get back to fiddling."

"Let's go listen," Abby said.

"I'm game," Kate said. "I want to do some more sketches."

"After we eat," John said.

Kate tore the sketch she'd made from her pad. "Here you go," she said, handing it to Patty Ann.

The girl studied the drawing and then looked up in amazement at Kate. "You're good, really good." She held it up for Ethel to see. "Look, Grandma, you've got an actual portrait done by an actual artist."

The old woman forgot to be embarrassed about her toothless state and smiled happily at Kate. "Patty Ann, you'll have to make me a frame for it. We'll hang it in the living room next to your grandpa's picture."

As always, Kate's talent amazed Abby. Her sketch of Ethel and Patty Ann captured their love for each other and, beyond that, their strength and pride. Ethel was still smiling at the sketch when they left, and her dog Brownie was still yapping.

CHAPTER 8

The Red Onion Restaurant was behind the inflatable Disney castle with its flock of laughing kids, which was why they had missed it earlier. When they stepped through the doorway, a blast of cool air hit them. Abby sighed in relief and vowed that no matter what was on the menu, she was staying as long as possible.

A waitress smiled and said, "Sit anywhere you like." John held the door for a pair of ladies coming in after them, and the waitress's smile super-sized. One lady had white hair permed high and wore a turquoise T-shirt adorned with rhinestone-studded birdhouses. The outfit looked like one the Old Dears would favor, and Abby smiled to herself.

"You want sweet tea, Bernice, Alma?" the waitress asked as she hurried past, the wooden floor creaking under her feet.

"You read my mind, Shireen," the birdhouse woman called after her. "We're parched."

The place was nearly full, but Ryan led the way to an

empty booth near the back. He stood while Kate slid in next to the wall, and Abby and John followed their lead. The artificial wood grain was nearly rubbed off the tabletop, but the seats were comfortable. The tall ceiling overhead was of vintage pressed tin and gave the room a quaint charm.

Abby looked around with interest. Three guys in matching work shirts and John Deere caps glanced her way but turned, almost shyly, back to their meal. She smiled at the young woman at the table next to theirs, who nodded a return greeting and went back to dealing out french fries to her three small children.

Kate handed everyone menus from the rack in front of her. Studying the selection, Abby made a bet with herself that Ryan would choose the chef salad as the least objectionable item.

"Oh, they've got corndogs," Kate said. But when the waitress returned, she ordered the chef salad after a regretful look at Ryan.

Abby went for the cheeseburger, and John chose a catfish sandwich.

"How can you eat that?" Ryan asked. "Do you realize catfish are scavengers, bottom feeders?"

John just rolled his eyes and smiled apologetically to the waitress while Ryan continued to frown over the menu. The waitress shifted from one foot to the other until Ryan finally looked up and said, "I'll have the chef salad also. With vinaigrette dressing. Only please bring the dressing on the side."

Abby awarded herself ten points.

"What are you smiling about?" John asked.

"I'm just happy," she said.

"Miss?" Kate said, "I wonder if you could help us?"

"Why sure," the waitress answered. "I'd be glad to if I can."

"I'm trying to find some relatives of mine. Do you know of any Greenfields around here?"

Putting her pen and pad back in her apron pocket, she cocked her head and thought for a moment. "I don't think so. Not in town anyway. You could ask Chief Logan. He knows pretty nearly everyone out in the hills."

"We already did," Abby said.

"Mayor Windham may know."

When the waitress left, Ryan scanned the restaurant with a sneer barely disguised as a smile. "Can you believe these hoosiers wearing their gimme caps indoors? Obviously no one taught them manners."

"Do you really think so?" John asked.

Kate seemed to be wearing blinders when it came to Ryan. Or maybe she was not the real Kate at all. Maybe all those stories about alien abductions were true. In any case, the Kate Abby knew and loved would never condone disparaging others.

"You might want to try the style yourself, Ryan," John said. "A cap covers a multitude of sins."

"What do you mean?" Ryan worriedly ran his hands over his hair and then rose suddenly. "Excuse me, Kathryn, Abby. I'll be right back," he said, heading toward the rear of the restaurant.

"John!" Abby said. "What is wrong with you?"

"Please don't tease him about his hair," Kate said. "He hates it if it gets messed up."

John made a face. "I know, I know. I'm sorry for acting so juvenile."

But it was hard to be too annoyed with John, since his comment had made Ryan leave. "So anyway, Kate, you asked where John and I were. Well, we managed to do a little time-surfing in the Methodist Church while you and Ryan were making goo-goo eyes."

"So it's working? Did you find Ned?"

"Yes, it's working. No, we did not find Ned. But we did hear Hickory Hill mentioned."

"The thing is," John said, "A guy named John Granger owned it—at least he did at one time."

"We saw the famous General Lawler too," Abby said. "He was related by marriage to Granger."

"We would have surfed more to see when the Greenfields lived at Hickory Hill, but Reverend Henderson came in and we had to leave."

"Quiet," Abby said. "Here comes Ryan."

"But what are we going to do next?" Kate whispered.

"I don't know. John and I will think of something. And, John? Try to behave, will you?"

"I promise. To try."

"Ryan, you got back just in time," Kate said. "Here comes our food."

Ryan picked all the ham out of his salad, and Abby wondered how he ever got enough protein to survive. Her burger was wonderful, much better than the one at McDonald's earlier, and she learned a new adjective to describe it when one of the cap-wearing customers thanked the waitress and told her his burger was "larrapin' good." She made a mental note to look that up and add it to her list of interesting words when she got home. She studied the chalkboard on the wall across from them where someone had listed the desserts. She was torn between chocolate pie, peach cobbler, and apple crumb cake.

Ryan dabbed at his lips, folded his napkin precisely, and placed it next to his plate. "So when do we set up the computer?"

Abby struggled to find an answer that wasn't a lie and finally settled for, "It's still a little too early for that."

"Why? We're getting nowhere without it," Ryan said.

"It's not exactly working right," Kate said, "But Abby and John found a clue about Hickory Hill. We need to do some more asking around."

"Is it working or isn't it, Kathryn? Because if it's not, there's no use sticking around here. Give me your keys and I'll drive. You can nap on the way home."

"Home? We're not going home," Kate said, making no move to hand over her keys. "And I'm not tired."

"Obviously, the day has been a complete waste," Ryan said. "And if the library and courthouse are as hoosier as everything else around here we won't find—"

"Well, I'm not going home until I've tried," Kate said.

"So, we're going to hang around here all day tomorrow doing what?"

"Asking about Ned Greenfield and Hickory Hill. Besides, it's picturesque. Think of it as a vacation."

"Why didn't we think to ask Patty Ann or her grandma?" John said.

Abby smacked the side of her head. "Duh. It didn't even occur to me."

Ryan heaved a sigh and got out his wallet. "Okay, let's go see if we have any better luck finding Mayor Windbag Windham than we did the library."

In spite of Abby and Kate's efforts to go Dutch, the guys insisted on paying. As they left Abby gave one last longing look at the list of desserts and followed them out onto the hot sidewalk.

"Y'all come again now," the waitress called after them.

The sun was lower in the sky than Abby had expected it to be. They'd have to get busy if the day wasn't to be a waste.

"You know, I think I'd better use the restroom before we go," she said.

"Okay," John said. "We'll wait for you here."

Abby willed Kate to look up, but she was smiling all gooey at Ryan again, probably trying to pacify him. So she cleared her throat and said, "Kate, are you coming?"

Kate snapped out of it and immediately got the message. "Oh. Yeah. Me too. I'll be right back."

Ryan heaved a sigh and looked at his watch. "All right. Try to hurry."

Abby and Kate hurried back into the Red Onion and edged past diners to the ladies' room in the back hall. As soon as the door shut behind them, Kate grabbed her arms. "Okay, what do we do now?"

"You take Ryan and ask around about Ned Greenfield and Hickory Hill. See if Mayor Windham's still around. John and I will try to get back inside the church. We'll meet up with you as soon as we can at the square."

"All right, but, Abby?"

"Yes?"

"I don't know how long I can hold off telling Ryan. I won't lie to him."

"I'm not asking you to do that. Just try not to give it away, okay?"

CHAPTER 9

The sidewalk in front of the Methodist church was clear, all traces of the earlier cakewalk removed. Unfortunately, this meant there was not a handy crowd there to blend in with. It also probably meant the church would be locked up.

As Abby expected, the door didn't budge. John seemed unconcerned. Checking to see no one was watching, he took her hand and led her around to the side of the church. "There's an exterior basement door. I noticed it earlier."

The church's foundation was made of hand-hewn limestone blocks, another indication the building was older than its facade implied. Matching stone stairs led down to a whitewashed wooden door for the church's walk-out basement.

"It will be locked too," Abby whispered.

"Probably. Although it looks so decrepit I could blow it open with one breath."

"John! You're not going to break in?"

He looked pained. "There you go again. Have a little

faith, girlie."

He started to sit on the bottom step, but Abby remembered she had a napkin in her purse and used it to wipe off some of the dirt and leaves. The steps were small and they were scrunched together, but she didn't mind. While the program launched, she took the opportunity to lean on John's shoulder.

"Do you think it will work?"

"I'm hoping we're close enough to the original building to pick up vibes."

A blur of images filled the screen and she got an immediate headache. "Oh, great," she said. "Just like at Shake Rag Corner."

John stood and went to hold the laptop against the basement door, which wiggled when he touched it, confirming that they could open it with little effort. The program snapped out of its funk into brilliant living color. Abby was grateful they wouldn't have to be tempted by the flimsy door.

It was nearly dark, and the broom Pauly carried was taller than he was. He took care to hold it close to his skinny chest so it wouldn't trip him on the icy stone steps. The door at the bottom wasn't closed all the way and he put his right eye up to it and peeked in. Two white ladies with lanterns were fussing over something in a crate. He heard Jim huffing behind him and jumped back guiltily.

Jim's black face was sweaty even though the December air was cold, and the tendons on his neck stood out as he wheeled the coal scuttle toward the steps.

"Get that door open for me, boy. Can't you see I'm coming?"

"They is ladies in there."

Jim eased the scuttle carefully down each step with a soft grunt. It wouldn't do to spill coal all over Preacher Farris's clean white snow right before the Christmas pageant. When he reached the bottom, he went to the door and took a quick look.

"They gettin' the Christmas doo-dads ready. We best wait 'til they go back upstairs." He sat on the bottom step and opened up his coat. "Come here, boy, else you freeze where you stand."

Pauly went to stand next to Jim and allowed him to fold him into his warmth. "Will they have a Christmas tree, do you think? I ain't never saw a Christmas tree, but Lil saw Miz Granger's last year up at the big house."

"Hush your foolishness, boy. That ain't for the likes of us." Jim dug into his pocket and pulled out a baked potato and handed it to him. "It's still warm. Put it in your pocket, and it'll keep your hands from freezing."

"Listen!" Pauly said.

Jim smiled and pulled his coat closer around the boy. "Ah, the choir's done started they practicing."

Pauly burrowed up out of Jim's coat and stood transfixed as the music floated down to where they waited in the gloaming to unload the coal. The words were clear as the crisp air, sung by ladies with high, pure voices, and gentlemen with low, mellow ones. Although he had no idea of their meaning, the words washed over him, filling him with happiness.

"What they be singin', Jim?"

"That song's called Joy to the World. Sounds like angels, don't it? When we get to Heaven we'll be a-singin' with 'em, I reckon," Jim said with a chuckle.

Pauly wiped the snot from his nose and looked up at Jim. "Don't you know, Jim? Negroes don't go to Heaven."

He patted Jim's arm. "Miz Granger, she say Negroes don't got no souls."

"You come here right now, boy." Jim frowned at him and Pauly was scared he meant to thrash him. Jim pulled him close and stared into his eyes. "You listen to me, Pauly. That's a big, fat lie, and don't you believe it." He shook him. "You got a soul just like them white folks, you hear? Preacher Edmunds need to give you a Jesus talk."

Jim set the boy aside, hauled himself up from the step, and went back to peek in the door. The ladies had left, so he opened it wide and then guided the scuttle over the threshold and into the church basement.

"Come along, boy. See that you sweep up all the coal dust."

Pauly blinked three times and then picked up his broom and followed Jim.

Flashing red and blue lights streamed down into the dark stairwell where Abby and John sat, and they looked at each other in alarm. While John closed his laptop, she crawled up two steps and looked out. One block down, Chief Logan was putting the orange barricades he had used to block off Lane Street into the trunk of his cruiser. Amazingly, all the vendors had cleared out while they were time-surfing. The only sign left of the Salt Festival was the yellow banner overhead and the sound of Eagle Creek's bluegrass drifting to them on the evening breeze.

The warm evening breeze. Abby rubbed the chill out of her arms and reminded herself that it was August, not December.

After shouldering his backpack, John joined her on the step. Chief Logan closed the trunk and got in the cruiser.

His brake lights came on, and then he turned onto Lane Street toward them. They ducked back into the stairwell until he was past.

"Come on," John said, taking her hand. "Let's go find Kate and Turner before they report us missing."

Abby pulled her hand out of his. "Wait just one minute." She dug in her purse for a tissue, but couldn't find one. "I need a second before I go charging back into the 21st century."

"Here." John pulled a genuine, old-fashioned handkerchief from his pocket and handed it to her.

Who knew they even still made those? She wiped her eyes and nose and then tucked it into her own pocket. John drew her into his arms, and they stood for a moment swaying to the distant music.

"Can you imagine?" She swallowed and willed herself not to cry. "Can you imagine being told you have no soul? How can people warp the Scriptures so out of shape?"

"And I thought it was bad when Mr. White told his wife that women weren't made in the image of God."

"You're a good man, John Roberts." She took a deep breath and expelled it. "Okay. I can do this now." She took his hand and they started down the street.

Patty Ann and the other members of Eagle Creek were just putting their instruments away when she and John got to the square. Most of the audience was gone. Others were folding their lawn chairs or already on their way back to their cars.

Kate and Ryan rushed toward them, their faces mirroring alarm. "Where have you been?" Kate said, taking Abby's arm.

"Looking for clues," Abby answered.

"Right." Ryan rolled his eyes and heaved a disgusted sigh. "Well, while you two were out looking for clues—

that's a new one—we lost our accommodations for the night."

"What do you mean, Turner? You reserved the rooms, didn't you?" John said.

"Ryan called the Shawnee Chief just now just to be sure. We missed the check-in deadline. They gave our rooms to other people."

"We'll find something else," Abby said.

"Apparently not," Kate said. "We checked. Unless we want to drive 49.6 miles to Carbondale, which would take over an hour. We might as well go back to Merri's for the night."

"You could stay with us." Patty Ann, Salt Festival Queen, held her instrument case in one hand, while removing her tiara with the other. "It's not fancy, but we've got room for you."

"That is so kind of you," Abby said. "But we couldn't just barge in on your family."

"Why not?" Patty Ann looked puzzled, as if everyone knew that the rules of hospitality included inviting perfect strangers into your home for the night. "My parents won't care."

"Won't care about what, sugar?" The man in the plaid shirt who had played the guitar next to Patty Ann came up, case in hand, and put an arm around the girl's shoulder.

"This is my dad Benjamin Frailey," she said. "Dad, these are the folks I was tellin' you about. They need a place to stay for the night."

"Okay, then," he said simply. "Why don't you go get your car and follow us. Stay close. The roads can be confusing at night."

Apparently, the rules of hospitality—at least in Gallatin County—did include inviting perfect strangers into your home for the night. Abby had a feeling the Fraileys would be insulted if they didn't take them up on the invitation.

John and the others didn't look thrilled, but what choice did they really have? "Thanks, Patty Ann," she said.

Mr. Frailey was right about the road. It grew increasingly narrower as it dipped and turned through the hills south of Equality. And the trees grew thicker and closed in on both sides of them as they entered the Shawnee National Forest. Abby reassured herself they'd be able to find their way back to civilization with the GPS on Kate's PT Cruiser.

The right taillight on Mr. Fraileys' truck was out. Now the truck's single working taillight gave the impression they were following a motorcycle.

Kate didn't seem to be bothered by the less-than-safe driving conditions. As she drove, she filled them in on what she and Ryan had learned while Abby and John had been time-surfing. It wasn't much. Mayor Windham had not known of any Greenfields in the area. When they changed the subject to Hickory Hill, his smile had grown chilly, and he told them the same thing Chief Logan had: "There's nothing there for you to see." Then he had hurried away, mumbling something about seeing to the vendors.

"What about you two?" Ryan asked. "What clues did you discover?"

Abby let John field Ryan's snarky question while she called Merri to fill her in on their discoveries. At least she would have filled her in, except she couldn't get a signal for her phone.

John was giving a creative version of their own investigative work when Ryan shouted and Kate simultaneously slammed on the brakes.

"Geez, Ryan, you nearly gave me a heart attack. It was just a little fox crossing the road." Kate goosed the car so she could catch up to the Fraileys' truck.

"That was no fox," Ryan said. "Did you see a bushy red tail on that thing? No, you did not. That was a cougar."

John snorted in disbelief, but he peered out the window all the same. "Calm down, Rye. We won't let him get you."

"Yeah? Well, who knows what all's out there."

"Well, obviously the Fraileys manage to survive."

Mr. Frailey slowed, and Kate followed suit. Their combined headlights picked out a doe and two fawns leaping across the road in front of the truck.

"It's a regular zoo out here," Abby said.

When the deer had disappeared into the dark woods, the truck picked up speed and Kate did as well. After a few more minutes, Mr. Frailey turned left onto an even narrower lane, which took them steeply down a hill, over a small bridge, and up until the trees fell away and they came to a white farmhouse and an unpainted barn nestled together at the foot of a steep hill.

The front porch light was on, sending a welcoming beam of light to the driveway. A woman sat on the porch railing strumming a guitar.

"Great. Now I'm sure we're reliving Deliverance," Ryan said. "If she were playing a banjo instead of a guitar I would not get out of this car."

"What's he talking about?" Abby asked John.

"Never mind," he said and kissed her cheek.

Patty Ann was out of her father's truck and at their car before they could get out. "Mom, we brought company," she called.

Mrs. Frailey put the guitar aside and came down to meet them. "Hi, I'm Darlene."

Patty Ann introduced everyone. Darlene told them she was an aide at the local nursing home and had just returned home. She was a mature version of her daughter and just as unflappable about unexpected guests, even though she had to be tired. She showed John and Ryan to a room that she explained belonged to Patty Ann's older brothers, both off in the Marines. Patty Ann led Abby and Kate to her own room and insisted she would be fine sleeping on the couch in the living room. She brought fresh sheets that smelled of sunshine, and Abby and Kate helped her change the bed.

The house was plain but clean, the furnishings shabby but comfortable, and the Fraileys made them feel welcome. Darlene popped popcorn in a pan on her stove. Abby had never seen it made without a microwave. Patty Ann poured glasses of homemade apple cider from a Mason jar.

Then Darlene smiled and said, "Let's go sit on the porch for a spell."

They sat in the dark so the bugs wouldn't be drawn to the porch light—Patty Ann and her mother on the swing, Abby and Kate on wooden chairs, and Ryan and John perched on the porch rail.

Declining popcorn, Benjamin Frailey took up the guitar and sat down on the top step to tune it. When he was satisfied with its sound, he began picking a lively tune. Then he and his wife and daughter sang a ballad about a girl who refused to marry a farmer because he was too lazy to hoe his cornfield.

When it was over, they all smiled their approval, even Ryan, because it seemed wrong somehow, in such an intimate setting, to clap. Then they sang old hymns that Abby had heard so long ago they seemed like dreams. She wished she remembered the words and could sing along. And she wished she could play an instrument, a guitar maybe. How freeing it must be to just pick one up and make music without being tied to notes on a page.

The inadequate sleep the night before and the long day filled with new sights and sounds began to weigh on her, and suddenly Abby realized she was exhausted, even a little disoriented. It seemed as if she had gone back to an earlier, better time than her own. She yawned, barely getting her hand in front of her mouth in time.

They all went in after that, and she slept soundly on Patty Ann's threadbare sheets that smelled of sunshine.

CHAPTER 10

It was a pleasant way to be awakened, much better than a blaring alarm clock. Sunlight streamed in around blue curtains, and laughter drifted in through the thin walls of Patty Ann's bedroom. A nasally voice announced, "This is WEBQ Radio bringing you the Baptist Hour, sponsored by the Otis Carter Hatchery in Eldorado." The announcer pronounced the town's name with a long A sound, causing Abby to wince. She stretched and started to turn over. Would it be rude to sleep a little longer? Then the scent of bacon—maybe sausage too—hit her, and she sat up.

"Wake up, roomie," she said, shaking Kate's shoulder.

She woke instantly and scrambled out of bed, a feat Abby had observed on more than one occasion. "We get breakfast, too?"

"Smells like it. We'd better hurry with our showers before John scarfs it all."

Everyone else was already seated at the table when Abby came into the kitchen, tucking her damp hair behind her ears. "I am so sorry," she said. "I hope you're not waiting for me."

Benjamin Frailey smiled at her from the head of the table. "Yup. Like one hog waits for another. Come on and sit down before Ryan eats all the biscuits. He just found out what sorghum's good for." Mr. Frailey wore a white shirt with a red tie and his hair was slicked back. Her brain finally came into sync, and she remembered it was Sunday.

"He's kidding," Darlene Frailey said. "I made plenty of biscuits."

"And, Abby, there's gravy too," John announced with something like awe.

"If you can cook, you've got it made, Abby," Benjamin said. "You know what they say about the way to a man's heart."

Abby's face heated, but she smiled and patted John's arm. "Yes, sir, I do."

"Kate was just tellin' us she's lookin' for her Greenfield relatives," Darlene said.

"That's right," Abby said. "We're hoping to find a connection to her ancestor Ned Greenfield."

"Well, y'all just come on to church with us, and I'll introduce you to Brother Alex," Benjamin said. "He might know, but—"

"Yes, he might know." Patty Ann wore a tiny smile and her eyes gleamed.

"Sorry, but I didn't bring dress clothes," Ryan said. "None of us did."

"Oh, y'all are fine just as you are," Darlene said. "Patty Ann, you stack the dishes while I go get dressed."

The day was already hot when they left for church. But the leafy canopy overhead tempered the sun, shading the road most of the way. This time, no animals came out of the woods to startle them.

When they walked into the small, humble building, Abby was surprised to find that Liberty Baptist Church: Friends of Humanity was a racially integrated congregation, about one-third of those present being African American.

Darlene Frailey had been right about them fitting in no matter what they wore. There was huge diversity in attire. Some men wore suits, some overalls. Some women wore silk dresses and fancy hats. Some wore denim skirts or jeans.

A flock of smiling women descended on them as soon as they entered the sanctuary. Their spokeswoman was of the hatted variety, a stout black woman who introduced herself as Sister Retha.

"Now, Sister Darlene," she said, "introduce us right this very minute to these nice young folks you've brought today." Sister Retha took Abby's hand in a firm grip and pumped it as if she were expecting to get a bucket of water out of her. "We are just so happy you're here."

Darlene introduced them, and then Benjamin said, "Thank you, Sister Retha. We better get to our pews. Brother Ron is fixin' to start the service."

The pews were hard, but they didn't have to remain seated in them for long. They stood while Brother Ron, a smiling man of about forty, led them in several rousing hymns, none of which Abby had ever heard before. But like the bluegrass music, the old hymns touched a chord in her heart, and she found herself catching onto them quickly with the help of the pianist, who pounded out the music on a battered upright piano.

Brother Ron prayed and then announced that Brother and Sister Blevins weren't there to sing the special number they had planned. "But the Frailey family is here," he said. "Would you'ns favor us with a song?"

The Fraileys didn't seem the least bit put out by the last

minute request. Patty Ann's dad thumbed through a hymnbook, and after a moment of whispered discussion they settled on a hymn and then rose and went to the platform. Abby turned in her own hymnal to the song they announced. She figured the pianist would accompany them since the Fraileys hadn't brought their instruments. But Mr. Frailey tapped his foot to set the tempo and then the three sang the hymn a cappella, their voices blending together in a tapestry of harmony:

Come, Lord, and tarry not;
Bring the long looked for day;
O why these years of waiting here,
These ages of decay?
Come, for Thy saints still wait;
Daily ascends their sigh;
The Spirit and the Bride say "Come,"
Does Thou not hear the cry?
O come and make all things new.
O come and make all things new.
O come and make all things new.
Build up this ruined Earth,
Come and make all things new.

Loud amens sounded throughout the congregation. Most people in her own church would have thought it unseemly emotionalism, but for the first time in her life Abby found herself softly calling out an amen herself.

Liberty Baptist's pastor was a huge black man. John leaned over and whispered that he looked like that actor in the Allstate commercials. Sounded like him too. And when he began his sermon she did indeed feel like she was in good hands. He started with a reasoned argument for Christ's deity that was so good she wanted to take notes, except she couldn't find any paper in her purse and they didn't have bulletins.

As it seemed the sermon would come to an end, he launched into a paean of praise for the One he had just preached about, his bass voice rich with feeling. It was not a prayer, not like any doxology Abby had ever heard, but a worshipful listing of Christ's names beginning with Almighty God, the Alpha and Omega, the Ancient of Days, continuing on through Emmanuel, Good Shepherd, the Holy One, and ending after at least two hundred other names with Word of Life. When it was finished, he took a handkerchief out of his pocket, wiped his face, smiled at the congregation, and said, "God bless you, my brothers and sisters."

The room fairly rang with amens, and the pianist began pounding out a reprise of Beulah Land. The Fraileys and the rest of the congregation stood and began to make their way to the door, chatting and shaking hands all around.

Abby found herself wiping her eyes with a handkerchief she only vaguely remembered John handing her.

"All I can say is wow," she said.

John looked as amazed as she felt. "I've never heard preaching like that before."

"Where's Kate and Ryan?"

"They left somewhere around Lord God Almighty," John said.

Sister Retha and her bevy of ladies took turns hugging them and telling them how happy they were they had come.

A small herd of children went racing toward the open door and she called after them, "Freddy, don't you be wallerin' in the dirt in your Sunday clothes." Without missing a beat, she turned back to Abby and John. "Y'all come visit us again, now, you hear?"

The line to shake the pastor's hand dwindled until only the Fraileys were left. "Come here, Abby, and meet Brother Alex," Benjamin said.

The pastor's hand dwarfed hers when he took it gently into his own. "I'm so glad you could worship with us today."

Abby smiled. "We did worship, indeed. I really enjoyed the service."

John shook the pastor's hand. "I'm embarrassed to say I've never been to an integrated church before. I'm glad we came."

Brother Alex's laugh carried through the whole church. "Bet it took some getting used to, huh? Liberty Baptist has a long history of being integrated, even back in the slave days. It was an important stop on the Underground Railroad. And folks in Eagle Creek didn't take it kindly when the Ku Klux Klan came riding in. They sent them on their way with their squirrel guns."

Abby looked at John and could see the wheels turning in his head. "How old is this building, then?" he asked.

"It's old, real old. I'm not sure when it was built. Of course, it's been remodeled and added onto over the years."

"Aren't you going to ask Brother Alex about the Greenfields?" Patty Ann asked with a sly smile. "Brother Alex Greenfield."

The pastor looked puzzled. Mrs. Frailey chuckled and shook her head. "Patty Ann, you're such a tease."

"We're helping my friend Kate—I don't know where she went off to—with her family tree," Abby explained. "She's looking for information about a relative named Ned Greenfield." She grinned. "Must be a different family."

Brother Greenfield chuckled. "Must be."

"He was born in Equality in 1834 at Hickory Hill,"

John said.

The pastor's expression went solemn.

"Do you know of any white families named Greenfield around here?" Abby asked.

"I'm sorry. The only Greenfields I know are related to me, and no one named Ned, as far as I can remember."

Mrs. Frailey invited Brother Greenfield to come for Sunday dinner, but he declined, saying he'd already promised the Brinkleys he'd go to their house. He invited Abby and John to come back to the evening service. Darting a look toward her, John told him they just might do that.

They found Kate and Ryan waiting beside the car. Kate explained that Ryan had begun to feel overheated. John rolled his eyes behind Ryan's back.

Mrs. Frailey had made chicken and dumplings ahead of time so she wouldn't have to cook on "the Sabbath." Afterward they helped her clean up the kitchen, and then Patty Ann took them on a tour of the farm, introducing them to her father's coonhounds Tuffy and Jeff, her cat Meow, and the sow and pigs in the barn. Mr. Frailey showed them his sorghum mill and explained how it worked.

Then Patty Ann led them up the steep, rocky hill behind the house. Ryan worried about the possibility of snakes until Patty Ann picked up a dead branch and handed it to him.

"Here," she said. "Your very own snake stick. If you see any snakes, whack 'em with it."

John wiped a grin from his face. "And it might help if you make lots of noise, Rye. So they hear you coming."

Abby smiled to herself at the sound of Ryan and Kate behind her on the path. He was enthusiastically hitting everything in sight with the stick while keeping up a steady stream of nervous chatter with Kate. It was actually quite a feat, because the hill was steep enough that Abby had to concentrate on finding toeholds for her feet and boulders to pull herself up with.

When John reached the top, he extended his hand and helped her up the last bit.

"I didn't expect this," he said. "It's beautiful." His voice and breathing were annoyingly normal in spite of the exertion.

Abby tried not to sound as if she'd just run a marathon.

A meadow covered the hill's summit, a single huge oak tree at its center. There was a small herd of red and white cattle, some grazing in the sun, others resting in the tree's shade.

"How do you get them up here?" John asked.

"There's a rough road over yonder," Patty Ann said, pointing across the meadow. "My grandpa used to make moonshine up here away from the revenuers. He'd truck it down that road and on into Shawneetown to sell."

"Really?" Kate said laughing. "Moonshine?"

"Yep," Patty Ann said. "He had other stills down in the hollows, too. Lots of folks around here did back in Prohibition days on account of Eagle Creek havin' the clearest, best water for makin' it. Not much else to do around here. It's too hilly for most crops. Some are still making 'shine, too, but I'm not going to mention any names."

They hiked across the meadow and Patty Ann led them out onto a rocky promontory. Hills and valleys lay before them. She pointed out Eagle Mountain to the south and Eagle Creek winding its way through the valley. In the bends of the creek were little, irregularly shaped fields that Patty Ann explained were corn and grain sorghum.

"It's an awesome view," Abby said.

"Worth the climb, wasn't it, sweetie?" Kate said, wrapping her arm around Ryan's waist.

"Sure."

"But not for long. Just beyond that last rise, Sherman has strip-mined off everything. Well, except for Uncle Charlie's farm. He's the last holdout over that way, but he'll have to sell soon. They blasted so close to his place that his well cracked. Contaminated groundwater seeped in and it's no longer fittin' to drink. They'd like to blow the top off this hill we're standin' on."

Patty Ann shaded her eyes with her hand and looked out across the hills and valleys. Then she swallowed and blinked as if trying not to cry.

Abby put a hand on her shoulder. "But like the hymn says, Patty Ann, God will make all things new one day."

"Can we see Hickory Hill from here?" Ryan asked, ever sensitive to the feelings of others.

Patty Ann turned and started back across the meadow. "It's over yonder," she called over her shoulder. "Nothing there for you to see."

"Is it far?" Kate asked. Patty Ann didn't answer, just kept walking back the way they'd come.

Abby shot a look at John and then hurried to catch up with her. "Wait."

Patty Ann stopped and stood there, kicking at the grass with her sneaker. She didn't look up.

"Could you tell us how to get there? You see, we have a clue about Hickory Hill. One of Kate's ancestors was born there. We'd like to see it. "

At last she looked up, wearing a mulish expression.

Kate and the guys had come to stand by Abby's side. She smiled engagingly. "Please, Patty Ann."

"She's the third person to tell us there's nothing there to see," Ryan said. "Which, I have to say, does nothing but make me more determined to see what is there." He took Kate's hand and tugged. "Come on. We'll find it on our own."

"All right," Patty Ann said quickly. "I'll show you."

"Really?" Kate nearly squealed.

"Come on, then." Patty Ann led them back down the hill, down the Frailey's driveway, across the road, and on into the deep woods on the other side.

At first it looked like an untamed jungle to Abby, but then she saw that they followed a faint trail. Even so, the going was rough. Kate and Ryan were next after Patty Ann, but the third time Ryan let a branch snap back at them, almost hitting Abby in the face, John took her hand and they edged past them.

"I think we'll go first for a while," he said with a pointed look at Ryan.

The path led down a steep bank, and Abby slipped on the thick leaves of the forest floor. John caught her before her rear hit the ground, and she smiled her thanks.

When they got to the bottom there was a little creek trickling over a pebbled bed. Dappled sunlight shone on green moss growing thick on boulders jutting from the ground.

"It looks like a good place for fairies," Kate said.

Patty Ann grinned. "Or snakes. You'd do well to keep your snake stick close, Ryan. I saw a copperhead here last week." She looked down at her arm and picked a black speck off and threw it away from herself. "And ticks. We'll have to check when we get back."

Talk of snakes hadn't really alarmed her, but the thought of blood-sucking ticks gave Abby the creeps, and she spent an anxious minute inspecting her arms and legs. When she was sure none had landed on her she sat on a boulder to rest.

"Do you come down here a lot, Patty Ann?" John asked.

"I've been exploring these hills and hollows since I was knee-high to a grasshopper," she said. "But if you mean this path, I go this way a couple of times a week." Then she stood and said, "If y'all are rested enough, it's time to tackle Hickory Hill."

By the time they reached the top they were all panting. The path ended at a sagging wire fence that could have easily been stepped over, but Patty Ann wouldn't let them. Abby pushed a tree branch aside and saw a glimpse of a faded red building peeking through a jungle of overgrown shrubs and trees.

"That's Hickory Hill?" she asked.

"The hill," Patty Ann said, "and the mansion on it. I help Miss Granger with cleanin' and stuff when I can."

"So that's where my great, great, great, however many greats grandfather was born," Kate said, studying the house with interest. "It doesn't look very…mansion-y."

"You're just not getting a good look at it," Patty Ann said defensively.

"Do you know anything about the Greenfields?" John asked. "When they might have lived there?"

"Nope. The Grangers have lived there for about forever. The first one leased the Half Moon Salt Mine from the government back when. It's over that way," she said, pointing to her left. "He got rich off it, which is how come he was able to build this place."

"It's huge," Abby said. "Cleaning it must take forever."

"It's not too bad. Miss Granger won't let me go up to the third floor. Thinks it's haunted. And she only has me clean on the second floor occasionally."

"So if the Grangers built the house…," Ryan said.

"That's what I heard. I'm not sure when, but it's really old."

"And a Granger lives here now," he continued. "then when did Ned Greenfield ever live here?"

"I couldn't say."

"Maybe the Greenfields owned the hill before there was a mansion," John said. "Although it seems strange they'd include that information in Ned Greenfield's birth records."

"Maybe the Grangers sold it to the Greenfields and then bought it back some time later," Abby said. "We'll have to check for deeds at the courthouse."

"Some people claim Hickory Hill was a stop on the Underground Railroad," Patty Ann said. "Bet that house could tell some interesting tales."

Abby glanced at John and found he was already looking at her. Even if the clue about Ned Greenfield turned out to be nothing, it would be fun to time-surf in a building so old.

"Cool," Kate said. "Dad would love it if Ned Greenfield were involved with the Underground Railroad. When I paint the mural I could put a train engineer's hat as his symbol."

"Or a gourd dipper like…some people hung on their front doors," Abby said.

"Can we go inside, Patty Ann?" Kate asked.

"No, it's not my day to help, and Miss Granger gets…upset when things don't go according to schedule. Besides, we're going to have to hurry back if we're going to be in time for the evening service."

Ryan whined that he didn't want to go to church twice in one day, and why didn't they just go on to Shawneetown? Abby could tell Kate was about to cave. And so when Ryan went on ahead down the path, she explained to Kate that they needed to get back to the church to time-surf in case they never got the chance to get inside Hickory Hill.

Kate came up with the excuse that she wanted to hear the gospel music again. It was lame because Kate didn't care one way or the other about gospel music, but amazingly Ryan didn't seem to notice.

CHAPTER 11

They were a little late getting to church, and the singing had already begun. John pulled her aside before they went into the sanctuary. "I'm going back to the car for my laptop. Go on in, but slip out like you've got to use the restroom. I'll meet you in that first Sunday School room."

"You're sure it's empty?"

"Yep. I scoped it out as we walked by."

Abby sat anxiously through the first song and then, mumbling her excuses, eased her way past Kate and Ryan into the center aisle. Nothing like being conspicuous. But no one seemed concerned about her departure.

The door was closed, and when she opened it, the room was completely dark except for the light streaming from John's laptop. He sat at a short table meant for small children. Glancing up, he said, "Come on. We'll have to hurry."

The sound of singing came to them as Brother Ron led the congregation in *Amazing Grace*. On the monitor an earlier congregation—the dial said October 12, 1849—was singing the same hymn in near sync with the congregation just down the hall in the present time.

She felt a moment of vertigo and rubbed her head. "Wow. What are the odds of that?"

John looked up and grinned at her. "Some songs just never get old." He turned back to the monitor and began to fast-forward.

They meant no harm—only good—but that didn't keep Ned from feeling nervous as the preacher and two other white folk from Liberty Baptist Church led him and Nelson down a short hall just inside the church door.

The preacher was a small, bird-like man, but Ned figured he had guts. He was one of the few who to let black folks into his church. "Right this way," he told them.

They came to a door, and the man they called Deacon Hayes opened it and looked inside. He was a tall man, taller than even Ned's pap, but skinny, bald, and pockmarked. "Here they are, Mr. Phillips," Deacon Hayes said.

He opened the door wide and Ned saw that a white man wearing a brown suit sat at a table. The man—Mr. Phillips—looked up from some papers in front of him. Light from the room's one window behind him made his gray hair and beard glow, and Ned had the sudden fanciful notion that they had been led to the Almighty sitting on his throne in Heaven.

He stepped into the room, and behind him, Nelson balked in the doorway as if he had had the same thought. Joseph, the young man with them, was fifteen and Nelson's true friend, even though he was white as flour. He smiled his encouragement and said, "It's all right. Go on in."

"Sit down, boys," Mr. Phillips said.

Nelson looked at Ned as if to ask if it was safe to sit in the presence of God. But Ned reminded himself that Mr. Phillips was only a man, although a white one. Too bad. They needed a miracle. Mr. Phillips told them to sit, and so he did.

Nelson and Joseph sat down beside him and the preacher sat across from them. Deacon Hayes closed the door and stood in front of it as if he planned to protect them single-handedly from anyone who might try to enter.

Joseph smiled again at Nelson. "We'll get them back. I promise."

Mr. Phillips didn't look as sure. "We'll try." He sounded sad. Or maybe mad. Ned couldn't tell for sure.

Joseph fidgeted. "But you're a lawyer, ain't you, Mr. Phillips? You'll tell the judge what happened and he'll make them—"

"Unfortunately, we don't have a case to take to court, Joseph. No witnesses. Truth is, even if these boys caught the kidnappers red-handed carrying away their family they can't testify in a court of law against a white man."

In spite of the ache in his heart, Ned almost smiled at the look on Joseph's face. First, surprise that he had lived there his whole life and not known this law, and then anger that there was such unfairness in the world.

Mr. Phillips coughed into his handkerchief. "No, our best hope is to offer a reward and see what turns up. Do you have the money yet, Reverend Edmunds?"

"Almost," he answered. "With this morning's contributions we have over ninety-six dollars."

"It will take the full one hundred for the reward, Eli," Mr. Phillips said.

Deacon Hayes dug into his pocket and pulled out a leather wallet. "Here, this should do it." He placed a golden half-eagle on the table in front of Mr. Phillips and chuckled softly. "With one dollar left over for your legal services, Mr. Phillips."

Ned had been amazed at the generosity of the congregation, but now his eyes widened in astonishment at Deacon Hayes' gift. Five whole dollars. And judging by his shabby suit, he wasn't a rich man. Ned wanted to say how grateful he and Nelson were. He wanted to ask why they'd do something like that, and what it was about these people that made them so different from other white folk. But a lump had formed in his throat and the words wouldn't come out.

"Then we're all set." Mr. Phillips was grinning. For a minute he didn't look so god-like, but then his expression turned somber and he directed his piercing gray eyes toward Ned and Nelson. He rested his hands on the vest covering his belly, then leaned back in his chair, and closed his eyes. "Tell me what happened."

Ned swallowed the lump away and pushed down the hopelessness that threatened to spill over every time he thought about what had happened. "Me and Nelson got in from the field same as always and—"

"That was the night of October 23?"

"It be last week, sir," Ned said. "I don't know—"

"That's right, Mr. Phillips," Joseph said. "Nelson came straight away and told me what happened."

"Go on," Mr. Phillips said without opening his eyes.

"They was gone, all of 'em." Ned closed his own eyes and saw in his head what they'd found. "They was mush cookin' on the fire like always. But Mama done let it scorch. Pap's blacksmith apron be hanging on the peg, but he weren't there."

Nelson wiped at his eyes with his sleeve. "We call and call. And look all over the place. Nancy Jane, Maybelle, and

Lizzie. They be stole too."

Mr. Phillips sat up in his chair and wrote something on the paper in front of him. "Maybe they ran, took a trip on the Railroad."

Nelson's eyes went wide, like he was just now thinking that thought and not liking it much. "But they wouldn't leave me and Ned behind." He turned to stare at Ned. "Would they?"

He wanted to reassure Nelson, but he couldn't get the answer out before Mr. Phillips started in with more questions. He looked fierce, like he thought they were lying to him.

"Your family lives up in the yard, right? Not down in the quarters with the others?"

"Yes, sir. No, sir."

"Mariah was John Granger's cook, and Charles was his blacksmith—a very good blacksmith," Preacher Edmunds said. "They've got a snug cabin in the yard. They were treated fairly well. Less reason to run than for most."

"Mama wouldn't leave without her necklace," Ned said. He leaned back in his chair and dug it out of his pocket, then held it out for everyone to see. Light from the window winked at the copper lady on it.

"No, sir," Nelson said. "Mama wouldn't leave without her necklace."

"May I see that?" Mr. Phillips asked.

Ned wanted to hide it away in his pocket again, but after a moment he handed it over to him.

"It's an 1843 penny."

"That be Lady Liberty, sir," Ned said.

"Your mama has kept her well-polished, I see." A smile flickered over Mr. Phillips' face. "I suppose your pap made the leather cord?"

"Yes, sir. Master give it to Mama when they was

celebrating up at the big house on account of Illinois bein' twenty-five years old. Mama said they was fireworks and a fine dinner. Lots of ladies and gentlemen from round about. Mama served champagne under the shade trees. Master tole my mama that he let her go when Pap's 'denture be up. She ax him how much longer. He say when Illinois be thirty-two, they go free."

"Is that so?" Mr. Phillips returned the necklace to Ned, and he put it safely back into his pocket. When he looked up, Mr. Phillips was looking strangely at Reverend Edmunds and Deacon Hayes.

"Why, that's next year," Deacon Hayes said.

"They wouldn't have any call to run," Reverend Edmunds said.

"No, they wouldn't, would they?" Mr. Phillips let out a grunt that wasn't very gentleman-like.

Joseph pounded on the table and Nelson jumped in surprise. "He did it! Why, he kidnapped them himself and then—"

"Now, Joseph," Reverend Edmunds said. "We don't know that. Let's give him the benefit of the doubt."

Mr. Phillips snorted and then dipped his pen in the inkbottle. "I need a detailed description of your family, Ned. The more information I get for the advertisement, the more likely we are to have success."

Ned frowned and tried to think of what to say. Joseph leaned over and whispered in his ear. "He means for you to tell what they look like. How old they are. Like that."

Ned nodded his thanks. "Lizzie be the baby. She six years old." He rose from his chair and held his hand to just above his waist. "She this tall."

"I would estimate that to be four feet tall." Mr. Phillips scratched words on the paper. "Go on. What about her complexion?"

Ned sat back down, and Joseph whispered in his ear again.

"She darker than me. 'Bout like a hickory nut."

"Any distinguishing marks?"

Joseph leaned in again.

"She have a mole on her head," Ned said, pointing to his own above his right eyebrow. He exhaled and looked down again. "And whip marks on her back."

Voices in the hall—Pastor Greenfield's, Kate's, and maybe Sister Retha's—sank in. Abby jolted out of 1849 and shuddered to present day awareness. Her breath seemed to be locked inside her lungs.

"They whipped her? A six-year-old girl?" John was nearly sputtering with indignation.

"John! Snap out of it," she said, trying to take control of the mouse. "Someone's coming."

The door flew open and Sister Retha reached in and flipped on the light switch. Pastor Greenfield came in after her, and then Ryan was there, Kate looking over his shoulder in dismay. Out of the corner of her eye, Abby saw that John had already shut the laptop.

"What's goin' on in here?" Pastor Greenfield asked. "Why are you here in the dark?"

Abby felt her face flaming and willed herself to look innocent. Judging by the expressions on everyone's faces, she wasn't succeeding.

John, failing completely, looked guilty of some vile crime. "We were just—"

"Gosh, you guys," Ryan said, "don't you have any respect for a church?"

"Oh, my," Sister Retha said. "Were you two—?"

"Please go on back in the hall, Sister Retha," Pastor Greenfield said and then turned back to them. "And I think it's time for y'all to leave."

Abby wanted to cry at the look of disappointment on his face, to protest that they hadn't been skipping church to make out in his Sunday School room. But the look John shot her warned her to be quiet, and so she let them think she was a defiler of churches.

Out in the hall, they said their thank yous and goodbyes to the Fraileys, who mercifully didn't seem to be aware of the incident. Sister Retha knew, but if Pastor Greenfield had done a good job of teaching that Scripture about not gossiping, maybe they never would.

"Thank you, Patty Ann, for everything," Abby said, squeezing the girl's arm. "I'm so glad we got to meet the Salt Queen."

"Y'all come again anytime you're down this way."

On the way out to the car, Kate pulled Abby aside. "I tried to keep them out. But Sister Retha was bound and determined to get her flannelgraph board from that room."

"Thanks for trying," Abby said. "I hate to imagine what they're thinking."

"Your faces were pretty red and you were breathing hard like—"

"I know, I know," Abby said. "But that's because Ned was talking about the whip marks on his little sister's back."

"What? You saw Ned Greenfield?"

"Yes. Not your Ned Greenfield, of course, but there is a connection to Hickory Hill, because apparently they were indentured servants for John Granger."

"What do you mean?"

"You know, they signed on to work so many years, seven I think, and then—"

"Not that, silly. Why wasn't it my Ned Greenfield?"

"He was black. But come on. We'll talk later. When we're alone."

When they got in the car Ryan entered the address for the Shawnee Chief Motel on Kate's GPS system, and she pulled out of Liberty Baptist's parking lot.

"Are you sure we still have our rooms, Ryan?" Kate asked.

"I'm sure."

Abby was amused by the voices Kate had programmed on the GPS. They alternated between Pooh, Eeyore, and Tigger—until Ryan took it upon himself to reset the voice to the factory default one.

"But I love Eeyore," Kate said plaintively.

"This is easier to understand, Kathryn."

Abby wished Kate would reach over and smack him, but she didn't, and the boring, robotic voice steered them faultlessly through the winding country roads onto Route One.

"I've been thinking," Abby said. "There has to be a road to get to Hickory Hill, doesn't there?"

"She's right," John said. "Why don't you try entering that, Turner?"

Kate slowed the car and pulled into a driveway. "I'll do it."

Abby unfastened her seatbelt and leaned over Kate's shoulder to watch as she cancelled the trip and then entered *Hickory Hill.*

The map adjusted, and then Hickory Hill Lane popped up on the screen. And it didn't look very far away. Kate squealed and turned to smile at her. "You're a genius, Abby."

Ryan sniffed. "It's probably nothing, Kathryn, but I guess we have to check it out."

As she pulled back onto the highway, the GPS advised

her to be ready to "turn. left. in. five. hun. dred. yards."

The highway was completely dark except for the occasional car coming toward them. "I can't see it," Kate said. "Help me look."

"There." John directed her attention to the left.

Kate put her turn signal on and waited for an approaching car to go by. As soon as she turned into Hickory Hill Lane her headlights picked up a metal gate across the road. A chain secured it to massive wooden posts. Thick trees on either side guaranteed no vehicle was going down Hickory Hill Lane.

"Obviously, it's a private lane," Ryan said.

It was more than obvious, Abby thought, giving in to the urge to roll her eyes. The large sign read *Private Property.*

"What does it say?" John asked.

"What? Are you blind? It says *Private Property*. Ryan said with a long-suffering sigh.

John exhaled loudly and Abby wondered if he were counting to ten. "I mean below that," he said patiently as he opened his door.

Abby got out, too. The gravel on the road was nearly boulder-sized and she focused on not tripping. They stood to the side so Kate's headlights would shine on the sign—*Trespassers Will Be Prosecuted.* Abby turned to go back to the car. When she realized John wasn't behind her, she spun around in time to see him ease past the fence post.

"John!" she called. "Are you insane? You can't go up there."

"Wait in the car," he said softly. "I just want to take a peek, see what's there." He started down Hickory Hill Lane.

Abby didn't want to trespass. But then again she didn't want to be a wimp and wait in the car while John went alone. She edged around the fence post and saw his light-colored shirt ahead in the dark. It was already getting harder to see it. She'd have to go fast to catch up with him.

A car's tires crunched the gravel, and Abby had the panicky thought that Kate was leaving them there. But when she looked back she saw that a car had pulled in behind the PT Cruiser. Its headlights blinded her, and she put her hand up to shade her eyes. Then red and blue lights joined in and her heart leaped up into her throat. Forget deer in the headlights. She felt like a convict caught in a prison guard's spotlight.

The car door opened and a man got out. "What's goin' on here?"

Abby stepped back onto the road. "Officer Logan."

Before she could think of anything to add to that, John came up beside her and took her hand, as if to say, "Leave this to me."

"Sorry, Chief," he said, grinning. "I had to use the facilities, if you know what I mean."

"Right." He shone his police-issue flashlight into Kate's car and then turned it back on them. "I suppose it was just a coincidence you decided to take a leak on the Granger property." Abby couldn't make out his face, but he didn't sound like Andy Griffith any longer. "There's nothing for you to see up there. You two just get in your car and move it on down the road."

"Yes, sir," Abby and John said in unison. They made record time getting back in the car.

"Whew!" Kate said. "I didn't know what he was going to do."

"Could this trip get any worse?" Ryan moaned.

"But did you see anything?" Kate asked.

"No," John said. "Just trees." He turned to Abby. "And just so you know, I didn't lie to Chief Logan. You know…about using the facilities."

Abby grinned. "I didn't doubt you for a minute."

Chief Logan backed his car onto the shoulder and when Kate pulled back onto Highway 1, he fell in behind them. And stayed there. All the way to the Shawneetown city limits. Finally, with a flash of his brights and a bleat of his horn, he made a U-turn and headed back toward Equality.

CHAPTER 12

It would have been difficult to miss the Shawnee Chief Motel even without the robot's instructions. The sign in front proclaimed it in vintage neon. Yellow tracer lights outlined a red Indian chief in full headdress. Apparently, the owners weren't into political correctness. Kate pulled off the highway and parked.

John and Ryan went to talk to the night clerk while Abby and Kate stood in the small lobby next to their luggage. When the guys turned away from the counter, Ryan held two large brass keys. He said something to John and handed one of the keys to him. John frowned as he took it, and then without answering came and handed the key to Abby.

"Here, you girls can have lucky room thirteen," he said. "Rye and I will be next door in fourteen."

Ryan frowned and, grabbing his and Kate's biggest bags, stalked off down the hall, Kate carrying the smaller one and scurrying to keep up.

"What's with him?" Abby asked.

"He's just cranky because he didn't get his nap today," John said.

"No, really, what's wrong?"

John took Abby's bag from her and started down the hall after them. "Well, it seems Rye had his heart set on coed room assignments."

Abby frowned at Ryan's retreating back. "What made him think we'd agree to that?"

"Apparently, our sleuthing has given him the wrong idea about how we've been spending our time."

Shaking her head, Abby picked up her cosmetic case and started down the hall. "I can't believe Kate's fallen for such a loser."

The room was clean, although it smelled of cigarettes. Paintings of matadors on black velvet hung over the beds. Indian chiefs on black velvet would have possibly been even more disturbing but at least have made sense theme-wise.

About midnight Abby and Kate heard noises coming from the room next to them that they'd just as soon not. It went on and on—so long that they started giggling, Kate so hard she snorted. Eventually, things quieted down, but Abby still couldn't get to sleep.

"Kate?"

"Yeah?"

"We're friends, right?"

"Of course we are, Abbicus."

"Can I ask you a question?"

"Sure."

"Did you and Ryan…you know…do it?"

"If you expect me to describe it, I won't. It was a

sacred moment and—"

"Well, of course it is. Which is why…well, we had a pact. We promised we would wait for marriage before we, you know…"

"Ryan said virginity is like a tamper-proof seal on a bottle of aspirin. It's meant for the man you're going to marry. And now that we know we're getting married, what's the point of waiting? You'll see when you're engaged, Abby." Kate turned on her side away from her. "Let's get some sleep."

Abby lay staring up at the blinking red smoke detector light on the dark ceiling, wondering if she even really knew her roommate any more.

Abby's eyes popped open. Noises were coming through the walls again—only this time from room fourteen, and the passion involved was the angry kind. There was a loud thump and muffled shouts. The clock said 1:35. She sat up and looked at Kate's shadowy form in the other bed. Another garbled shout came through the thin walls.

Kate bolted upright and turned to look at her. "What was that?"

Abby turned the sheet back and slipped out of bed. "I don't know. Either the guys are duking it out or someone broke into their room and is murdering them."

"Should we call the front desk?"

Abby felt around in the dark until she found the shirt she'd worn earlier and pulled it on over her pajamas. "Only if they're being murdered. I'll let you know." She grabbed the room key, and then slid the deadbolt and stepped out into the hall.

She put her ear to the door of room fourteen. The voices came again, clearer this time. Definitely assault and battery, but apparently not perpetrated by an outsider. She knocked on the door. "John? What's going on?"

After a pause, the door opened just enough for him to poke his head out. "Nothing, Abby. Go back to sleep." He turned and shouted into the room, "I mean it, Turner."

Kate came up beside her and pushed the door open. "Ryan? Are you all right?"

Ryan jumped up from the room's small desk and stood there looking like a little boy caught with his hand in the cookie jar. "Kathryn? What are you doing here?"

"We heard loud noises. We woke up."

John went to stand in solidarity beside Ryan in front of the desk. Neither seemed to be aware that they wore only boxer shorts. "It's nothing," John said. "We're fine. You can go on back now."

Abby walked over to them and stood waiting for John to get out of her way so she could see what was on the desk behind them.

Kate, not so polite, shoved herself between the two guys. And then Abby saw that John's laptop was open, which of course was not at all unusual. The fact that she and Kate were frozen on its screen—dressed in their pajamas—was.

Abby blinked and felt her heart break a little. "John?"

"I can explain, Abby. Trust me. Please."

Kate seemed to snap out of it first. She shut the laptop and glared first at John and then at Ryan.

"Kathryn, you won't believe what I just saw." Ryan tried to put his arms around her, but she shoved him away.

"Oh, I can imagine what you just saw."

"It's the program, Kathryn. It's much more than a house tour thing. It's awesome what you can do with this."

Kate continued to glare at him. Apparently, Ryan was familiar with that old adage, a good offense is the best defense.

"But you already knew, didn't you," he said angrily. "You knew Abby and John have been going back in time with this thing. Why did you keep it from me?"

"They made me promise, Ryan."

"Did you show him, John?" Abby asked.

"Heck no, Abby. Please trust me."

"Just tell me what happened."

"I woke up and there was Ryno pilfering my laptop."

"I just wanted to see if I could make the program work. We weren't getting anywhere with the genealogy and—"

"And for some reason, it's working here tonight," John said. "Even though the Shawnee Chief can't be that old."

"Maybe it was built over an older building."

"Anyway, Ryno was sitting there with his mouth open watching the thing, and I figured I might as well explain it to him. So I was showing him how we can go backward—"

"And apparently forward," Abby said drily.

"Yes, I ran forward in time more than I expected, and then there was this maid, so we followed her, and she went into room thirteen, and then you and Kate were there, and—I tried to stop it, but Ryan wouldn't."

"I was just figuring it out, practicing so we can use it to find your relatives, Kathryn. Just think what we can do with this."

"Like create your own private porn channel, Ryan?" John said. "It's just like I thought. If this gets out, no one will ever have any privacy again."

Kate put her arm around Ryan's waist and stood facing Abby and John. "He was trying to help. We just need to explain about our rules."

John exhaled loudly and crossed his arms over his

chest, looking like an angry bear in boxers.

"I'm sorry we didn't let you in on it, Ryan," Abby said. "But don't you see John's right? This thing is powerful. If it fell into the wrong hands…well, we just can't let that happen. So promise you won't tell anyone else, okay? We all agreed never to time-surf alone. And never in people's bedrooms or bathrooms."

"That includes motel rooms, sweetie," Kate said.

"Speaking of porn," Ryan said, "this actually would work—I mean, not that I would, but some people might really like—"

"Ryno, I am going to sock you in the mouth," John said.

"All right, all right."

Kate went up on her tiptoes and kissed Ryan's cheek. "Okay, then. Let's get some sleep. I can't wait to try this thing out with you tomorrow."

"Let's concentrate on old-fashioned research first," Abby said. "Maybe we'll find something at the library or courthouse tomorrow."

She started for the door and John hurried after her.

"Abby?"

She cupped his face with her hands. "I told you before, John. I trust you."

He leaned down and kissed her.

She slipped under his arm and went to the desk. "But not necessarily you, Ryan." She picked up the laptop and took it back to lucky room thirteen.

CHAPTER 13

John was calling her name. He wanted her to go with him to warn Merri that the recipe for snickerdoodles only called for a teaspoon of cream of tartar, not a tablespoon. Then Abby opened her eyes and realized John really was calling her. She scrambled to get her phone from the nightstand and flipped it open just as Kate sat up, mumbling incoherently.

"Hello?" her voice came out in a croak.

"Open the door, Abby," John said. "Or we're going to get arrested."

Abby pulled the cotton blanket off the bed and wrapped herself in it as she went to the door.

John and Ryan stood there fully dressed and looking intense. "Can we come in?"

Yawning through her fingers, Abby opened the door and waved them in.

"What's going on?" Kate mumbled from the bed where she sat looking part zombie and part sleepy toddler. "What time is it, anyway?"

"It's three o'clock. Let's go, Kathryn." Ryan went to her open suitcase and began pulling things out. "Here, put this on," he said, handing her a random shirt.

"Hey, stop that."

"So how soon can you be ready?" John said. "You don't have to put on makeup or anything, do you?"

"I'm not going anywhere until you explain," Abby said.

"Now that I know what this program can do, we're going back to Hickory Hill," Ryan said.

"Obviously," Abby said just as Ryan did.

Kate had claimed she wasn't awake enough to drive and given the keys of her Cruiser to Ryan. He pulled the car into Hickory Hill Lane as far as the gate would allow and doused the lights.

Abby didn't feel fully awake either. Until they got out and the humid night air smacked her in the face. Something was blooming nearby, giving off a sweet scent, and a million tree frogs were making a racket in the woods. The moon, nearly full, cast its silvery light over them and everything not shaded by the trees.

"Be careful," John whispered. "Remember how rough the gravel is."

"Yes, I do remember, John. But what I don't remember is what's beyond the gate. Oh, wait. That's because we have no idea what's up the road. And we're walking—trespassing—up the road in complete darkness. And by the way, if Chief Logan shows up again, I will disavow all knowledge of you."

"Come on, Abby," Kate said. "Be spontaneous for once. We're having an adventure."

A part of her was excited to have a middle-of-the-night adventure. The other part of her realized that this would probably go down as the stupidest thing she had ever gotten involved with in her whole life.

"Besides, the moon is so bright we can see the road just fine."

"Well, don't come crying to me, Kate, when you fall and break your neck."

"If we stick to the road, we'll be fine," Ryan said.

"Trust me, I'm not leaving this road," Kate said. "No telling what creatures are roaming around in the woods at night."

"Oh, good," Abby said. "Now I'll be thinking about zombies."

"Zombies, Abby? Really?" John laughed and took her hand. "Here, see?" He flipped on a small flashlight and trained it over the road and the trees surrounding it. "No worries."

"What are you, a Boy Scout?" Ryan said. "You brought a flashlight along?"

"Never leave home without it," he said, unperturbed.

Although the gravel was rough, at least there didn't seem to be any potholes to worry about. But the lane was steep and seemed to go on forever. After a while Abby's quads started to complain. They passed the ruins of an old barn, its roof caved in and door hanging open. Old farm implements sat rusting in front of it. John shone his light over it briefly, but they didn't stop to explore.

And then, after they came around a curve in the lane, the house rose up before them, bathed in moonlight. Its windows were completely dark, but when they got closer Abby saw that a dim light came through the panes of the front door. Maybe Miss Granger had a nightlight on.

"Come on," John said. "We can sit on the porch and

try from there. No one even has to know we're here."

"So how does this program work?" Ryan asked.

"My brain is still mushy," Abby said. "It will be easiest to just show you."

Ryan wasn't satisfied and asked a million questions until John gave in and explained most of the features. The program came up right away, and John adjusted it to 1849. He was trying to take them into the interior of the Hickory Hill Mansion when a man came through the front door and stood looking out at the landscape.

Ryan gasped and jerked away as if to hide from him.

"It takes a little getting used to, doesn't it, sweetie?" Kate said. "But don't worry. The man can't see us. He doesn't know we're here."

Ryan sniffed and settled back against the porch. "Obviously," he said, apparently recovered from the shock. "Who is he?"

"It's Mr. Granger. John and I saw him at the Methodist Church in Equality. His daughter married the famous General Lawler. Well, he wasn't a general at the time. We saw him before the war when he was younger."

"I think he was also Granger's lawyer. They were discussing some business deal."

John Granger took a cigar from his pocket, clipped the end, put it to his lips, and began to puff.

"I can smell it," Ryan said.

"Just wait until we go virtual," John said. "Everybody ready?"

"Do it," Ryan said.

Abby saw John's teeth gleaming in the darkness and knew that he was grinning. "Okay," he said. "You asked for it."

It was a beautiful morning and John Granger looked out from his little mountain with satisfaction. The dogwood and redbuds were blooming in his yard and lane, and green hayfields blanketed his acres at the bottom of Hickory Hill.

He wished, not for the first time, that his salt mine was visible from where he stood, even though it would have marred the pleasant vista before him. The hills and trees screened it from view, but in the distance he saw a wagon on Shawneetown Road carrying barrels of his salt.

He imagined the barrels being offloaded at the Ohio River by his Negroes and carried away by steamboat, eventually to be sold in other cities and towns, some as far away as New Orleans. And in his mind's eye he also saw his money piling up in the big bank in Shawneetown.

He smiled at his fancifulness and then took out his pocket watch. It was time to get to work. Just as he thought it, Jim came around from the back with the carriage. The boy hanging on the back—he couldn't remember this one's name—jumped down and hurried to lower the step for him.

And then they were off down his lane. He spent the time it took to get to the salt mine considering the current crop of problems that his overseer Tom Yancey had brought to him. One of the barrel makers had been injured last week, and now according to Yancey, the wound—on the man's hand, drat it—had become so infected he was no longer able to work. He was their best barrel maker, too. When he got to the salt mine, he would check the supply of barrels to decide whether he should hire someone new or if he had the luxury of waiting around to see whether or not the man's hand had to be amputated. Perhaps he should just go ahead and fire him for being stupid enough to cut himself in the first place.

And then there was the fuel situation. Yancey and the other overseers had been after him to make a decision. The timber was being depleted faster than he had thought possible, and they were going farther and farther afield to acquire it and thus taking longer and longer to get it to the furnaces. If he didn't want production to fall, he would soon have to have more woodcutters and wagon teams to bring the fuel to them. One solution was to pump the saline to the source of the fuel. That would necessitate hiring carpenters to hollow out logs to create the pipeline and more masons to build more brick furnaces.

Yancey insisted they should switch to coal. Granger didn't know much about coal—either mining it or burning it. But he suspected the furnaces would have to be modified to accommodate it.

There was no getting around it. He needed to hire more trained craftsmen, which would mean a hit on his profits. And he'd have to get more Negroes for the rough work. They were always getting themselves killed one way or another.

Even though the salt mine wasn't visible from his porch, it wasn't truly far away, and Jim drove the carriage into the mine yard before he had time to finish considering his options.

He was struck anew with wonder at the bustling hive of activity. Negroes worked to keep the furnaces stoked. Others stirred the brine in the iron evaporation kettles. When the crystals formed on the sides of the kettle they ladled it into baskets overhead to drain and then hauled it to the drying sheds to become beautiful, white salt. There, other Negroes filled barrels and loaded them onto wagons for the trip to Shawneetown.

Granger recited the numbers to himself for the sheer enjoyment of it: fourteen furnaces, each with fifty kettles and manned by thirty Negroes, working seven days a week to make fifteen bushels of salt a day, each of which sold for two dollars. It took two hundred gallons of brine to make one bushel of salt. As it stood so far, it took forty Negroes to cut the wood and fifteen wagon teams to haul it. With the carpenters, cooks, blacksmiths, masons, barrel makers, and the five overseers, Granger was in charge of over five hundred men.

He allowed himself a small smile of satisfaction as he got down from the carriage. He would hear reports from his overseers first off. But before he got far, the beauty of the morning was ruined by screaming coming from somewhere down the line. Tom Yancey hurried up to him. "Sorry for all the caterwauling, Mr. Granger. One of the niggers tripped and fell into the boilin' brine."

Granger's face grew red and he cursed. "There goes another one. I trust that not too much spilled."

The front porch light came on and Abby went catapulting back into the present. She covered her eyes and scooted over closer to John. A rattling sound came from the door, telling them someone inside was trying to open it.

She didn't wait to be told, just scurried off the porch with its revealing light and down the dark driveway. She heard panting and the crunch of gravel and was relieved to know the others were right behind her. When she was sure they were far enough away, she looked back and saw that a tiny, white-haired lady stood at the half-opened door.

"Who's out there?" she called in a wavering voice.

A jolt of guilt hit Abby at the note of fear she heard. "This wasn't supposed to happen, John."

Taking her arm, he led her farther down the lane. "She must have heard the man screaming."

The woman stuck her head farther out the door and

looked cautiously around. At last, muttering something about the "blasted coyotes," she went back in and shut the door.

"Well, that was a complete waste of time," Ryan said. "Why didn't you time-surf inside the house instead of following Granger to the salt mine?"

"I had it set to *Interior*, but the program locked onto him instead."

"Let me try next time," Ryan said.

"You can try, I guess, but the program sometimes seems to have a mind of its own about what it wants us to see."

"That's ridiculous."

"Nevertheless…"

"Come on," Kate said. "Let's go back to the motel and get as much sleep as we can."

"We're going to be so tired tomorrow," Abby said.

CHAPTER 14

They were tired, but not as tired as Shawneetown looked. Under the bright light of day, the town, like an aging woman, showed every sag and wrinkle. According to the brochure Abby had picked up in the motel before they headed out to find breakfast, Shawneetown was established after the Revolutionary War to serve as the center of government for the Northwest Territory. Other than Washington, D.C., it was the only town in the country to be chartered by the United States government. The first federal land office as well as the first bank in Illinois were built in Shawneetown. The bank pictured in the brochure was an impressive five-story, neo-classical Greek monument to finance. And pride. When the fledgling town of Chicago had come asking the bank to buy its civic bonds, the bank had turned them down, saying Chicago would never amount to anything. After all, it didn't have access to a major river.

Shawneetown was located on the Ohio River, but that

blessing was often offset by flooding. Its citizens were used to floods, but then in 1937 one came that was so huge it took the town away. Determined to persevere, they rebuilt the town on higher ground.

But even New Shawneetown looked old, dying actually. It obviously wouldn't be winning the governor's award for best little town in Illinois any time soon. And yet Abby found its stubborn unwillingness to give up appealing. She didn't consider herself fanciful, but a sense of time and history pressed in on her as they drove slowly around town on the lookout for golden arches or other fast food signs.

They didn't find any, but they did find the courthouse and library, right next to the Dollar Store just as Mrs. Barnett, the soap woman, had described. And a block down from that they found Belle's Diner. The food was good, the service friendly, and even Ryan found nothing to complain about.

"Anyone want more coffee before we go?" Abby asked. "We should probably hurry. No telling how much time it will take to find anything useful."

They sat there looking at each other's tired faces. John was the first to voice what everyone was obviously thinking. "Why should we waste time digging through dusty historical files when we can live it at Hickory Hill?"

"Let's go," Kate said. "Maybe Miss Granger will let us in. If not, we can do more surfing from the porch."

"We have to be getting close. Everyone help me look for the road sign," Kate said.

It should have been easier to spot Hickory Hill Lane in the daylight, but everything looked so different from the night before.

"I must have gone too far," Kate said. "I'm going to turn around."

"Try the GPS, Ryan," Abby said.

"How hard can it be to find? It has to be close."

"Just do it, Rye," John said.

"Oh, all right."

Kate pulled into a driveway and then headed back north. When they came around a bend in the road, she gasped and then stomped on the brakes, causing her passengers to screech as loudly as her tires did. Fortunately, no one rear-ended them, although a driver laid on his horn and shot them a dirty look as he went around them.

"Kathryn!" Ryan said.

Kate pulled onto the shoulder. "Look. There it is."

Trying to calm her racing heart, Abby lowered her window and studied the Granger mansion standing in isolated glory on the tall hill before them. They had caught only glimpses of the back of it with Patty Ann. And last night, no matter how bright the moon, they hadn't seen it clearly. Now in daylight it was magnificent, even if a little strange-looking. Judging by its relative size at the distance they were from it, it had to be huge. It was painted a rusty red with white trim. Twelve pillars supported first and second-story verandas, giving it a faintly Greek style like some weird version of the Parthenon.

"See if we can get a closer look, Kate," Abby said.

Kate pulled back onto the highway without terrifying them any further, and then after about a half mile, she found Hickory Hill Lane. The house wasn't visible because even in full daylight the trees were too dense to see more than a little way up the curving lane.

But today, the gate stood open, the *No Trespassing* sign no longer screaming its warning at them.

"Hurry, Kathryn," Ryan said. "Drive on up a little and

get us off the highway."

"At times like this, I wish I didn't have such a distinctive license plate. It makes me a clear target if Chief Logan would happen to drive by."

"The way I read it," John said, "the absence of the no trespassing sign means 'hey, come on in for a visit.'"

Kate chuckled and after a quick look around began to ascend Hickory Hill. The trees grew close, creating a dense shade. The car's engine labored, and Abby wondered if it had the power needed to make it to the top. They passed the old barn they had seen the night before, then after a bit they came out of the trees into sunlight, and the mansion rose up before them. Kate stopped the car, and they sat staring at it.

"Should I go on? Or what?"

"A little more," John said.

She pulled closer to the house and stopped again.

John got out of the car. "You guys stay here. If we all go to the door, it'll look like an invasion of book salesmen."

"Don't flatter yourself. They dress better," Ryan said.

Abby opened her door and got out. "No matter how cute I think you look," she said with a grin, "you'll look less threatening with a female presence."

John sighed. "Okay. You may be right." He took her hand. "Cute, huh?"

Beige sheers covered the front door's two windowpanes. They weren't sheer enough for Abby to see into the dimness behind them. Tinny music came from inside, so garbled she couldn't make out what it was. The doorbell was a brass knob engraved with a curling letter *G*. It clicked when Abby turned it but didn't produce any other sound that she could hear. After a minute had passed, John rapped on the windowpane.

The curtain pulled back, and a little, wizened face

haloed in stringy white hair popped into view. Abby jumped in surprise and came down on John's foot. He yelped and caught her arm to steady her.

The door opened and the tiniest and oldest lady Abby had ever seen looked up at them suspiciously. She wore a floor-length black dress, frayed and faded, that looked more like something Mary Lincoln would have worn than any twenty-first century woman. Although it looked nothing like a wedding dress, Abby suddenly thought of Miss Havisham and felt a totally inappropriate urge to laugh.

Instead, she coughed into her hand. "Hello, ma'am. We're here because—"

"Did you bring my cheese crackers?"

"No," Abby said, glancing at John. He looked back at her as if to say the ball was in her court. The hall behind the woman was paneled in some dark wood, and she got a glimpse of a similarly dark staircase. The tinny music seemed to be coming from an upper floor.

"Ma'am, I'm Abby Thomas and this is John Roberts." She paused to allow the woman to volunteer her own name, but she only adjusted her glasses and continued to study them. "We're doing family research for a friend. Her relative is connected to Hickory Hill."

"I don't care much for the kind with peanut butter."

"We're trying to find the Greenfield family, ma'am," John added.

The woman smiled suddenly, revealing tiny, yellowed teeth. "Abraham Lincoln came to Hickory Hill. Not while he was president. I wouldn't try to fool you about that. He and Mr. Lamborn had a debate over at the courthouse in Equality while he was campaignin' for President Harrison. Mr. Lincoln told us how the crowds sang *Tippecanoe and Tyler Too!* Afterwards, we had a party. The servants set up tables under the trees yonder. They barbecued at least three hogs.

And then that night there was the ball. Oh, you should have seen the ladies dressed in satin and lace! And the gentlemens dressed so fine, too. We danced the Virginia Reel all evening long. Mr. Lincoln danced well for such a tall man. He was quite in demand with the ladies. I kept hoping he'd ask me to dance again, but he spread his charms among all the ladies present. In the ballroom upstairs. Would you like to see it?"

The old woman opened the door a little farther, but Abby felt rooted to the front porch. She did some fast calculations. Sure, the woman looked ancient, but she'd have to be nearly two hundred years old to have danced the Virginia Reel with Abraham Lincoln.

The hair on the back of her neck stood up, and she glanced over at John. He was scratching his head. His laptop was still in the car. But even if he had booted up *Beautiful Houses* right there on the porch, the program wouldn't actually take them physically back in time. Nevertheless, Abby spun around to check that Kate's car was still there. Yep. They were still in the twenty-first century.

Patty Ann's voice came down the hall staircase. "Miss Granger," she called, "I'm fixin' to turn on the vacuum sweeper, okay?" After a beat, the vacuum came on and blended in with the tinny music. And then the rattling sound of it being dragged back and forth over bare wood floors joined the mix.

"Could we please come in and—" In sudden concern, John stooped to look at the old woman's face.

Miss Granger's eyes were wide with what looked like terror. Slapping her hands over her ears, she turned and looked fearfully up the stairs. "All those girls," she moaned. Bird-like, her head swiveled back to them on her thin neck and she grabbed Abby's arm in a surprisingly strong grip.

"Do you hear them cryin'?"

"It's the vacuum, Miss Granger," Abby said, patting her hand.

The old woman's face cleared a bit. She released Abby's arm and shoved her back. "You all go on. There's nothin' to look at here." The door slammed in their faces, and the lock turned. The vacuum continued, overlaid with the sound of Miss Granger weeping.

"Well," Abby said as they stepped down from the porch. "We sure made her day."

When they got back to the car, Abby told Kate and Ryan what had happened.

"Isn't there something we can do?" Kate asked.

"I'm going to try again to make it take us inside the house." John grabbed his backpack and started back toward the house.

"It's worth a try," Kate said.

"But she was crying, John," Abby said. "She's upset and thought that—"

"If we keep low she won't even notice we're out here."

"Don't you want to find Ned Greenfield?" Ryan said. "For once I agree with Roberts."

Kate opened the door and got out. "I don't mean any disrespect, but she's wacky, Abby. She's probably forgotten all about us by now."

Abby sighed. "Well, if you're sure she won't see us."

"I'll move the car back down the lane a bit," Ryan said. "In case she happens to look out."

They moved up the porch steps as quickly and quietly as they could and then sat down under the window where they wouldn't be seen from inside. John opened his laptop and it began booting up.

He was able to take them inside the house this time and they watched the Granger family living rather boring lives.

The daughters did a lot of embroidering or writing in their diaries. Mrs. Granger spent hour upon hour playing a huge mahogany piano. The sons and Mr. Granger were seldom there, presumably off amassing more money at their salt-making business.

Guests visited from time to time, which probably went a long way to break up the monotony of their lives but did nothing to help them find the information Kate needed. And they had parties. Abby had just spotted a guest that looked a lot like Abraham Lincoln, only without the beard, when a noise from the present intruded.

Chief Logan stood glaring down at them. "What in the cat hair are y'all doin' here disturbin' Miss Granger? I told you there wasn't anything here you needed to see."

"We didn't mean to upset her," Abby said.

"We just wanted to ask her a few questions," Ryan said. "It's a free country, isn't it?"

Naturally, Ryan's attitude annoyed Chief Logan—as it did everyone except Kate. "Guess you folks didn't see the No Trespassing sign." He smiled, but not in a friendly way. "But wait. I seem to recall discussing that with y'all last night."

"But the gate—"

"John," Abby said quickly, "don't go there, okay?"

"You and you," Chief Logan said, pointing to John and Ryan, "are coming with me. If you ladies want your young men back, you'll have to follow along to the station in your car."

CHAPTER 15

Abby had to keep reminding Kate the whole way into town that they were following a policeman. They couldn't break the speed limit or tailgate no matter how much of a hurry they were in to get the guys back. The chief had already gone in by the time they pulled up to the Equality Municipal Building. It was newish and brightly lit. A pretty receptionist, who looked no older than they, was apparently waiting for them. John and Ryan had already been whisked out of sight.

"I hear you're writing about our town," she said.

"No," Abby said. "We're doing research."

"Family research," Kate added.

The receptionist looked unconvinced. She probably heard all manner of excuses from felons. "Well, you can have a seat in the waiting area until Chief Logan gets it all sorted out."

They sank into the hard plastic chairs and looked around. Signs indicated the building housed offices for the utility company, the mayor and city clerk, and the police department. Abby wanted to go back to the counter and ask the receptionist whether John and Ryan had been taken to a cell or to be photographed and fingerprinted or what. But the young woman had already gone to her desk and begun typing about two million words a minute.

Wherever they were, the guys weren't with Chief Logan. The window blinds on his office were open, and they saw him reclining in his chair, talking into a telephone he held under his chin.

"Why doesn't he say something?" Kate asked. "How long is he going to make us sit here?"

Abby looked up at the clock on the wall. "You realize it's only been six minutes? Calm down. And try to look innocent if Chief Logan turns our way."

A door across the lobby opened and a frowning policeman came out. He walked briskly toward them, his police-issue shoes squeaking on the gray linoleum floor. Abby's heart rate kicked up and she felt faint. Would he be the one to take them to be fingerprinted? But he passed by them without speaking and went into the chief's office, closing the door behind himself.

"They'll get to make a phone call, won't they?" Kate asked. "Or is that only on TV?"

"I think so." Abby got out her phone and saw that the reception was terrible. Only one bar showed. She tried to decide whom she should call before she got taken to a cell. Her parents would go spastic, but there really was no other option. Her best friend was sitting next to her, in just as much in hot water as she was. She took a cleansing breath and put her phone back in her purse. Maybe this would all get worked out and they wouldn't have to know about her run-in with the law. At least not for a very long time.

But somebody ought to know where they were, just in

case this whole thing turned out to be like that movie where the sheriff murdered outsiders who came to his town. Abby took out her phone again.

"Who are you calling?"

"Don't worry. Just Merri." Sure, she was only eleven, but she was smart and solid. She angled herself away from the receptionist's desk and Chief Logan's window as best she could but still felt like she was in a fishbowl.

Merri's home phone rang six times and then went to the answering machine. Abby mumbled a garbled message about finding Hickory Hill and Ned Greenfield, only not the right one, and in case she didn't call back in a few days Merri should consider calling the Equality Police Station, only it wasn't serious. Probably. And Chief Logan seemed nice. So she shouldn't worry about them because they would surely be the only inmates. Probably. Because how many hardened criminals could a town the size of Equality have anyway?

Abby hurriedly signed off when the frowning policeman came out of Chief Logan's office with some official-looking documents. He walked over and handed them to the receptionist, and after a whispered conversation with her, went back out the door he had come from.

"Do you suppose those were arrest warrants?" Kate asked.

"Maybe," Abby said.

The big clock on the wall said it was ten-twenty.

Mayor Windham came out of his office, looked around, and then zeroed in on Abby and Kate. He put up a finger and said, "Wait right there." As if they had a choice. He went back into his office, then came out again after a minute and strode over to where they sat, carrying a stack of tourist type brochures.

"Here." He handed Abby one titled Guide to Southern

Illinois Fishing and one to Kate called Native American Artifacts in the Saline River Basin.

"Thanks, Mayor Windham," Kate said.

His face fell at Kate's lackluster response. "I've got even better ones," he said eagerly, flipping through the stack in his hands. "Southeastern Illinois Clean Coal: Fueling Better Lives, Shawneetown Bank State Historic Site, Ohio River Scenic Byway: River to the Nation, Garden of the Gods: Gateway to the Shawnee National Forest, Gallatin County Songs and Folk Tales. Oh, and this one's good: Fluorspar: The Official Mineral of Illinois. Of course, Patty Ann already told you all about salt, but just in case you need to refresh your memory, here's one called When Salt Was King. I know you'll want to get your facts straight. And I'd be glad to repeat the stuff about Little Egypt if you want to take notes this time."

"That's all right. I think we're good," Kate said.

"Thanks," Abby said. "This will keep our minds busy while we wait."

"Okay," Mayor Windham said. "Don't be afraid to ask if you need any more information." He hurried back to his office and shut the door.

"Wow," Kate said. "They sure are nice to convicts."

"And committed to education, apparently."

Kate must have sensed the panic rising in Abby's chest, because she reached over and gave her a hug. "Don't worry, Abbicus. I'm sure we'll just be fined or something."

But would it go on their permanent records? Would she and Kate be kicked out of Ambassador College? Would she be reduced to a career in hamburger flipping? Worse yet, would her parents wear that same look of disappointment that Brother Greenfield had?

Abby straightened in her chair. "You're right, Kate." She picked up a brochure and began to read. Might as well improve her mind. When she finished the last of them, having learned more than she ever wanted to know about the trees, rocks, rivers, and minerals of the area, she stacked them on the chair beside her and looked up.

The clock on the wall said ten-fifty. The receptionist was still typing, and Chief Logan was still on the phone, although he had straightened in his chair and was writing something on a yellow legal pad.

Kate nudged her arm. "Hey, Abby, did you know that we have a state mineral?"

"Fluorite. Merri told me."

"Well, did you know that they get fluorspar from it, which is used to make a ton of stuff. And did you know that 80% of the U.S. production of fluorspar comes from Illinois?"

"I do now."

The outside door opened and Shireen, the waitress who had served them at the Red Onion, came in carrying a white paper bag. The receptionist stopped typing and came and looked inside it. "You didn't bring the kind I like."

"Hey, friends don't let friends do donuts."

"Thanks. I owe you."

"I hear you're going to need prisoner lunches today."

The receptionist glanced over at Abby and Kate and said. "I'll call you when I know how many."

"It's terrible the way they're stirring up trouble around here. Why do reporters always want to write about nasty things anyway?"

The receptionist lowered her voice and said something that caused Shireen to look their way.

"Oh. Well, I've got to get back, Monica. See you."

The receptionist took what looked like a cherry Danish from the bag, put it on a paper plate, and went to the chief's office. After a quick rap on the door she went in. The smell of the pastry followed her.

When she came out, Abby said, "Excuse me, Miss?"

"Yes?"

"Does that waitress—Shireen—think we're reporters?"

"No."

"Oh, good, because we're not."

"She thinks you're journalism students from SIU. But I set her straight. When will your book come out?"

"Book?" Kate asked.

"We're not writing a book," Abby said. "We're down here to do research."

"Oh, right," she said with a wink. "Research." A phone rang and she hurried back to her desk. After a brief conversation she went back to typing.

The frowny policeman came and picked up the paper bag from the counter and took it with him. Abby's stomach growled, and she pictured the Red Onion's menu. If they ever got out of here she'd order a corndog to celebrate—and one for Kate too, no matter what Ryan thought.

The street door opened and Patty Ann Frailey stepped inside the lobby. After a slight hesitation she went up to the counter. The typing stopped and the receptionist stood. "What can I do for you, Miss?"

"I need to see Chief Logan," she said. "Quick."

"He's on a call right now, but you can wait over there."

Patty Ann turned to where she pointed and saw them. "Oh," she said, rushing over to them. "I got here as soon as I could. I'm sorry. I didn't realize Miss Granger had called the police. It took me a spell to get her calmed down enough to talk."

"Miss?" the receptionist called. "You can go in now."

"I'll do the best I can," she said with a concerned look at them. She went into the chief's office, shutting the door behind herself. Chief Logan smiled at Patty Ann, but then a range of emotions, most of which Abby couldn't identify, passed over his face. One, however, was clearly annoyance. He looked toward where they sat, and she lowered her eyes. After a second, Abby risked another look and saw that Chief Logan had picked up the phone and was dialing a number as Patty Ann recited it to him. He talked into the phone for about five minutes. Then the door opened and he ushered her out.

"You go on back and finish up at Miss Granger's, Patty Ann," he said. "And as for you two ladies, it's time to have a little chat." He motioned for them to go into his office. "Mr. Roberts and Mr. Turner will be joining us shortly."

Abby stuffed the brochures into her purse because there was no sense adding littering to her rap sheet, and then she followed Kate into the lion's den.

CHAPTER 16

They wasted no time leaving the municipal building after Chief Logan finished yelling at them.

Kate put her head on Ryan's shoulder. "Was prison awful, sweetie?"

Ryan smoothed his hair back and let out a huff. "Yes, but I'm all right, Kathryn."

"Yeah," John said. "It was pretty awful. Ryan didn't have a mirror, and all the donuts with sprinkles were gone by the time we got ours."

"Well, I'm glad you guys were having a fun time, John," Kate said. "I was worried sick. I kept remembering this movie I saw where a small-town sheriff arrested strangers passing through. He hacked them to death with a machete and then buried them in back of the police station."

"You saw that, too?" Abby said with a shudder.

John laughed. "Chief Logan was pretty mad. No telling what would have happened if Patty Ann hadn't talked Miss Granger into dropping the charges."

"And speaking of our hero." Abby waved at Patty Ann who was just coming out of the post office across the street.

She smiled and hurried over to them. "I had to mail a letter for Miss Granger." She nodded at the paper bag she held. "And pick up a few things from Anderson's."

"Thanks to you," Abby said, "the guys are out of the slammer."

Patty Ann let out a huff. "Yeah. Well, I'm not so sure I did the right thing. Miss Granger was already as nervous as a cat in a room full of rockin' chairs when I got there this morning on account of the coyotes keeping her awake last night."

Abby darted a look at John. He looked as guilty as she felt.

"Then you guys really set her off. Of course, I never should have vacuumed upstairs when she was having one of her spells. I thought I'd never get her settled down."

"I'm sorry we upset her," Abby said. "We just didn't realize."

"Well, if y'all are so all-fired anxious to talk to Miss Granger, I'll take you."

"We wouldn't want to worry her," Abby said the same time Kate said, "Would you?"

They stood out of sight on the porch while Patty Ann knocked on the door. She put her face to the window and tried to see past the curtains. "I hear her coming," she said softly. "Remember though, I'm not going to let you in unless she's feeling all right."

"Of course not," Abby said.

"Just try, okay?" Kate said.

The door opened and Patty Ann smiled. "Miss

Granger, I brought some of my friends for a visit."

"You're not dressed, child." Miss Granger's voice sounded serene. "Come on in and I'll find you something pretty to wear. But we'll have to hurry. The dancin' is about to start."

Patty Ann stepped through the door, extending her hand back so they could see the wagging movement she made to indicate it was iffy whether Miss Granger was up to their visit or not. Then she turned and mouthed the words, "Wait here."

"Well, at least she's not shrieking," Ryan said, checking his watch. "Obviously, we'll need to keep track of the time, or we'll be stuck in the armpit of the nation for another night."

"Obviously," John said.

Abby took her phone out of her purse and saw there were thirteen missed calls. Merri picked up on the first ring and shouted in her ear. "What's going on, Abby? Are you guys all right?"

"We're fine, fine. As I thought, it was no big deal. I'll tell you all about it when we get home."

"You said you found Ned Greenfield, but he's the wrong one?"

Abby chuckled. "Definitely. This Ned Greenfield is black. But we did find Hickory Hill. We're standing on the front porch right now. I'll take a picture to show you when we get back. Speaking of which, it might be late. Hopefully, the old lady who lives here will let us time-surf, and we'll get our answers sooner rather than later."

The front door opened, and Patty Ann waved them in. "Come on. I think it's goin' to be all right."

"Sorry. I've got to go now, Merri," Abby said into her phone. "I'll call you when we're on the road." She clicked her phone off and followed the others into the house.

Patty Ann led them down the dim walnut-clad hall, past the dark staircase, and into a living room straight out of Dickens. Miss Granger sat primly on a gold brocade loveseat, smiling pleasantly in a way that said she didn't remember them. "Welcome to Hickory Hill. I'm delighted you could make it."

"Thank you, ma'am," John said. "I hope we're not disturbing you."

"Certainly not. Please be seated."

The room, a cross between a funeral home and a museum, was crowded with a hodgepodge of overly ornamented tables and oversized stuffed chairs. A huge mahogany piano with massive carved legs took up one end of the room. A shiver went down Abby's spine; it was the same piano they had seen John Granger's wife Martha playing.

Everyone sat down and looked around the room. Whoever had designed the wallpaper had managed to make pink roses and magnolia blossoms look ugly. But it didn't matter because most of it was hidden by portraits of Miss Granger's grim, unblinking ancestors hanging on the four walls around them as if they were supervising their visit.

Straight across from where Abby sat was the man they had seen last night on the porch. She stood and went to look at his portrait. John Granger and his wife made a handsome couple. In fitting with his status as a successful businessman, landowner, and upstanding member of the church, he wore a fine suit with a velvet-trimmed vest. Martha wore a dark dress with lace collar and hair covering. He looked satisfied with life. She looked resigned.

Kate came and studied the portrait and then whispered, "Yep. That's John Granger." They went back and sat down.

"We heard that another family also lived in this house," Kate said. "The Greenfields."

"They're related by marriage to General Lawler," Miss Granger said.

"Really?" Kate said.

"You might have seen his statue in the town square."

"Yes, we did," Abby said. "He was quite famous, wasn't he?"

"Indeed, not to brag, my family is more so. My great, great grandfather owned the salt mine and was quite wealthy. Patty Ann can tell you all about how important salt was, can't you, dear?"

Patty Ann blushed. "I already told them more than they want to know about salt, ma'am."

"Do you recall the name of the Greenfield who married into the family, Miss Granger?" John asked.

She frowned and fidgeted with the buttons on the front of her dress. "You're mistaken. It was the Lawlers that married into the family." Then she smiled vaguely and rose from the loveseat. "Well, Patty Ann, let's go make tea." She turned back in concern. "You are staying for tea, aren't you?"

"We'd love to," Abby said, glancing at the others. "If it's no bother."

Patty Ann took Miss Granger's arm and led her to a door at the end of the room. "We'll have a tea party, won't we?"

John had already slipped his laptop out by the time the door closed behind them. He pushed aside a leather-bound book on the coffee table to make room for it and launched *Beautiful Houses.*

The book appeared water-damaged, the cover stained and wavy, preventing it from lying flat. Abby picked it up and opened it. The pages were densely covered with spidery words in faded brown ink. It was a diary, a very old diary. It was surely too old to be Miss Granger's, but all the same, she felt embarrassed to be handling it. She shut it quickly and set it at the end of the table.

"Okay," John said. "We're in."

"And here we are," Kate said. "This same room."

"Yeah, some of the same portraits on the walls," Ryan said. "Same piano."

Abby glanced at the kitchen door. "You'd better turn the volume down."

CHAPTER 17

Elizabeth sat in the light from the front window embroidering pink roses on a pillowcase for her hope chest. "Mother, make him sit down. He's driving me ma—" She glanced over where her sister Mary sat writing furiously in her diary. "He's driving me to distraction."

Eyes closed, Martha played on with no need to refer to the hymnal in front of her. Oh Come, All Ye Faithful was her favorite Christmas carol. She smiled, thinking of Reverend Farris' compliment after church. She had a real musician's touch, he'd said. Her playing would make this year's Christmas pageant a complete success. Why, she could be a concert pianist if she had a mind to be.

"Mother!" Elizabeth said again.

"Thomas, please quit pacing the room like a race horse," Martha said without looking up.

"Is it any wonder I do?" He swore viciously. "It's Sunday! Why does he have to do it on Sunday?"

"Some business has to be handled right away, dear.

Even if it is Sunday. The Scriptures allow a man special leave to break the Sabbath if his ox is in the ditch."

Another muffled cry came down from the third floor. Mary looked up from her diary, her pale blue eyes gone wide. She darted a look to the door that led out into the hall and then bent back to her writing.

Martha transitioned into *Hark, the Herald*, already considering what she would play when that song came to an end. Maybe *Go Tell it on the Mountain*. It was a favorite with the Negroes. Although why she should try to cheer them up when they were being so obstinate was a mystery.

The door opened and Lil, eyes downcast, came in carrying a tea tray. The cries from upstairs were clearer. "Shut the door, for mercy's sake," Thomas said.

Lil leaned against the door until it shut and then brought the tray and eased it onto the credenza against the wall.

Martha opened her eyes at last. "Oh splendid! Look, children. Lil brought Christmas cookies."

Mary's diary lay open in her lap. A tear fell from her tightly closed eyes and blotched the ink. Elizabeth thrust her embroidery frame away and went to sit by her sister. "Hush, Mary dear. It'll be over soon."

Martha changed her mind and began playing *Joy to the World*. It was not her favorite Christmas carol, but it was loud. "Come on, children, sing with me."

"We're getting nowhere," Ryan said, snapping them back to the present. "This is going to take forever, wading through all this to find him. If there ever was a Ned Greenfield here."

John paused the action and ran a hand through his hair

before turning to him. "Okay, I'm going to take it off virtual and browse through the whole century."

"No need for that," Kate said. "Concentrate on just one decade. According to the census, Ned Greenfield was living here in 1850, but he's not mentioned in the 1840 census."

"Good to know," John said. "That will save us a lot of time."

Abby picked up the diary on the table. Inside the front cover in a bold script was written, "To Mary Granger from Mother." It was the diary they had just seen the young woman nervously writing in. Abby had assumed Miss Granger's "spells" were because she was getting a little senile. But perhaps "wacky" ran in the family. She closed it and put it back on the table.

"Okay," John said. "I've got it set for 1840."

"Surf's up," Kate said, grinning.

The door swung open and Patty Ann stood there holding a silver tea tray. "After you, Miss Granger."

"Oops," Abby said. "Not now."

Miss Granger became tired, and so they had no choice but to leave after tea. They stood on her porch trying to decide what to do next.

"Let's go eat," John said. "I'm starving."

"You just had cookies and tea," Abby said.

"And donuts before that," Kate said.

"Can't help it," John said. "Being incarcerated makes me hungry."

"Well, I'll be seeing you around," Patty Ann said.

"Don't be silly," John said, "You're coming with us."

The Red Onion was bustling with the lunchtime crowd. Shireen hurried to wipe off a table for them. "I'm glad you didn't get thrown in the pokey. I'll be back to take your orders."

"I'd like to pray, if that's all right with everyone," John said.

"That's something we could all use," Kate said.

John's prayer included thanks for the food and their new friend Patty Ann—and a mumbled apology for trespassing.

Abby responded with a heartfelt but silent amen.

When Shireen came to take their orders, Patty Ann said, "I'll have a small Coke, ma'am."

"Nonsense," John said. "You've got to be hungry. Order anything on there. My treat."

"Really? Thanks." She reopened the menu and then looked up at Shireen. "Could I have a cheeseburger, ma'am?"

"You sure can, darlin'."

"Bring her some fries, too," John said.

"And I want a corndog." Abby looked over at Kate. "Make that two."

The others ordered and Shireen hurried off toward the kitchen just as a man in paint-splattered clothes rushed up and stood next to their booth, twisting his hat in his hand.

"I have something to say to you'ns."

The noise in the room went down a few hundred decibels and heads turned toward them.

"You'ns come down here and make a big stink, the tourists will stop a-comin', and The General Lawler Bed and Breakfast won't even get off the ground. Nobody's more in favor of the First Amendment than me, but I'm just saying you'ns shouldn't stir up things best forgotten. That's all I got to say."

He turned away and headed toward the door. A man two tables over from them called out, "Can't you see he's just trying to make a living?"

Abby felt her eyes go wide and her face grow hot. "What's he talking about?"

"Guess the word is already out that you went and disturbed Miss Granger," Patty Ann said. "We're kind of protective of her."

"I noticed," John said.

"But what does that have to do with him?" Ryan asked.

"Everyone seems to think we're writing a book," Abby said.

"The woman at the police station is convinced we're journalism students in town to investigate—"

"Can we talk about that later?" Patty Ann asked, glancing around the room.

"Sure," Abby said. Maybe she was right. It felt like the whole room was focused on their table. Shireen refilled everyone's drinks. They chatted about the weather and anything else but what was most on their minds.

The door opened and Brother Greenfield came into the Red Onion. Beside him a stooped elderly man shuffled in, leaning heavily on a cane.

"Come sit by us," Patty Ann called.

Abby cringed. He surely wouldn't be happy to sit by them. Were they about to get another public scolding, this time for profaning a church? She glanced at the people eating nearby, hoping they weren't the type to carry their pitchforks to lunch.

But thankfully Brother Greenfield was not one to hold a grudge. A smile lit up his face and he gave them a little salute. His elderly friend politely removed his straw hat, and together they started slowly toward their booth. They were the only African Americans in the restaurant, and Abby had a new sense of how it must feel to be so conspicuous as a minority.

"I heard y'all were still in town," Brother Greenfield said when they finally reached their table. "I was hoping I'd run into you."

Shireen wiped the table next to their booth, and he and his friend sat down. The old man held his cane out for them to see. "Alex gave it to me. It's my birthday, you know."

"It's quite stylish, sir," John said, grinning.

"It is, isn't it? But I'm grateful for its usefulness too. I'm not as spry as I used to be, you know. Or as tall, for that matter. Why I used to be taller than Alex here, although not as tall as Cousin Clyde. Huge men, the Greenfields are."

Shireen stood waiting politely with her pad and pen. "What can I get you gentlemen?"

Brother Greenfield smiled and patted the old man on the arm. "My Uncle Henry had a hankerin' for Coca-Cola to celebrate his 89th birthday. Miss, we'll have two of your largest."

"Congratulations, sir," John said.

"Clyde promised to guard the cemetery whilst I'm gone," Henry said.

"He means the one down by Half Moon," Brother Greenfield explained. "Sherman Coal Company has no qualms about blasting cemeteries off the face of the earth. Of course the Eternal Judge knows where everyone's buried and come Judgment Day he'll raise them up. Won't he, Uncle Henry?"

"That he will, Alex. But no sense making it any harder for the Lord than it has to be."

Brother Greenfield's expression turned serious. "I hear y'all had a spot of trouble this morning. Glad to see that everyone's here and accounted for. How's Miss Granger, Patty Ann?"

"She's all right. Now. I took them back and introduced her. We had a little tea party. She's restin' now."

"You're lucky. Miss Granger doesn't much care for company." He smiled sadly. "Or at least for 'colored' company. I got the chance to talk to her about Jesus one time, but she was too scared to listen much. Satan's got her locked up tight. Convinced her she's got to pay for her sins herself. Hers and her whole family's. Makes me so sad I can't help her more—other than praying, that is." Then he smiled at Patty Ann. "But God's using you to work on her, honey. He'll break through those chains binding her one of these days."

Henry propped his cane against the table, closed his eyes, and began humming. Brother Greenfield patted his frail back. "Don't go to sleep there, Uncle Henry. These folks want to know about Ned Greenfield."

The old man's eyes popped open and he looked surprised to find himself there. "Ned Greenfield, hey? Well, he got took away. Kidnapped. Sent down the river. The whole family got carried away." He chuckled and looked at everyone with twinkling eyes. "Well, except for one Greenfield. Wouldn't be here otherwise."

Abby shot a look at John and Kate. It had to be the same Greenfields they had seen even if the story was a little off.

Brother Greenfield chuckled. "It's funny, Kate, that we'd both have a Ned Greenfield in the family."

Kate smiled. "What are the odds?"

"Grandpa always talked about it," Henry said. "He'd scare the living daylights out of all us children, warnin' us about the bad men that would carry us away to Kentucky if we weren't good. Said it happened to his Grandpa Nelson.

Said Grandpa Nelson was always sad wonderin' where they had taken his family, 'specially his brother Ned. He always wondered what happened to Ned."

Shireen came then and set the drinks down in front of them. Brother Greenfield helped Henry get his straw unwrapped. "There you go. What do you think?"

Henry took a long swig of his Coke and then smacked his lips and grinned. "Ah, that's good. Don't care who you are."

"Let me out, John," Abby said. "I need to use the restroom."

"Say please."

Abby sighed in mock disapproval. "Please let me out."

He stood and Abby scooted out of the booth. She stared at him, and he got the message and followed her down the hall to the restrooms.

"What's up?" he said.

"I think we should tell Brother Greenfield," she whispered. "Ask him for permission to time-surf in the church. There's got to be some connection between the Ned Greenfield we saw and Kate's Ned Greenfield, the one born at Hickory Hill. If we lock onto him maybe we'll find out what it is.

"I'd love to have the chance to explain we weren't getting it on in Brother Greenfield's Sunday School room, but that means another person in on this deal. And if we tell anyone, it ought to be Patty Ann. If she could get us back inside the Granger mansion, I know we'd find something."

"I don't know. Miss Granger is really fragile. I wouldn't count on her cooperating. Besides, he's related to Ned Greenfield. He deserves to know what happened to him."

"Okay. I guess if you can't trust the Allstate man, who can you trust? We can ask. But if he says no…well, my trespassing days are over, just so you know."

"Agreed."

When they got back to the table, Uncle Henry was looking anxious. "We'd better hurry, Alex. It's gettin' late."

"We've got plenty of time, Uncle Henry. Go on and finish your Coca-Cola."

"What's your hurry, Mr. Greenfield?" John asked.

"Wouldn't do to be late," Henry answered and went back to sipping his Coke.

Brother Greenfield looked at his watch. "It's not even two o'clock, Uncle Henry. Quit your fretting. He smiled apologetically to the others. "He doesn't like to be in town late." He took out his wallet.

Shireen stopped by the table carrying a tray. "Put your wallet away, sir. Clara said to tell y'all it's on the house, seein' as how it's the old gentleman's birthday and all."

"Why, that's very kind of you, ma'am. Isn't that kind, Uncle Henry?"

"It's my birthday," he said with a grin. "I'm eighty-nine years young."

John took his wallet out, and Shireen nodded at him and said, "You young folks too."

John looked perplexed. "Thanks. But why?"

Shireen set her tray down on the edge of their table. "Clara says to tell you....Well, she wants to know if you could leave out that stuff about the Red Onion in your book. You know, about the Red Onion bein' a speakeasy—well, actually more like a whorehouse."

Abby looked around the restaurant. "You mean this is a..."

She laughed. "Oh, no, miss. Not this Red Onion. I mean the original one down in the holler by Half Moon."

John heaved a sigh and looked Heavenward for patience. "Please tell Carol—"

"Clara."

"Clara. Tell Clara we're not reporters—or even journalism students—and we're not writing a book." His voice rose on the last, and he aimed it at the whole restaurant. Several diners near them looked up and then studiously went back to eating.

"We're doing family research. That's all," Kate said.

"Oh, that's a relief. I'll tell her." Shireen looked apologetic. "In that case, here's your ticket. You can pay at the counter." She picked up her tray and walked away.

Brother Greenfield sent a look at each of them in turn. "But there's more to it, isn't there?"

"Yeah, there kind of is," John said. "We wanted to talk to you about it. Only you've got to promise not to tell anyone."

"I'm not a priest, but the rules of confidentiality work the same. Go on, son."

John looked at Abby and she glanced over at Kate and Ryan. "You see," Abby began. "We have this computer program that…" She lowered her voice to just barely above a whisper. "It sounds crazy, I know, but with the program we are able to go back in time—"

"Just virtually," Kate added.

"It seems to work in conjunction with old buildings," John said. "Like Liberty Baptist Church, for example."

"Oh, I get it," Patty Ann said. "That's why you've been so fired up to see the Granger mansion."

"Abby and I were trying it out in the church Sunday night."

"And we saw Ned Greenfield," Abby said. "Back in 1849."

"Ned Greenfield." Henry slurped his straw. "Grandpa always wondered what happened to him."

Brother Greenfield closed his eyes and sighed. Abby steeled herself for a sermon on lying. But when he opened them, his eyes were shining. "Hallelujah. Praise the Lord. I've always wanted a WABAC machine like Mr. Peabody's so I could go back and see what it was like in the olden days."

Patty Ann playfully poked his arm. "Speaking of olden days, that cartoon's from the sixties. I've seen it on Cartoon Network."

Brother Greenfield chuckled and then turned eagerly to John. "How does it work?"

"You mean you believe us?" John said. "Just like that?"

Brother Greenfield laughed. "'Blessed are they that have not seen, and yet have believed.' Our God is omniscient, omnipotent, and omnipresent. Hallelujah! If he wants to give us a gift like that, he can."

"We're not sure how it works," John said. "And it only works part of the time. It has controls where you can zoom in, change the perspective, lock onto characters, and go back and forth through time."

"Best of all," Kate said, "is when you go virtual. It's like being inside their heads."

"It's hard to explain," Abby said. "Would it be all right to go to the church? We could show you."

"Sure." Brother Greenfield retrieved the cane and helped his uncle to stand. "Come on, Uncle Henry, you're about to get the best birthday present ever."

When they stepped out onto the sidewalk, Henry looked up at the sky in surprise. "Why, sundown's a long way off!" he said. "Can we go back in and get another Coca-Cola?"

Everyone laughed, except Brother Greenfield, who wore a funny expression. Abby wondered if they had offended him by laughing.

"I'm sorry," she said, putting a hand to his sleeve. "We didn't mean—"

He smiled kindly at her. "No, no, Abby. You didn't do anything wrong. I was just embarrassed that he brought it up like that. He still worries."

"I don't understand," she said.

"You know, the Sundown Law," he said and looked at each of them. "Well, I suppose you're too young to know about that. You see, there used to be a sign at the edge of town that said…it said…"

"Nigger, don't let the sun set on you in Equality," Uncle Henry said. "Sometimes I forget that sign's gone." He turned to his nephew and grinned. "Did I hear somethin' about another birthday present?"

"I'll meet y'all at the church," Brother Greenfield said.

Abby blinked back tears as she watched them walk off down the sidewalk.

CHAPTER 18

Abby paused the action on the monitor. Hearing Ned's recitation of his little sister's distinguishing scars a second time was no less traumatic than the first. She still wanted to cry. Or hit someone. Wordlessly, John handed her his handkerchief and she wiped her eyes. She wondered if he had an endless supply of them.

Even if it were only a movie it would be distressing to watch. But knowing it was the lives of real people unfolding made it nearly intolerable. Knowing it happened to a relative had to be ten times worse. When Abby had her face under control, she turned to look at Brother Greenfield.

His eyes were liquid with tears, and he was mopping his face with his own handkerchief. "So that's what you two were watching last night. Sorry I jumped to conclusions about what you were up to." He put his handkerchief in his pocket and shook his head in wonder. "Lord have mercy. Those poor, poor boys are my grandpa and uncle with who knows how many greats in front."

Patty Ann's eyes were huge. "Wow. Wow. Wow."

"I wish that were only a made-up story," Kate said.

"Times were really hard for blacks around here back then," Brother Greenfield said. "Even for free blacks. Kidnapping was a common occurrence. You heard what Uncle Henry said."

"Okay." Abby turned back to the monitor. "I'm going to lock onto Ned and see if he goes to Hickory Hill."

Ryan made a production of looking at his watch. "What's the point? Obviously, this is the wrong Ned Greenfield and…"

"Because, Ryan, it's not all about me now." Kate turned to smile at Brother Greenfield. "I'm sorry. Of course you'd like to find out more about your Ned Greenfield."

"It would be wonderful if we could. Although it's going to kill me not to be able to tell the family how I found out."

An acorn landed on his head, and Ned looked up into the oak tree he and Nelson hid behind. A jay screeched and flew off. Ned's stomach was as nervous as if that jay was hunting acorns in it. They'd pay dearly if anyone discovered they had left the farm. The November wind whipped through his shirt, and he put his hands under his arms to warm them. The sun was sinking fast.

"Don't worry," Joseph said. "He'll come. He always goes into town of a Saturday night."

Ned took a deep breath and looked over at his brother. Nelson looked back at him, his face a mask of fierce determination. "We get 'em back."

Joseph looked as certain. "I'll make him tell us."

There was a noise, and a sorrel mare pulling a black buggy came tripping down the lane from the Granger mansion. There was no mistaking the barrel-chested man holding the reins.

"Joseph...." Ned pulled his arm. "You don't know that man."

"Don't worry about me. Just don't let him see you." Joseph hoisted his squirrel gun and stepped out of the trees onto the road.

The mare reared furiously. John Granger let out a loud stream of foul curses and sawed on the reins. "You crazy fool! Are you trying to get us both killed?"

Joseph grabbed the mare's halter and rested his gun on his shoulder. "Where are the Greenfields, Mr. Granger?"

"I have no idea what you're talking about, young man."

"Just tell us where. St. Louis? Paducah?"

"Us? Who else is with you?"

"No one. It's just me. Now tell me what I want to know."

Ned held his breath and told himself all they had to do was keep quiet. Even that man couldn't see through solid oak. Nelson's eyes were wild, and Ned put a steadying hand on his shoulder.

"Get out of my way, or I'll run you down, you fool."

Granger brought his carriage whip down on the mare's back, and she shrieked in fear and rose up again. Joseph fell back and the gun went off. Nelson moaned and pulled away from the tree. Ned grabbed at his shirt but missed. Nelson stumbled from behind the tree, and Ned made another grab for him.

Granger whipped the reins, and the mare took off, Joseph scrabbling to get out of the path of her hooves. Granger looked back over his shoulder and drilled a look of pure hatred at them. He shouted something they couldn't make out. It didn't matter what. The meaning was clear.

"He'll kill us, sure," Nelson said.

"That done it," Ned said. "We got to run."

"Where will you go?" Joseph asked.

"Better you don't know nothin' 'bout that." Ned grabbed his brother's arm. "Hurry. We got to go afore he come back with his gun."

Nelson grabbed his arm and stared at him wild-eyed. "Mama's necklace."

No matter how foolish the idea, Ned found he couldn't deny his little brother that one thing. "I'll get it," he said. "Say your goodbyes to Joseph." He released Nelson and took off running into the trees, past the salt works, and out to Master Granger's farm.

At their cabin he stood in the doorway just looking. The wind whistled through the cracks, and the roof leaked when it rained, but Mama had always done her best to make it a home. He gasped and doubled over with the pain of their loss. Somehow he still expected her and Pap and the girls to be there even though his head told him they were long gone.

It was past quitting time, almost time for supper. By now his Mama would have ended her long day up at the kitchen and be making corn mush and frying up salt pork for their supper. His Pap would come in from picking greens in the little patch he worked by lantern light after his own long day smithing for Master Granger. He'd be telling them stories of where they'd go and what they'd do when his indenture was up. Only a little more time, he'd say. Only a little more time.

Nelson barreled past him where he stood at the doorway. "I made Joseph go on home," he said.

Ned blinked. He went to the ledge on the wall by Mama and Pap's cornhusk bed and got the penny necklace. Lady Liberty was still shiny, and he'd have to remember to keep her polished like Mama had. He looked at it for a moment and then thrust it into his pocket.

"Hurry, Nelson," Ned said. "Grab the blanket and let's—"

Something bashed into the back of his head, and he fell to the floor. He watched through a blood-red haze as Sheriff Dobbs stepped over him and aimed his shotgun squarely on Nelson. "Tie him," he said, and Ned realized other men were there crowding into the cabin. He felt himself being hauled to his feet, and a blinding pain streaked through his head, causing everything to go black for a bit.

They tied him to the back of a horse with a length of rope. When the horse took off, Ned stumbled but remained standing, surprised to find he could trot along, although each step made it feel like someone was chopping at his head with an axe. He tried to see where Nelson was, but the other horses were in the way, and blood kept dripping into his eyes.

It wouldn't be long now. There were plenty of good hanging trees in the woods behind the barns. And then his legs went boneless, and he couldn't trot anymore. He felt himself being dragged over rough ground, and then the blackness came again.

"I've lost him." Abby clicked on the controls but it was no use. They were back in the present and the houses were doing their slideshow again.

"What do you mean?" Kate asked.

"The lock on Ned. Do you think because he passed out that had anything to do with it?"

"Maybe. Try again."

Abby looked at John and grinned. Sometime during

their time-surfing, Uncle Henry had fallen asleep in his chair and was leaning against John's shoulder.

"Sorry," she said. "It's all gone. The church isn't even available."

"Did he pass out, or did he die?" Kate asked.

"If they're going to lynch them, I don't think I can watch," Patty Ann said.

Ryan snorted. "They didn't lynch them—at least not Nelson. Obviously, Henry and Alex wouldn't be here if they had."

"That took place in November of 1849," Abby said. "And Ned was living at Hickory Hill when the 1850 census was taken."

John looked at her and then over to Patty Ann. "Do you think you can get us back into Miss Granger's house? If we had a little time, I'm sure we could find out more."

"I can try. It depends on how she's feelin'. But…" Patty Ann looked apologetically at Brother Greenfield.

"You all go on," he said. "No sense me scaring the poor woman with my big, old black self. Only you have to promise to tell me what you find out." He grinned and leaned over to shake the old man sleeping against John's shoulder. "I've got to get Uncle Henry home anyway."

"Okay," Patty Ann said. "I'll go back and—"

"Wait," Abby said. "Aren't we forgetting something?"

"The library and courthouse," Kate said.

Ryan looked at his watch in horror. "If we don't hurry, they'll close and we'll have to spend another night in this God-forsaken place." He had the grace to look embarrassed. "Oh. Sorry."

"But maybe we won't need any of that. We could just time—"

"We have to go anyway, Kate," Abby said. "Remember? We never checked out of the motel." "

CHAPTER 19

By the time they had retrieved their stuff from the Shawnee Chief and convinced the desk clerk not to charge them for a second day, it was three o'clock. That meant they had only two hours to find any useful information.

They went to the library first. A woman carrying an oversized tote bag was unlocking the door of the tidy brick building. She turned to smile a welcome as they walked up the sidewalk. "I hope you weren't waiting long." She removed a paper sign from the door that said *Back at 3:00*.

"No," Abby said. "We just got here."

"I had to slip out for a minute to drop my dog off at the vet. Lucy's got a nasty abscessed tooth that needs pulling."

"That's too bad," Kate said. "My mom's pug had the same thing."

"You're not from Shawneetown, are you?"

"No," Kate said, "We're not."

John hurried to get the door, and the woman flipped

on the lights as she passed through it and went to set her things on the counter. "Now," she said. What can I do for you? I'm guessing you're not here to check out a book."

Abby pulled her steno pad and pen out of her purse and the librarian's eyes latched onto them. A smile bloomed on her face. "Oh, I get it! Although I'm surprised the Gazette sent four of you. Then again it's not every day we get a famous author here in Shawneetown. But I'm sorry, you've got the time wrong. The book signing isn't until seven p.m., and even then, I thought it would only be polite to give her time to catch her breath before she got interviewed. You're welcome to stay until then, of course. Did they tell you? She was born just over in Eldorado. She didn't grow up around here, but her dad's folks lived in the hills near Equality."

At last the barrage of words came to an end, but before Abby or anyone else could correct her mistaken idea, the librarian had turned her attention to her tote bag on the counter. "I brought refreshments," she said. "And I found the cutest paper plates with strawberries on them at the Dollar Store."

Abby suddenly realized she was the only one still standing there and wondered when the others had slunk away. "Over here," John called softly. They stood looking at a bookshelf against the far wall. She gave the librarian a little wave and hurried over to them.

"Is this the genealogy department?"

"Heck, we found the entire history department," John said with a grin.

Ryan snorted. "All six shelves."

Kate sighed in disappointment. "Let's go check out the courthouse, then."

"Hey, don't look so glum, roomie," Abby said. "It's small, but who knows what clues we'll unearth. No doubt the local historians have already done a lot of the sleuthing."

Abby scanned the shelves. "Ah, good. Here's an obituary index and several cemetery indices. Here, hold these." Abby pulled them and started loading Kate's arms. "And quite a few church histories. Good."

"There's one about our famous General Lawler," Kate said. "On the third shelf."

"I think I've heard about all I can take about him," Ryan said.

"Yes, but since he's related to the Grangers…," Abby said.

"And here's one about the history of Shawneetown," John said. "And Gallatin County. And several histories for the surrounding counties."

"This is going to take hours," Kate said. "And we still have to get to the courthouse."

"Don't be silly, Kathryn," Ryan said. "Obviously, we won't read the books in their entirety."

"Just scan their indices," John said.

"Oh. Right," Kate said.

They carried the books to a table, divided them up, and started thumbing through indices and tables of contents. None of them listed any Greenfields.

The librarian rushed up to where they sat, smoothing her hair. "I am so sorry. I got everything set up. I hope our author likes chocolate chip cookies. I see you found something to keep you occupied while you wait. Looks like you have an interest in history. That's wonderful. Let me find you something a little more interesting. I've got a book on the river pirates down at Cave-In-Rock, and Elizabethtown has an interesting history. Did you know it has the oldest hotel in Illinois?"

"Actually," Kate said. "We're here to do genealogical research."

"Oh. Why didn't you say so?" She went to the shelf and pulled out two books with industrial green covers from the bottom shelf. "We've got both 1840 and 1850 for Gallatin County, Illinois."

"The U.S. census," Kate explained.

"A transcription of it."

"Obviously," Ryan said.

"As I said, Ned Greenfield isn't in the 1840 census, but Mom and I found him in the 1850." Kate looked in the index and then turned to the page it indicated. "Here it is. I have to say this transcription is easier to read than the original."

Abby leaned over her shoulder as Kate pointed to an entry for a household headed by John S. Granger. Beneath his name, Martha A. Granger was listed, then Thomas, Elizabeth, and Mary Granger. Below that were fifteen other individuals with various last names. Kate ran her finger down to Ned Greenfield, born 1834, Hickory Hill, Gallatin, Illinois.

"This is the Ned Greenfield Mom and I traced back to," Kate said.

"Wow. What a large family," Abby said. "With so many different last names. Were they cousins, or foster children, or what?"

The librarian chuckled. "I don't think so. All but the first three children were colored. Including Ned Greenfield. Look." She pointed to a B in the fourth column. "That stands for black."

Kate's mouth dropped open. And then Abby realized hers had too. She closed it and stared at the librarian.

"I've heard that that mansion on Hickory Hill was part of the Underground Railroad," the librarian said. "That would explain the huge number listed at that household. Maybe they were on their way north."

Abby didn't want to contradict her, but that theory didn't make a lot of sense. No one would report runaway slaves to the census taker. People risked huge fines and even imprisonment for aiding and abetting them. Charlotte Miles had been well aware of the dangers she faced in her work in Miles Station.

The librarian smiled kindly at Kate. "Sorry. This is the wrong Ned Greenfield, honey."

"Obviously, this is Brother Greenfield's relative," Ryan said and then barked out a laugh. "You should see your face, Kathryn. You're as white as a ghost." He laughed harder. "That was even funnier than I realized. White as a ghost! Don't worry," he said, taking her arm. "You're as white as I am."

Kate blinked and then turned to frown at her fiancé. "That's not it at all, Ryan. There would be absolutely nothing in the world wrong with having African blood in the family. I'm just disappointed this is a dead end."

Chuckling, he put an arm around her shoulders. "Okay, Kathryn. Maybe we'll find something at the courthouse. And if not we'll go back to Chicago and start all over again."

Abby smiled at the librarian. "Thanks for your help."

"Keep in mind that sometimes slaves took on the surnames of their masters. Your Ned Greenfield may have owned this slave at one time."

"Is that supposed to make me feel better?" Kate muttered when they were out of earshot.

It wouldn't, Abby thought. But it might be the connection they were looking for.

CHAPTER 20

Signs posted in the courthouse led them down narrow halls, past the courtroom, and eventually to the Office of Records. The clerk at the front desk was eating a late lunch. Or early dinner. She wiped her mouth and smiled apologetically up at them.

"So there is a Mickey D in town?" John asked, looking with interest at the white and yellow McDonald's bag on her desk.

The woman grinned. "Sorry. If you've got a hankerin' for a Big Mac, you'll have to go over to Kentucky for it. What can I do for you?"

Kate explained once again about her genealogy project, and the woman abandoned her hamburger and led them to a room behind her office. The walls were covered with floor-to-ceiling bookshelves, each packed to near capacity with books of various sizes and colors. In the center of the room a slanted chest-high counter was provided for those who wished to study the books.

"All the volumes in this room are indices," she explained. "They'll tell us which record books to look in next door. Let's start with births. What year are we looking for?"

"I don't really know for sure. I mean, I thought I did. My mom and I traced my family back to a Ned Greenfield. In the 1850 census his birth date was listed as 1834."

"Okay, that's a start," the clerk said.

"But now I know he's not the right Greenfield, so I have no idea on the birth date."

"Well, let's see what we can find. Ned is usually a nickname for Edward, Edmund, Edgar, or even Edwin." She pulled a faded gray ledger from a shelf, plunked it down on the counter, and thumbed to the G section. The only name that came close was Greely. She looked next in the Index of Gallatin County Marriages, and Abby's eye zeroed in on an entry for a Nebo Greenfield and she felt a rush of excitement. Maybe his given name had been entered wrong. Only on closer examination, she saw the date was 1923. If he was related there was no way to see how.

Nevertheless, Abby got out her steno pad to copy the information in case it led to other Greenfields. But before she could, the clerk whisked the ledger away to make room for the Index of Deaths, the Index of Criminal Records, and three others for which Abby didn't catch the names. In some, the name Greenfield was entirely absent. In others it was associated with a completely wrong date. None of the variations of Ned showed up as a given name.

The clerk saw Kate's long face. "Don't give up. We're not done yet." She lay another huge volume down on the counter and opened it to the G's. "This is the Soundex Index. It will give us surnames with variant spellings. Clerks in years past were notorious for their creative spelling of people's names. Of course, sometimes they had to come up with their own spelling if the person they were recording was illiterate."

The Soundex Index listed Greenfeld, Grenfell, and Grenfold as variants of Greenfield, but none of them were Edwards, Edmunds, Edgars, or even Edwins, much less Neds.

"It's so frustrating," Kate said. "The 1850 census shows him right here in Gallatin County."

"Let's check the Registry of Deeds. If he or his family owned property we can find him that way."

They struck out completely for any property deeds for the years 1800 through 1899.

"Okay, so much for our theory that the Greenfields once owned Hickory Hill," Abby said. "What about rentals? Would there be any kind of record for that?"

"Hickory Hill?" the clerk asked.

"Yes," Kate said. "The census record says Ned Greenfield was born at Hickory Hill, 1834, Gallatin County."

The clerk looked at Kate for a long moment. Then she whisked the ladder over to the far bookshelf and quickly scaled it. Taking a book from the top shelf, she came down the ladder and placed it on the counter and then looked at each of them in turn. "It's probably not in here, but...well, it wouldn't hurt to look, would it?" After a while, she snapped it shut and said, "Wait right here."

After only a minute or two, she returned with an ancient-looking ledger. They got a brief glimpse of the scarred leather cover, a shade of brown that reminded Abby of her dad's cordovan dress shoes. A musty smell wafted out when the clerk opened it. Pushing her glasses into place on her nose, she bent and studied the pages of hand-written information closely.

"There," she said at last and pushed it over in front of

Kate. "It's faint. But look closely. John Granger registered a baby born in his household. Ned Greenfield, born 1834, to Mariah, his cook at Hickory Hill. The father's name is Charles."

Kate peered at the page for a moment, and then holding her place in the book, closed it on her hand to see the title: Slave Registry, Gallatin County. She looked up at the clerk.

"They were indentured servants," Abby said. "Not slaves, right? After all, Illinois is a free state. It always has been."

"You didn't know?" the clerk said. "There were slaves in southern Illinois as early as 1719. The French brought them—"

"We're not concerned with what the French may or may not have done before Illinois became a state in 1818," Ryan said.

"Well, yes," the clerk said cautiously, "Illinois came in as a free state. The state constitution forbade slavery. And, yes, most of them were indentured servants. Technically. But since they were held indefinitely—in perpetuity—you'd have to say it was slavery."

"Most of them?" Abby said.

"Well, at the salt works…there they had outright slavery. You see, salt was so important to the whole economy—of the state and the nation. Why, at one time, one-fifth the state's revenues came from salt, and—"

"But the Constitution? What about the Constitution?" Abby realized she was sputtering and tried to calm down.

"Well, you see, the state of Illinois paid the United States Treasury thousands of dollars annually for a special exemption to use slave labor at the salt works. How else would they have been able to keep production up?"

"So you're saying John Granger owned Ned

Greenfield?" John said. "He and the others were his slaves?"

"That can't be right," Ryan said. "Everyone's been telling us Granger's house was a stop on the Underground Railroad."

"Maybe he changed his opinion about slavery later," the clerk said.

Abby couldn't think of what to say, and Kate looked shell-shocked.

Fortunately, John managed to smile and thank the clerk for her help. "We'll let you get back to your lunch. And sorry. It's going to be cold by now."

"Not a problem."

They left the records department and went single file back down the narrow hall. When they came to the courtroom, this time the door was open. The juror boxes were empty and the judge had already left, but lawyer-types in summer-weight suits were still there gathering up their files at the tables for the defense and prosecution.

Abby was about to continue walking past when she noticed that what she had thought was the wall behind the judge's bench was slowly rolling up like a huge white projection screen. A courtroom official was working a control switch in the far corner of the room.

As the screen lifted, a mural painted on the wall beneath it was revealed. The title, on a banner at the top of the mural, was History of Gallatin County. Dozens of people were portrayed, representing the early civil and military leaders and ordinary citizens—farmers, laborers, and housewives—who had played roles in the development of the county. Prominent in the center of the mural were wooden barrels labeled *Salt*. Beside them black slaves labored at the industry upon which the Gallatin County economy had been founded. In the sanitized depiction before them, the slaves wore simple but glowing white shirts and trousers and happily worked away, apparently content to expend their lives for the benefit of the citizens of Illinois. A status they had no hope of attaining.

Abby's heart did a strange gallop, and she thought she might vomit. She had to get outside. Quick. She started to edge past John, but an elderly black man wearing a green uniform stood behind her, broom in hand, watching the courtroom. Seeing Abby's panicky attempt to leave, he stepped aside and released a dry, rusty chuckle. "You look a mite upset by our famous mural. I'd venture to say you're not from around these parts."

"It's disgusting," Ryan said.

"Yeah. Well. You know." He chuckled again. "At least they cover it up when court's in session," he said philosophically as he pushed his broom down the hall.

They sat on the steps of the First Bank of Illinois, grateful for its shade, while they watched the Ohio River roll by a short distance away. Abby had read about the bank in the brochure. But when they had followed Route One down for a quick peek at Old Shawneetown before leaving, she still hadn't been prepared for the sight of the colossal bank sitting all alone on the abandoned street. The bank had once held the money made by the sweat and blood of slaves. Mighty King Salt, Abby thought and then remembered Shelley's poem.

'My name is Ozymandias, king of kings:

Look on my works, ye Mighty, and despair!'
Nothing beside remains. Round the decay
Of that colossal wreck, boundless and bare
The lone and level sands stretch far away.

She realized she'd quoted it aloud when John gave her a look. No sand around, of course, just a muddy riverbank and an empty road that dead-ended where the town once sat. A tugboat pushing a barge upriver tooted as it passed under the Kentucky bridge just downstream from them. She imagined herself further back in time, before the bridge, when, according to the brochure, an enterprising pioneer named Barker had made a living ferrying people across the Ohio in his boat.

Earlier in the summer Abby had learned that Alton, a Mississippi River town on Illinois' western boundary, had been an important entry point for slaves escaping from Missouri. Hundreds, if not thousands, had been conducted through Alton on the Underground Railroad north to safety, helped by the Miles family, among many others.

But here on the eastern boundary, slaves coming from Kentucky and points south had the Ohio River to contend with. Had they sighed in relief to be in the free state of Illinois only to find themselves re-enslaved at the salt mines of Gallatin County? How long had it taken them to find out they weren't safe? Not yet. A worse thought came to Abby, and she struggled to get her head around the idea. Ned Greenfield was born a slave in the land of Lincoln. If she were to go down to the riverbank and cup the water in her hands for a drink, would it taste salty? The Saline River emptied into the Ohio. But how many tears of fear, anger, pain, and disappointment had also added their saltiness through the years?

John picked up a flat pebble and skimmed it across the

empty street. Abby snapped out of her reverie and turned to Kate. She was still watching the barge being pushed up river. Her eyes were red and her hair blew unnoticed into her face. Ryan was patting her ineffectually on the back.

"Don't worry, Kate," Abby said. "We'll go back and time-surf back until we find out the connection between them."

"Sorry, Abby," John said. "But that theory the librarian had about the white Ned Greenfield owning the slave Ned Greenfield? Well, it doesn't make a whole lot of sense if he was born at Granger's Hickory Hill mansion."

Seeing Kate's misery, John's expression softened. "We'll figure out something."

Ryan took Kate by her shoulders and looked into her face. "Kathryn, I don't think there's any connection between that slave and your ancestors. You and your mom just got the wrong Greenfield, that's all. Maybe he's not even named Ned. Let's just leave before we waste any more time in this place. When we get back to Chicago I'll—"

"No, not yet. Let's try a little longer."

Abby flipped her phone open. "I'll call Patty Ann and see if she had any luck with Miss Granger."

The phone number Patty Ann had given Abby was to their landline. She didn't own a cell phone. She left a message on the answering machine for her and decided to call Merri while she waited for her to call back.

Unlike Patty Ann, Merri picked up on the first ring, as if she had been waiting by the phone.

"So when are you getting home?" Merri asked. "Mom said we can call out for pizza again tonight."

"I'm sorry, Merri, we won't be there in time for pizza. We've been following the wrong Ned Greenfield, a black slave. We're going to do a little more time-surfing and follow him in case he leads to the right Ned Greenfield that connects to Kate's relatives in Chicago."

"Hey, maybe you'll meet up with that guy from Charlotte's attic," Merri said. "He was going to Chicago."

"I don't know what you mean. Have you been time-surfing?"

"No, it's not working, dang it. You know? The man we saw when we time-surfed with Kate."

Abby's phone chirped. "I've got to go, Merri. I've got a call coming in."

"Okay. Call me later."

Abby switched over to Patty Ann. "Hey, we're almost back to Equality. What did you find out from Miss Granger?"

"She seems to be fine," Patty Ann said. "So y'all can go see her. Only don't go in until I get there."

"Good," Abby said. "Because we didn't find any more information in Shawneetown. Except, did you know that the salt mine used to be worked by slaves? The free state of Illinois actually used slaves to—"

"Of course, I know that," Patty Ann said. "Everyone around these parts knows that. But no one in Equality wants you writing about all that horrible stuff. It'll ruin any chance we have for tourism."

"We are not writing a book," Abby said. "We're only trying to—"

"You know that and I know that, but lots of other people don't know that. Why do you think everyone's so worked up? I've got to hang up so I can get over to Miss Granger's before you beat me there."

"Okay, see you in a few minutes."

CHAPTER 21

Abby looked up from where she sat on Miss Granger's loveseat as Patty Ann came in from the kitchen. "Any luck, you guys?" she whispered.

John paused the action. "Look," he said, pointing to the monitor, "We found Ned again. The sheriff brought him here."

"He looks terrible."

"At least they didn't lynch him," Abby said. "There's no sign of his brother Nelson."

"Are you sure you want to do this?" Patty Ann said. "As horrible as what we saw at the church was...well, it's nothin' compared to what you might find here."

"It's the only way left to find the right Ned Greenfield," John said.

"Well, then you better hurry with it. Supper is almost ready."

"It was really sweet of her to invite us to stay for

dinner," Abby said.

Patty Ann grinned. "Yeah, well, you may change your mind when you taste it. I'll stall as long as I can."

John Granger opened his front door and stepped out onto the porch with his lantern. When he saw the boy looking lifeless at the end of the rope he cursed and came forward. "You fools! I told you to take it easy. He won't do me any good if you've ripped it off of him." He tipped him over onto his back with the toe of his boot. "All right. He'll do."

Sheriff Dobbs got down from his horse and tied the reins to Granger's porch. "Where do you want him, John?"

"Have your boys take him upstairs."

Dobbs nodded and his men untied Ned. One man took his feet and another his hands and carried him over the threshold. When they started up the stairs, Ned's head bounced over the first few steps.

"For crying out loud. Watch his head," Dobbs said, adding a curse.

"Well, give us some help here. He's huge."

Dobbs went up the steps and grabbed Ned's waistband. The man at his head adjusted his grip on Ned's shoulders, and they lugged him up to the second floor. A door opened, and Martha stuck her head out, her dark hair primly covered with a lace nightcap.

"You go on back to sleep, dear." Granger shut the door in her face and turned back to the sheriff and his men. "We've got to get him up another flight of stairs. There at the end of the hall. Here, let me go first with the light."

Patty Ann came to the door again. "Supper's ready. You'll have to stop for now."

John closed the laptop and rose from the loveseat, apparently eager to eat again.

Kate went to Patty Ann. "Do you think it's possible…would Miss Granger allow us to go upstairs?"

"Maybe," she answered. "You could ask to have a tour. Brag on the house. She's very proud of it."

They sat at one end of a huge mahogany table meant to seat twenty. Patty Ann brought chipped china bowls of chili and distributed packages of cheese crackers. And their choice of water or sweet tea.

"Patty Ann," Miss Granger said, "you say the blessing, why don't you? It won't do a bit of good if I do it."

She bowed her head and thanked God for the gift of salvation and asked him to bless the food, Miss Granger, and her new friends.

When Patty Ann finished, Miss Granger smiled at each of them in turn. "Eat up, everyone. There is plenty more chili in the pantry. Patty Ann gets it at Anderson's for me."

"It's delicious," Abby lied.

"I don't like the kind with peanut butter."

"Nope," Patty Ann said and patted her arm. "I always get the cheesy crackers for you."

"Did you know I once danced with Abraham Lincoln? Right here at Hickory Hill. In the ballroom upstairs. The walls are made to fold back whenever we have dances up there. We all wore our fancy dresses and—"

Patty Ann frowned and took the woman's hand. "Now, Miss Granger, you know the doctor said it wasn't good for you to read the diary anymore."

Her smile was watery. "I'm sorry. I get confused

sometimes."

"I know you do. But you're fine now," Patty Ann said. "I've got a good idea. After supper, why don't we make brownies for your guests?"

"That's a superb idea, Patty Ann."

Kate smiled her best smile. "Miss Granger, we really love old houses."

"We do," Abby added.

"Your house is wonderful," Kate said. "Would you mind if we looked around?"

"Why, certainly. This house has been in my family since 1834. Lincoln once visited here and—"

"That's great." Kate stood and began to gather their bowls.

"Oh, no," Miss Granger said. "You're our guests."

"Y'all go on." Patty Ann waved them away with a speaking glance. "We'll let you know when the brownies are done. It doesn't take long, you know. To make brownies."

"Okay," Abby said. "We'll hurry."

CHAPTER 22

The second floor of the Granger mansion was much the same as the first. The wallpaper was just as garish. Other than that, the walls looked ordinary, and Abby couldn't imagine them folding back to form a ballroom. Either that was a figment of Miss Granger's imagination, or someone had renovated the walls. Not wanting to take advantage of Miss Granger's hospitality, they only peeked in the rooms. The six bedrooms were filled to capacity with the same dark, over-sized, and over-ornamented furniture.

"Let's just sit here in the hall to time-surf," Abby said.

"The sheriff took Ned to the third floor," John said. "Only I don't see any stairs."

"They must be in one of the bedrooms," Kate said.

"They wouldn't put the staircase in a bedroom," Ryan said. "It would be in the hall. Obviously." He walked down to the far end of the hall and entered the bathroom. "But if the bathroom was added later—since obviously they didn't have indoor plumbing in 1834—then maybe…"

Abby and the others crowded together at the door to look in. Like everything else, the bathroom was oversized. It was paneled in boxcar siding that at one time had probably been painted white but was now yellowed with age. Just inside on the left was a small door of the same material set flush with the wall. A padlock dangled, unlocked, from a bracket high on the door.

Ryan removed it and opened the door, smiling smugly. "And there you are."

Inside was a dark, narrow staircase, not nearly as grand as the main one to the second floor. John pulled out his flashlight and aimed it up the stairwell. A thick layer of dust covered the steps, indicating no one had swept them for a very long time. Footprints in the dust meant someone had been using them recently.

John started up the stairs. They creaked loudly, but Kate followed gamely after him. Ryan politely offered Abby the chance to go next, but she waved him on.

The third floor was one open room, a garret really. Although there was plenty of daylight left outside, the room was dim because the windows in the gables of the roof were boarded up.

Even so, they provided enough light to see what the third floor held. Ryan cursed and then Abby saw why.

Twelve sets of chains with manacles were set into the walls at equal distances. And chains hung also from the three support posts in the center of the room. Abby went to the one nearest her and knelt. At the end of the chain was a rusty neck collar resting on the floor.

"What is this place?" Kate asked, her voice hollow and strained.

John grimaced and his nostrils flared as if he had picked up a disgusting smell. "Ned Greenfield's new home." He opened his laptop and launched *Beautiful Houses*.

The lantern flickered over the walls and low ceiling. A chain hung from a post in the center of the room. "Bring him closer," Granger said.

The sheriff and his men lay Ned beside the post and Granger pulled the chain up until he found the wide collar at the end of it. He knelt beside the boy and lifted his head to slip the collar in place. When he turned the key the lock clicked loudly.

Ned's eyes opened. "Master Granger?"

"You'll be all right, boy. I'll take care of you." Granger drew up Ned's shirtsleeve and squeezed his bicep. "Just look at all that muscle. I've been watching you grow, boy." He stood and looked proudly down at him. "Just look how big he is, Dobbs. Big all over, I'll just bet."

The men snickered and slapped their knees. "You fools go on down," Granger said. "We've got to let Ned rest up."

"Nelson? Where's Nelson, Master Granger? Is he hanged?"

"Why in Hades would I waste a good man? I'll put him to work at Half Moon. Soon as he's healed up."

Ned groaned and put his hands up to cover his face.

"Didn't you hear me, boy? He's not hanged." Granger's face and teeth were yellow in the lantern light. "But I daresay you'll find your new job more…pleasurable than he does his."

Master Granger moved away and the door closed. The key grated in the lock and the footsteps grew soft and were gone.

Ned wept until he had no more tears. When he opened his eyes, the moon shone in from a window high on the wall. Even that soft light hurt his eyes, so he closed them again. His head still felt like an axe was buried in it, but even so, he could think now.

No sense denying he was scared. But mostly, he decided, he was surprised he wasn't hanging from a tree, swaying in the wind. Unless they'd lynched him and he was too stubborn to know he was dead. He reached up to feel for rope burns and found instead a metal collar. Yes, he remembered. Master Granger had put it on him.

A whispered voice came to her, and for a moment Abby was confused about where she was—or rather when she was.

"Abby? John? It's me, Brother Greenfield. I'm coming up. I don't mean to startle you."

It was much darker, most of the light gone from the windows. Only the glow from the computer showed Abby where everyone was. Then she saw Brother Greenfield as he reached the third floor. Patty Ann came in behind him.

"Hello." John paused the action and shown his flashlight at the feet of the newcomers.

"Miss Granger went on to bed. I think she forgot y'all were here. So I called Brother Greenfield…."

Matching expressions of horror played over Patty Ann and Brother Greenfield's faces the moment they spotted the chains.

"There have been tales that Granger kept his kidnapped victims on the third floor," Brother Greenfield said. "I had no idea the evidence of it would still be here."

"So this wasn't part of the ,Underground Railroad, then," Patty Ann said.

"No, honey," Brother Greenfield said. "I think that rumor got started because it made for better PR around town. In the black community, the story is that John Granger was part of a network that kidnapped free blacks and sold them into slavery in the South."

"A Reverse Underground Railroad," John said.

"She has to know this is here," Patty Ann said. "That's why she's been so set on me not cleanin' up here."

"She knows," Brother Greenfield said. "I think it's part of what's got her so tied up in knots."

Ryan looked at his watch again. "Well, let's get back to time-surfing."

"We were watching your Ned Greenfield," Kate said. "It was awful. Granger had him chained to that post. Are you sure you want to watch this? If you want, we could tell you what we find out."

"Oh, honey, I was just thinking the same thing about y'all. I hate for you to see what went on up in this room. But as distasteful as it will be, I want to know what happened to Ned. It would set Uncle Henry's mind to rest."

"Are you sure?" John asked.

"Go ahead."

Ned stretched out his arms and legs. They moved sure enough, but hurt like demons were gnawing on them. His shirt was torn to pieces from the rough ground he'd been dragged over. He ran his hand over his chest and belly and found wounds there, but at least the blood was sticky and not running.

Nelson! He gasped and fire wrapped around his ribs, which made him gasp all over again. Then he remembered Master Granger said he wasn't dead. Said he put him to work at Half Moon. Ned groaned. He might as well have said Nelson was dead.

He had walked past Half Moon many times. The salt slaves lived in even rougher huts than Master Granger's field workers. Was Nelson bleeding in one all alone?

He'd seen them working and knew there were lots of ways to die making salt. He'd heard about a man being crushed by a wagon loaded with salt barrels that got away from them. Another man was hit by a flying axe-head as he cut down trees to keep the furnaces fed. Another was burned when a boiling saltwater kettle tipped over on him. They had heard his screams out in the fields as they chopped weeds in the corn. They said it took him nearly a week to die.

The slave graveyard was down that way. And plenty of times when he walked past it, there was a fresh-dug grave with a fresh-carved wooden marker. It had to be easy to carve the words in the wood. But there weren't near as many of them on the slave markers as there were on the granite ones in the Granger family cemetery. They put the slaves' names on the markers, surely. But did they put how they died on them? Did they say where they came from? Who their families were?

Oh, Nelson!

Mama had picked the name Greenfield for them because Master John promised her that her children would work the fields and not ever make salt. Master loved Mama's cooking that much. That other thought tried to wedge its way in, but Ned wouldn't let it get a hold in his head. It was Mama's cooking that Master liked.

Oh, Mama!

Pain streaked through Ned's chest, and he put his hands to his heart to keep it from ripping in two. Pap and Nelson and Nancy Jane and Maybelle, and Baby Lizzie. Where were they this lonesome night? How would he ever find them now he was chained to a post like a dog? At least

Mama wasn't there to see it. And that her other boy was working the salt after all.

Metal scraped against metal, and he knew that someone was working the lock in the door. Lantern light streamed into the darkness and he covered his eyes. He tried to sit up, but an explosion of pain in his head put him right back down on the floor. The door was relocked and he heard a soft shuffle of footsteps coming toward him.

"I'm here to tend you," a female voice said. She set the lantern by him, and he turned his face away when the light threatened to burn out his eyeballs. Mercifully she moved it away and he turned back. She was not as young as her voice had sounded. She was blacker than he was and, except for her calico head covering, melted into the darkness. She looked ten kinds of sad, but her face was set like she was determined to get a bad thing over and done with.

He heard water trickling and then he saw that she had set a bucket of water next to him. She wrung a rag out and wiped his face with it. The warmth of it was soothing and he tried not to flinch.

"Who you be, ma'am?"

"I don't be no ma'am, that's sure. I be Master John's house gal Lil." Water from the rag ran down his neck behind the iron collar, and he wondered if it would rust away given enough time. She opened the shreds of his shirt and began dabbing at the wounds on his chest. He tried to pull his shirt back. His mother was the only woman that had ever touched him and that had been years ago.

"You just lie still. Master John say to clean you up. He say to tell you…he say to show you what your new job be."

"I'm not going to Half Moon then?"

"No, you goin' stay right here. He say if you be nice he take off this thing." She thumped her finger against the iron collar. "You'd like that right enough, I 'spect."

"Yes, ma'am—I mean yes."

"Master John, he don't got enough mens to make the salt. He say he ain't to get no more from Kentucky, not Missouri neither. Master John, he got gals though. He tell them gals if they make fifteen babies they can go north." She held up her ten fingers. "That's this many." She closed her left hand, leaving her right fingers extended. "And this many." She put the rag back in the bucket and then took up her lantern and aimed its light around the room.

Ned rolled onto his side and followed the lantern's light with his half-shut eyes. A dozen chains hung from the walls. Near each was a narrow sleeping pallet and a lidded pot.

"Master John, he pick the strongest gals and bring them here soon as they ready." Her voice was as rusty as a nail in the rain. She wiped at her eyes and stood there looking down at him. "Master John, he say I got to show you how."

As her meaning sunk into his skull at last, he pulled himself to his feet, his head near cracking open, and backed away from her. "Why you talkin' that way, Lil? I'm the one with a broken head, not you."

She followed him until he reached the end of the chain. His eyes went strange again and he felt himself starting to fall, but she took his arm and eased him back to the floor.

CHAPTER 23

John was stomping across the floor when Abby snapped back to the present.

"Did I say Reverse Underground Railroad?" He held his clenched fists close to his sides and stared up at the window in the eaves. The sky showing through the boards was black now, the clouds shutting out most of the light from the moon and stars. "More like Perverse Underground Railroad."

Abby closed the laptop and went to him. He turned and pulled her into his arms.

"Why did you shut it down?" Ryan muttered. "It was just getting interesting."

"Do you really think so, Rye?" John said, his voice dangerously quiet.

"Ryan!" Kate said.

Brother Greenfield pulled his handkerchief from his pocket and wiped his eyes.

Ryan seemed to suddenly remember he was there and

mumbled an apology. "Anyway, I was right. This Ned said that his mother made up the Greenfield name. They didn't have a white master named Ned Greenfield. She made it up. See, I was right, Kathryn." He took her into his arms and tried to spin her into a dance.

She struggled until she had freed herself. "Ryan, stop it."

"Don't you get it? He's the wrong Ned Greenfield. I was right all along. Admit it."

"Or maybe it proves the exact opposite. If there was no other Ned Greenfield, then he's the one I'm related to."

Brother Greenfield snorted a laugh and held his black arm against her white one. The contrast was obvious. Only hers showed up in the dim light. "Not likely, honey."

"Well, we still need to follow him," Kate said. "To find out if he goes to Chicago."

"I thought I could watch this, but I was wrong." Brother Greenfield turned to go.

"You won't have to watch it," John said coming back to the laptop. "You all turn away. I'll fast-forward until I see when he leaves here."

"Why do you get to watch, Roberts?"

"Turner, could you please just…just…shut up?"

Ryan huffed and crossed his arms across his chest. "Well."

"Okay, here goes," John said. "I'll have to slow it down from time to time to check. I'll let you know when it's safe to look."

Everyone turned away, although Kate had to tug at Ryan's arm. The sound of the computer whirring was the only thing Abby heard for several minutes.

Then the whirring stopped and John said, "Dang it."

"What's wrong?" Abby said.

"You can look now."

It was all gone—Ned and Lil, the third floor room, Hickory Hill itself. The *Beautiful Houses* slide show was in full swing.

"You went too far forward, Roberts," Ryan said.

There was a shuffling sound from the stairs and then Miss Granger was there. She reached up and flipped a light switch none of them had noticed. The ugly yellow light made the room even more horrible. She was wearing another museum-quality long dress, this one a midnight blue studded in matching sequins on the hemline and mutton sleeves.

"I heard the music," she said, smiling gaily. "We're gettin' an early start on the dancin', aren't we?"

Patty Ann went to her and took her arm. "Miss Granger, I thought you'd gone to bed."

"I couldn't sleep. At first I thought it was the girls cryin' again. But then I knew it was the music."

She pulled away from Patty Ann and went to Abby. "I'm delighted you could make it." She held out her hand and Abby shook it gently. "And your charming young man." She smiled up at John and put her hand on his arm. Then she frowned and patted her left wrist. "I seem to have misplaced my dance card." She laughed again. "But never mind. I saved a dance just for you."

He took her arm. "Miss Granger, I think you'd better go with Patty Ann."

Turning away from him, she stumbled. Brother Greenfield extended a hand but then pulled it back as if he thought his help would be unwelcome.

Miss Granger seemed to notice him for the first time. Her eyes went huge and she put her hands to her cheeks. "Why did you have to come back?"

"Miss Granger? It's me, Brother Greenfield."

She moved her hands from her cheeks to her ears.

"The girls. All those girls. Do you hear them crying?"

"They're not crying anymore, Miss Granger," Brother Greenfield said. "All those horrible things are long past."

Miss Granger wiped her eyes with the backs of her hands and then turned to Abby and looked earnestly into her face. "Don't ever call them niggers or they'll cut off your ears."

"Miss Granger, there's no need to be afraid. I'd never hurt you, no matter what you called me."

She began sobbing and would have fallen except Brother Greenfield caught her. "Oh, ma'am, don't cry. I'm Alex, not Ned. And you're not John Granger. But even if you were, I'd forgive you."

"How can you?" she sobbed.

"How can I not after all the Lord's forgiven me? Do you have a Bible, Miss Granger?"

"Yes, Patty Ann gave me one, bless her heart."

"Then let's go downstairs. I want to read you one of the Lord's parables—the one about the wicked servant."

"I'll get the Bible," Patty Ann said and followed them down the stairs.

Ryan looked at his watch. "Now can we go, Kathryn? We can be back in Chicago by midnight or one if we leave right now."

"Merri," Abby said. "I forgot to call her back. She wanted to know—" Abby shut her mouth and then opened it again. She probably looked like a fish. "The man in the attic. She was trying to tell me about the man in Charlotte's attic. Remember? The one with the iron slave collar?"

"What are you talking about?" Ryan asked.

"Charlotte told him to go to Chicago," Abby said. "To look for a man named Moody."

"Maybe," John said. "After all, he was only sixteen or so when he was brought here. He'd have changed."

"What man?" Ryan said.

"You know," Abby said. "The slaves we saw in Charlotte's attic the night you and Kate arrived in Miles Station."

Ryan snorted. "Guess I missed that trip," he said sarcastically.

"Oh, sorry."

"And if he did make it safely to Chicago…," Kate said slowly. "Where my Greenfield ancestors all came from. Well, that's just wild."

"We're back on the trail," John said. "Come on. Let's go."

CHAPTER 24

Merri was sitting in the dark on her porch petting Kit Kat when they finally got back to Miles Station. She jumped up and came down the sidewalk to hug Abby.

"You should be in bed, Merri Christmas," John said, ruffling her hair on his way past. "It's after one."

"Are you kidding? After you called, I tried it and it's working again. Come on, I've got it all set up."

"Okay, kiddo," Abby said. "Show us what you found."

"Everyone be quiet on the stairs, okay? Mom went to bed with one of her headaches."

"And, Lord, please bring Mr. Bartlett to us soon, and protect those under this roof from those who would do them harm. And, dear Lord, give me the strength—and time enough—to get everything done that needs doing. Amen."

Charlotte rose from her knees by her bed and hurried from the room. It was too cold to dawdle. In the kitchen she stoked the stove and then made a trip out to the smoke house for a slab of salt pork. She sliced it and then mixed up a batch of cornbread batter in her blue bowl. She put the cornbread on to bake in one iron skillet and the salt pork on to fry in another.

Someone knocked on the back door and then opened it before Charlotte could finish wiping her hands on her apron.

"Lucinda Brown, what are you doing here so early in the morning?" At twenty-five, Lucinda was four years older than Charlotte but her dearest, best friend.

"Early, late, and middle of the day. I'm here, Charlotte, to lend my assistance if you're going to be foolish enough to continue conducting passengers on the Underground Railroad while also tending to the passengers of the Chicago & Alton."

"Well, I expect I've got railroading in my blood." Charlotte peeked into the oven and saw that the cornbread was coming along nicely. "As if you and your father don't do the same thing in Brighton. And how is Doctor Brown?"

"He's well, thank you. And besides him I've got a sister and two brothers to help with the cause. You have no one."

"Don't let Joshua hear you say that."

"Well, yes, of course, dear Joshua." Lucinda took her bonnet off and hung it on a peg by the back door. "Where is the boy? He can bring my case in."

"You're serious about staying?" Charlotte said.

"You know me. I'm always serious."

Charlotte hugged her friend in relief. "That's wonderful, Lucinda. So would you keep watch down here while I take breakfast up?"

"Certainly. I aim to please."

"If anyone should happen to stop by—"

"Don't worry, Lottie, I know what to do."

They loaded the food in a basket and Charlotte took it up to the attic. The morning sun shining through the small windows painted stripes on her guests, making them look all the more like the prisoners they were.

Sally and her boys Solomon and Little Frank smiled and thanked her when she set the cornbread and salt pork down for them.

Charlotte had plenty of work waiting for her downstairs, but she knew it was pure agony for them to be confined there with nothing to do but wait another whole day, hoping that Mr. Bartlett would come for them.

"How would you boys like a story while you have your breakfast?"

Eyes sparkling, they nodded excitedly.

"Once upon a time, there were three little pigs," Charlotte said. "The first little pig …"

"Oh, for crying out loud," Ryan said. "Skip past the fairy tales and get to the guy you say is Ned Greenfield."

Merri glared at him. "I'm trying, Ryan. Besides, I happen to like watching Charlotte."

"She's right," Abby said. "You ought to know by now how easy it is to go too far forward or backward."

Ryan sniffed. "Just try to skim past all the unimportant stuff. If you know how."

"He's there. Just be patient," Merri said.

"I am in earnest,'" Charlotte read from The Liberator. "I will not equivocate—I will not excuse—I will not retreat a single inch—and I will be heard." She rose from her seat on the wooden trunk and folded the newspaper. "There now. What do you think about that?"

"That be fine talking," Sally said, nodding her head wisely.

"Did you understand what Mr. Garrison means?"

Sally looked down and patted her sons' heads as they lay drowsing next to her. "Not rightly, ma'am."

Charlotte had not expected that Sally would understand much of it. But she had known somehow that the man in the corner would. She couldn't make out his face in the shadows, but she saw that he sat leaning against the wall, alert.

"When Mr. Garrison says 'popular but pernicious doctrine of gradual abolition,' he's arguing that slavery should be done away with right now. Not gradually like many people want."

Charlotte returned the newspaper to the trunk. "I've got to go downstairs for a while, but it's getting dark. If Mr. Bartlett's coming tonight, he'll be here soon. You won't have long to wait now."

Just as she was about to descend the stairs the man in the shadows spoke at last. His voice was still croaky, but a bit stronger.

"For Mr. Bartlett—or for freedom?"

Charlotte smiled sadly. "For both, I pray."

Just before she shut the door at the bottom of the stairs, she heard Sally softly singing a mournful song about being a poor wayfaring stranger.

She had hoped that Mr. Bartlett would come take them on to their next stop the evening before. Something must have made him nervous. It didn't pay for a conductor to get careless. But he'd come when it was safe.

Joshua would have gladly taken them on, but her father and husband had made him swear an oath on the Bible that he would never leave Charlotte alone. They hadn't thought to tell her not to take in runaway slaves and would be upset to know the risks she took. But knowing what Proverbs said, how could she look the other way? She had memorized the passage and recited it softly to herself:

If thou forbear to deliver them that are drawn unto death, and those that are ready to be slain; if thou sayest, Behold, we knew it not; doth not He that pondereth the heart consider it? and He that keepeth thy soul, doth not He know it? and shall not He render to every man according to his works?

When she and Joshua brought the evening meal, the attic was completely dark. But her guests didn't complain. They knew it was too dangerous to have a lantern.

"It won't be long now," Charlotte said into the darkness. She wished she could see their faces one more time. "Solomon, do you still remember John 3:16 like I taught you?"

"Yes, ma'am."

"Say it for us then, please. One more time."

"For God so loved the world that he gave his only begotten Son, that whosoever believeth in him should not perish but have everlastin' life."

"And you and Little Frank will remember that verse means everyone, won't you?"

"Yes, ma'am," they whispered together.

"And, Sally, do you remember where you're to go? If you can?"

"Chicago. Mr. Moody's there at the White Swan."

"That's right. He'll help you."

There was a noise outside, and Charlotte hurried to the stairs. "It's surely Mr. Bartlett," she told them, "but everyone keep quiet while I find out."

When she got to the parlor, she saw that Joshua had cracked the front door and was looking out. He moved aside so she could see. A pony cart was coming down the lane.

"I don't recognize him, do you?"

Joshua picked up the shotgun he had leaned against the wall. "Not the pony, the cart, nor the man driving it."

But as he got closer, Charlotte realized the driver was whistling Amazing Grace, one of the code songs she and the other conductors in the area had decided upon.

"Indeed," she said, "how sweet the sound." She opened the door and stepped out onto the porch, Joshua beside her, his gun cradled in his arms.

"Hello," she called cautiously.

"You must be Miss Miles?" the man said.

"I'm Charlotte Miles McGuire."

"I'm Joseph. Mr. Bartlett sent me."

Charlotte let out a deep breath. "Then welcome, sir."

The man got down from the cart and tied the pony's reins to the hitching post. When he lifted his hat, the moonlight revealed that he was not a full-grown man after all, but a young lad about Joshua's age.

"Mr. Bartlett said to tell you he was sorry he couldn't come," he said, wringing his hat. "I'm to take the passengers on."

"You're doing a brave thing, Joseph."

"Mr. Bartlett said to tell you they're usin' his wagon for the harvest, but he found this old pony cart."

"I don't think all my passengers will fit."

Lucinda came out onto the porch. "It'll work, Lottie.

The big man isn't ready to travel yet anyway. Those feet of his…"

Joshua led Sally, Solomon, and Little Frank down from the attic and Charlotte hugged each one as they got in the pony cart. "Don't forget what I told you."

"We won't never forget, ma'am," Sally said.

Joshua secured the canvas over them, and then Joseph clucked, and the pony cart started down the lane. Charlotte stood on the porch between Joshua and Lucinda praying them on their way.

"Obviously, we have to get back into the attic," Ryan said. "if we're ever going to find Ned Greenfield."

"Obviously, Ryan. That's what I'm trying to do," Merri said. She fast-forwarded a bit more and they watched as Charlotte went back up into the attic.

"Stop there, Merri," Abby said. "This is where three new men arrived. Merri and I saw them and heard their stories earlier this summer. One man named Lucky," she said, using air quotes, "struck his master with a hoe when he found him whipping his six-year-old daughter. She hadn't washed his shirts to suit him. Lucky had to leave her behind and flee to save his own life."

"Some of the stories they told weren't as bad as that one," Merri said. "The second man Wilson said he'd never been whipped his whole life. And the master's wife taught him how to read and made her husband let him go."

"It's the third man I'm interested in," Abby said. "He might be our Ned."

"He's large enough," John said, studying the monitor. "But he doesn't look much like him. Besides he's not wearing a slave collar.

"They were trying to get it off him," Abby said. "Maybe they finally did."

"Write in the book that the Lord done delivered me from bondage in plain daylight, Ms. Charlotte. I walked out of Kentucky and no one told me no. Just like when the chains fell off Saint Peter and he walked out of jail. Write that in the book."

"How did you manage that?" Charlotte asked.

"Well, see, when the gentlemens go about in they carriages, they always make a nigger run along behind so he can help him with the carriage steps. Brush the road dust off his coat and such like."

Samuel and Lucky sat there calmly listening to the story as if this were an occurrence they were familiar with as well. Charlotte frowned but continued to write in her journal. "Go on."

"So one day, I got it in my head to trot on down the road just like I's followin' Master Lewis' carriage. I got a long way down the road before anyone thought to ask me my business. When the man say, 'Where you goin,' boy?' I say, 'Have you seen Master Lewis' carriage go by?' He say 'no' and I say 'I gots to hurry on.'"

Charlotte chuckled. "That was quite clever of you."

He hung his head. "But I done tole a lie, Miz Charlotte."

She thought about it. Sin was sin, even if the slave owners' sin far outweighed this man's lie to survive. "The Lord will forgive you if you ask."

"Oh, I did. I did."

"So what happened after that?"

"Well, I just kept on a-goin'. I had to ask the Lord's

pardon four more times afore I got to the Ohio River and the ferryman rowed me over to Illinois."

"How did it feel to know you were in a free state at last?"

"I fall down on my knees and thank the Lord right on that muddy bank just like it be the River Jordan. Then I go on a little ways. I slept in an old horse trough that night. I didn't care. No ma'am. But the next mornin'...that be when things got troublesome.

"I start on down the road, and before long an old man, standing in his cabin door, tole me to stop. And then he started in throwing rocks at me. I seen from the look on his face that he weren't much interested in my story, so I just lit out runnin'. He call out, and then other fellas come and chase me fierce."

"What did you do next?" Wilson asked.

"Yeah, how you get away?" Lucky asked.

"Well, the Lord done hid me in the cleft of the rock. Write that in the book, Miz Charlotte. See, there be this holler with a crick runnin' through it. I clumb down and hid under a big rock that stuck outta the bank. Them fellas kept on a-looking for me. And I kept on a-hiding under that rock."

"It must have been terribly frightening," Charlotte said.

"Well, Miz Charlotte, while I waited for them to go on, I had time to ponder things under that ole rock. I tole myself the Lord done led me that far, and he was sure to keep at it until he led me out of the wilderness into the Promised Land. And another thing come to me under that rock: Illinois sure ain't no Promised Land. No offense, ma'am."

"None taken," Charlotte said, grinning.

"After they gone, I got back on that road. I heard it be called the Goshen Road, and I knew I be a-goin' the right way. Then Mr. Jemmy found me and took me along—"

"Okay, okay," Ryan said impatiently. "He's obviously not Ned Greenfield. And we can't sit here listening to every story she writes in her book."

"Well, maybe we should," John said. "They went through so much. Isn't listening the least we can do?"

"So read about it in a book or something. On your dime."

"The book!" Merri said. "We could look in the book."

"What book?" John asked.

"Charlotte's book," Merri said. "She had the stories published."

"I thought about it, Merri," Abby said. "But there's no index, and it takes forever to turn the pages."

"Maybe for you," Ryan said. "Where is it?"

"We don't have an actual copy, Ryan. But I downloaded it from the State Archive website."

"So do we wait for more slaves passing through?" Kate asked.

"He's there already," Merri said, taking the mouse. "We just need to fast forward a bit more to see him."

"Are you talking about the man in the corner who never talks?" Abby said. "Because, kiddo, he's too old to be Ned Greenfield."

"I never got a clear look at him," John said.

"I did," Merri said, taking the mouse. "He's wearing a slave collar. And I'm sure Charlotte called him Ned."

"Then why did you just waste our time on all that other stuff?" Ryan asked angrily.

Merri continued fast forwarding, unfazed by his attitude. At last she paused the action.

"Sorry I wasted five minutes of your life, Ryan. Anyway, here he is."

CHAPTER 25

"Thank you for telling me your stories."

"Thank you, ma'am, for writing the book," Samuel said. Andrew and Lucky mumbled shy thank-yous as well and then settled onto their pallets to wait.

The silent man in the corner blended into the darkness, but Charlotte saw that he was watching her. "How about you?" she said. "Can you tell me your story? I'd love to include it in the book."

Charlotte didn't hear what he mumbled but got the answer to her question when he lay back down facing the wall. She put her things away and went to the stairway. "Then I'll see you all later."

After the woman left, he lay there thinking for a while about the stories the other men had told. On the other side of the room they already snored, resting easy with their pasts. He thought of his and tried to remember how to pray.

"Well, is that Ned Greenfield, or not?" Ryan asked, looking at his watch.

"I don't know," Abby said. "I couldn't see him well enough."

John let out a huge yawn and stood to stretch. "Maybe we should pause it here and wait until morning. I can hardly see the screen anymore."

His yawn was contagious. When Kate finished hers she said, "Let's watch him a little longer. See him in daylight."

"Yes, why stop now?" Ryan said. "We're finally making progress."

Merri smothered a yawn. "Because it's two-thirty in the morning?"

"Okay," John said. "A little longer. But don't go too fast, Merri. He surely didn't stay in Charlotte's attic too long. If we miss his departure, it will just take more time to go back and find the right spot."

"Well, then stop talking so she can do it," Ryan said.

Stifling another yawn, Merri began fast-forwarding again.

"Stop," John said. "Go back. Just a little."

"You're right. He's on the move," Kate said.

"Finally," Ryan muttered.

The huge man had gone to the trunk where Charlotte kept her writing things. He took out the journal and walked soundlessly past the sleeping men to the stairs.

"See, Ryno, this is why we have to wade through all this. He's leaving and we would have missed it if we hadn't been watching so closely."

"Okay," Abby said. "I'm going to lock onto him and go virtual again. Everyone ready?"

"Keep your fingers crossed that it's Ned," Kate said.
"And that he's on his way to Chicago," Abby said.

When he got to the bottom of the stairs, he tapped on the door and whispered, "Miz McGuire?" He tapped again, a little louder. Then someone grabbed him from behind and he fell onto the steps with a loud grunt, taking his attacker with him.

"We got him, Miz McGuire. Don't worry."

Pulling on her dressing gown, Charlotte unlatched the door and opened it. In the scant moonlight from her window, the tangle of arms and legs on the steps looked like a nest of corn snakes.

"Samuel? Is that you?"

"Yes, Miz McGuire.

"And Lucky," another voice mumbled.

"And me, Andrew. Don't be afraid. We got him."

"What on earth? Let him up this instant." Charlotte went to her bedside table and lit the lantern there. Her four guests sorted themselves out and stood at the attic doorway looking anywhere but at her.

"He was stealing your book, ma'am," Samuel whispered angrily.

"I seen him get it out of your trunk, Miz McGuire," Andrew said.

Lucky glared at the man, who remained silent, his head hanging low. "Weren't right for him to steal the stories. Here, Miz McGuire," he said, handing her the journal with a sideways glance.

Charlotte craned her neck to look up into the face of the man who towered over her. As always, his eyes never met hers, but seemed focused on something just over her left shoulder.

"I weren't stealing it, ma'am," he said at last. "I be bringing it to you so's you could..."

"You want me to write your story after all," Charlotte said. "That's good. In the morning—"

"I'll be gone in the morning, Miz McGuire. I can't stay in that attic no more."

"But your feet."

He didn't answer, but his face said he was determined to leave.

"All right," she said turning toward her bedroom. "Let me get a pen."

"I brung it," he said, taking her pen and ink bottle from his pants pocket.

She took them from him and turned to the others. "The rest of you go on back upstairs and get some sleep."

"You sure?" Samuel said. "We can stay right here in case he gives you any trouble."

"I'll be fine, Samuel. Go on."

After several dubious backward glances they clomped back up the stairs. Charlotte prayed Joshua wouldn't hear them and come running. His presence would probably send the man running before he told his story.

Charlotte led him to the kitchen and set the journal on the table. She indicated for him to sit there. But he ignored that and went to the back door. Opening it part way, he stuck his head out and looked into the night. Satisfied no one was out there, he stepped out onto the porch and sat on the step. It was a clear night and moonlight silvered his head and broad shoulders. He turned his gaze to the sky and breathed in great gulps of the brisk air as if he were savoring his release from the attic.

"You should wait for Mr. Bartlett, you know. He'll have something to get that collar off."

He didn't comment.

"You remember what I told the others. If you get to Chicago, look for Mr. Moody. At the White Swan."

He mumbled something that led her to believe he understood.

Charlotte wrapped her dressing gown closer against the cold draft coming in the open door and busied herself finding food to send with him. There was a chunk of cheese and half a loaf of bread, which she wrapped in brown paper and set on the table. She went and sat down and opened her journal.

"Will you come in now and tell me your story?"

He didn't answer, just sat looking out into the blackness of her back yard. After a long moment, he said in a low and rusty voice, "My name is Ned Greenfield."

Kate squealed. "It's him!"

Merri smiled smugly. "I told you so."

"He sure looks older," John said.

"Oh, I'm so glad he escaped," Kate said.

"At least he made it this far," Abby said. "The question is, Kate, did he make it to Chicago and tie in with your relatives?"

"Let's get this over with and go to bed. I'm tired."

"You don't have to watch, Ryno," John said.

Ryan sighed deeply. "Just run the program."

Charlotte dipped the pen in the ink and wrote his name on a fresh page in the journal. "Good. Go on, please."

"I was born in Equality, Illinois. At Hickory Hill. My mama and pap was owned by John Granger, and so he owned me too."

"In Illinois?" Charlotte looked up. "But, that's not possible. Slavery's illegal in Illinois. The state Constitution clearly says so."

"That piece of paper don't mean much down in Equality, ma'am. Least ways, not at Half Moon."

"What's Half Moon?"

"That the salt mine, ma'am. Master Granger owns it."

Charlotte huffed. "I wonder if my father and husband know about this. Go on, Mr. Greenfield. Tell me."

He seemed taken aback by her use of his rightful title. After a pause, he said, "My pap was a blacksmith—a good one he was too—for Master Granger. Mama was his cook. I don't mean for Half Moon. I mean she his cook at Hickory Hill. Master Granger—"

"You don't have to call him master, Ned. Never again."

He took in another deep breath. "No, ma'am. I don't. Anyway, Granger told my mama he goin' to free her alongside my pap when his indenture up in 1850. They was real happy about that."

"What are their names?"

"My mama was Mariah. My pap was Charles. They didn't have no last name. When I was born my mama gave me the name of Greenfield on account of Granger promised her that her children wouldn't never have to work at Half Moon like the other slaves. Didn't neither. Worked in his fields."

"When were you born, Ned?" Charlotte said.

"Round about 1834, then my brother Nelson. Then come Nancy Jane, Maybelle, and Lizzie. When the indenture almost done, they was kidnapped, the whole fambly 'cept me and Nelson. That be my mama and pap's story. And

Nancy Jane, Maybelle, and Lizzie. For your book, Miz McGuire."

When Charlotte finished getting that down, she looked up from her journal. "What about you and your brother?"

"Granger put Nelson to working at Half Moon."

"Did you work there, too?"

"No, ma'am, I didn't never work in the salt mine."

"What happened then?"

"Me and Nelson knew Granger was the one that done kidnapped the fambly. Nelson's friend Joseph brung his shotgun and the three of us waited for Granger to come along down the road. Joseph made him stop his buggy and told him to tell what happened. Somehow his gun went off, and Granger drove off all mad. That night the sheriff come and took Nelson away."

When he didn't say more, Charlotte asked, "What about you and Joseph?"

"He a white boy, so nothing happen to him." Ned stated it with no bitterness. It was just a fact of life. "Sheriff hit me over the head with his club."

He rose from the step and glanced briefly into the kitchen where she sat. "That's all. You write that in your book, Miz McGuire."

"Wait," Charlotte said. "I want to write your story too."

He stood on the porch looking at the sky. "Not fittin' for you to hear, ma'am."

"Did you go to prison?"

He didn't answer.

"Ned, you can tell me. I've already heard so many sad stories."

"Not fittin' for you," he said again.

"But we need to hear, no matter how distressing. Most of the soldiers who come through here on the train have no idea what they're fighting against. When this war's over and they come home wounded and scarred they'll need to remember what it was all about."

Ned sat back down on the step. He rested his forearms on his knees and hung his head. "You axed me if I been in prison? Well, I sure enough was. Granger chained me in his attic. Said I was a strong young buck, big for my age and he had a new job for me to do. Easy job. But my head hurt where the sheriff busted it, and my eyes wasn't working right. I couldn't tell at first what they was talking about."

Ned stopped and the only sounds were the crickets and Charlotte's pen scratching on the page. "There's the North star, Miz McGuire," he said, pointing to the sky. "I didn't see it for so long."

"Can you go on, Ned?"

He took a shuddering breath and let it out. "Lil say I have to make babies, lots of babies for Master Granger on account of he can't get enough slaves to keep the salt mine working. She say she have five children and if she get ten more babies Mr. Granger let her go free."

Charlotte felt a sudden wave of nausea and put her pen down. She swallowed until she was sure she wouldn't vomit.

"I hadn't never been with a gal before, but that Lil, she be all over me that night. My head didn't want to do it, but my body…it did it anyway. Then Granger brought more gals. He say if I make two hundred babies, he let me go north. He chained the gals in the attic with me til they take. Then he send them back to the farm and bring more gals. Some gals he brought were like Lil. Other gals…"

He stopped talking and Charlotte kept her eyes glued to the journal. "How did you feel about…your new job?"

She heard Ned moving and glanced up to find him looking at her. He turned away again and lifted the back of his shirt. "Here's how I felt about it, ma'am."

Light from the lantern picked out dozens of

intersecting ridges of scar tissue on the black terrain of his back. She gasped and closed her eyes to block out the sight. Then, taking a deep breath, she picked up her pen again.

"What about the other girls?"

"Them other gals… be young and untried. They cry in my ear and fight me. I tell Master Granger I'm not making babies on those gals."

"So you ran away?" Charlotte prompted.

"I be going now, Miz McGuire." Ned rose wearily and stood there looking at the floor.

She got up from her chair and took the food out to him. He nodded his head and stepped down from the porch.

"Wait. Please tell me. You ran away so you wouldn't have to hurt the girls, right?"

"When them gals don't take, Mr. Granger, he say niggers is always dying in the salt mine and maybe Nelson like to go back to working the fields."

Ned limped across the yard, stopping at the tree line to turn and look back at Charlotte. "I made the babies, Miz McGuire. Two hundred babies I made." And then he faded away among the trees.

Charlotte realized that tears were streaming down her cheeks. She didn't know which were for the poor girls and which were for the boy who'd spent twelve years of soulless existence chained in the attic with them.

"God bless and keep you, Ned Greenfield," she called softly into the night.

The screen went black and Abby snapped into the present. Merri had fallen asleep, and her head landed against the monitor's power button.

"Merri! We've got to lock onto Ned."

Merri lifted her head and squinted at her. "Whaaa?"

Abby turned the monitor back on and rewound until Ned re-appeared. Sighing with relief, she paused the action and then allowed herself to process what she'd just seen.

"That poor, poor man."

"I never thought I'd sympathize with a rapist," Kate said. "Do you think he ever got over it?"

"You have to wonder," John said. "But I don't think I can bear to watch more right now."

"You've got to be kidding, Roberts," Ryan said. "We are finally getting somewhere and you want to go to beddy bye?"

"Look around you, Rye. Everyone's exhausted."

"Then let me try."

"Please, Ryan," Kate said, taking his hand. "No telling how long it will take to follow Ned all the way to Chicago. We can start again first thing in the morning. But let's grab a couple hours of rest."

John scooted over in front of the monitor. "There's no need to follow him from here. Now that we know where he's going."

"Moody," Abby said. "The Bible Institute that he founded is not far from Ambassador College. You know, Kate, over on La Salle Street."

John entered D.L. Moody into the search engine and then clicked on a website that gave the history of his ministry. "According to this, he started out preaching on the North Side among the poorest of the poor. Guess what? He bought an old tavern called the White Swan, and it grew into Illinois Street Church."

"I wonder if it's still there," Abby said.

"So, John, could you lend—?"

"No, I'm sorry, Kate."

"Please. I promise we'll be careful with it."

John grinned. "Are you serious? I'm going with you."

"If it's all right with Merri's mom, we'll all go. But we'll have to leave early so we can get back in one day."

"Thank you, thank you, thank you," Kate said.

Merri's eyes popped open, and she and tumbled out of her chair. "We're going home?"

"At last," Ryan said.

CHAPTER 26

When Abby came out of the bathroom after her shower early the next morning she heard a startled cry from downstairs. Sort of a yelp. She hurried to find out who had made it.

The scene in the living room was odd. John stood staring grimly at Kate's distinctive pink phone. Next to him, Merri was holding Kit Kat and hopping, trying to see whatever held his attention on the phone. Kit Kat did not look pleased. Neither did Kate. She slouched in a puddle of depression on what had been Ryan's bed on the couch.

Abby wasn't sure if the yelp had come from Kit Kat or Kate, but she sat down next to her friend and put an arm around her shoulder. "What's wrong?"

Kate looked up, her face all wobbly, but didn't answer.

John handed Abby Kate's phone. "Ryno scarpered off with my laptop. That's what's wrong. See for yourself."

"Let me see, too," Merri said.

Abby read the text message and then handed the phone

to Merri.

"When did he leave?"

"I don't know," Kate answered miserably.

"I vaguely remember hearing something around five o'clock," John said. "I figured the Ryno was getting up to go to the bathroom."

"I'm so sorry, guys. I don't know what came over him," Kate said. "He won't answer his phone, but I'll text him back and talk some sense into him. I promise."

Merri handed Kate her phone and sat down next to her.

John began pacing the room. "I can't believe the idiot thinks he can sell it out from under us."

"I know. Ryan shouldn't have done that," Kate said. "But like he says, this thing is bigger than any of us. Think of the benefits to mankind."

John snorted. "I'm sure Ryan is thinking of the benefits to Ryan."

"He said it wasn't about the money," Kate said, sounding as if she was trying to convince herself. She composed a short message and sent it to Ryan, frowning the whole time.

"But we talked about this, Kate," Abby said. "It's so dangerous."

"He's just thinking of all the good it will do, you know?"

John snorted again. Abby shot a warning look at him. "But, Kate, what if the people he sells it to are unethical?"

"Who knows what kind of a shyster he's found," John said. "And how did he find a buyer so soon anyway?"

"He has lots of contacts in Chicago."

"But how did he make a deal without us knowing?" Abby asked.

"I noticed him making several phone calls yesterday, all

secretive," Kate said. "I thought he was planning a surprise for me. He does that a lot."

Kate's phone chirped and she grabbed it, her face a mixture of hope and worry. "All he says is that he's sorry he had to leave without talking to us. The buyer wants it right away." The phone chirped again and she looked down at it. "And that my car is at the Amtrak station."

"That's good," John said. "If he took the train, we have a chance of catching up with him. You know how many stops they make."

"But he'll never tell us where he is," Abby said.

"It's got to be Chicago," Kate said. "But that would be like looking for a needle in a haystack."

"That's all right," John said, taking out his own phone. "This baby will tell us where he is."

"What do you mean?" Abby asked.

"Timmy Tech put a tracer app on my phone. In case my laptop ever got stolen." After a moment, he smiled sourly and held his phone for Abby and the others to see. "And there's Rye. Come on. We're going to Chicago."

Ryan hadn't lied about Kate's car being at the Amtrak Station. They took it and left John's Mustang there, having decided that he, Abby, and Merri would take the train back when they finished in Chicago.

John offered to drive and Kate, still an emotional bowl of Jello, let him. Merri kept him company in the front seat, and Abby and Kate sat in the back where they could talk. Not that Abby felt like talking.

It was only a little after eight o'clock when they left Alton. But even if they drove non-stop, Abby calculated it would be one o'clock before they reached the outskirts of the city. There was no way to know whether it would be soon enough to prevent Ryan from selling *Beautiful Houses.*

The tracer app Tim had installed on John's phone was working fine, and they were able to watch Ryan's movements, or rather those of the laptop, in nearly real time. The app was another example of Tim's technical brilliance, but it wasn't by any means up to Mission Impossible standards. It didn't give them Ryan's current address, only a rough idea of where he was in relation to where John's phone was.

The blinking dot on the phone's screen stopped periodically, and every time it did they wondered if Ryan was making the deal with his buyer. But then the dot would start moving and they would resume breathing.

Meanwhile, Kate continued texting Ryan. His replies were all about the good things the program would accomplish, the creative ways it could be used to help people.

"But Ryan's forgetting one important thing," Abby said. "The program only works with old houses."

"So far," Merri said. "But who knows what it will decide to do."

In between texting Ryan, Kate regaled Abby with nauseating stories of his all-around wonderfulness. She was about to list all the imaginary stars he had earned on her imaginary "Marriage Material Chart when Abby shushed her so John wouldn't hear and start wondering if he had a similar chart.

And then a text came in from Ryan that had Kate yelping again. She shoved her phone into Abby's hands. "Please don't say I told you so."

"I promise," she said as she turned to read Ryan's text.

Kathryn, if you won't consider all the ways it will help

mankind, just think of the money the program will bring us. We can get a house like that one we liked in Hawaii. And travel anywhere we want. When we want, since we won't have children to worry about.

"But, I thought you wanted to have children."

"That's just it. I do. And he does too. Why is he talking about not having children?"

Kate took her phone back and texted Ryan again. When his response came in, she read it without comment, put her phone back into her purse, and turned toward the window as if the flat, flat farmland they drove through was the most interesting landscape she'd ever seen.

"What did he say?" Abby asked.

Kate turned back, her face pure misery, and put her head on Abby's shoulder. "He said… obviously we wouldn't want… to have children because…" She broke off and sobbed broken-heartedly. It was a while before she could continue. "Because…what if they turned out to be…kinky-haired throw backs."

The car swerved and John frowned murderously in the rearview mirror. "I should have punched him when I had the chance. I knew I should have."

"I'm so sorry," Abby said, patting her arm. "Oh, Kate, don't cry." She wondered if it would help to tell her that none of them had liked Ryan from the first moment. Probably not.

"Let's call the cops," Merri said. "After all, he did steal your laptop, John."

"No," he said. "If we call in the police the laptop would be held as evidence for who knows how long, and news of the program would be bound to leak out.

Ignoring their discussion, Kate lifted her head from Abby's shoulder and resumed staring at the cornfields outside her window. "I know it's wrong. We're supposed to forgive those who hurt us. And I will try to." She sniffed. "Eventually. But right now…."

"Hey, here's an idea," Abby said. "We'll get John to hold him—after he has a turn at him—and then you, Merri, and I can kick him. We'll wear our pointiest shoes."

"No, cut off his precious hair," John said.

"Oh, no," Abby said. "Don't cut it all off. Just give him a really bad haircut."

"A mullet," John said.

"A permed mullet," Abby added.

"And a tattoo that says I am a jerk," Merri said.

"And another one that says Obviously." Kate snorted a laugh, which quickly turned into another sob. "How could I have been such a fool?"

Abby tried to think of a kind answer and came up blank.

After what seemed like a century, they exited the freeway and pulled into a Casey's to refuel and grab what food they could find to eat in the car. Kate wore sunglasses to cover her swollen, red eyes. They were back on the road by twelve-fifteen. John said it beat his all-time record for shortest pit stop by thirteen seconds.

"What's Ryan doing now?" Abby asked.

"He's still stopped," Merri said, studying John's phone. "We're getting pretty close to him."

"Can I see that a minute?" Kate asked.

"Sure." Merri handed the phone back to her.

The screen on John's phone was tiny, and Abby couldn't make out much detail on the map. But after a moment, Kate looked up. "I think he's at his parents' home in Oak Park. It's the only thing that makes sense."

"So you think he set up a meeting with a buyer there?" John asked.

"But he would know you'd come looking for him there,

wouldn't he?" Abby asked. "And even Ryan isn't such a jerk that he would involve his parents in some shady deal. Is he?"

Kate studied the phone again. "Which explains why he's moving again."

"Here, let me see," John said.

Kate handed his phone to him. He glanced down at it and then gave it back to Merri. "Hold it where I can see it, kiddo."

"Sure thing," Merri said. "Does this mean I'm the navigator?"

"That's right. Let me know if he changes directions."

"He just did. Right is east, right?"

"Huh?" John looked down at his phone. "Right you are, navigator. He's moving east, Kate. Any guesses where he could be heading?"

"Straight downtown to the Loop."

"What's his parents' address, do you know?"

Kate told him and John entered it into the GPS. When the map came up, he grunted in satisfaction. "Show them my phone, Merri. Compare the map on it to the GPS map."

"He's on Eisenhower Expressway. I'd bet on it," Kate said. "Take I-90, John, and we'll intersect with him."

"We're close. Really close," he said. And then when he exited onto Interstate 90 north they realized they were in front of Ryan.

"What's he driving?" John asked.

"A white Prius—or Pious, as I secretly thought of it," Kate said. "And slow down, John. Ryan may be a bigot and a thief, but he's a straight-arrow when it comes to obeying the speed limit."

"He turned again," Merri said. "Left. I mean north."

"He left the freeway," Kate said.

"Dang it," John said. "I lost him."

He took the next exit and backtracked until eventually they were behind Ryan again on Wells Street heading north. It was a commercial district, but certainly not the Loop. They passed restaurants, a bookstore, and numerous other small businesses.

"He's turning, John," Merri said. "There on Illinois Street. Wait, he stopped."

"Good." John pulled over, parked, and then smiled. "We did it. High-five, navigator."

Merri complied and then looked thoughtful. "Isn't this the same street that the—"

"Hurry, everybody. I don't want to lose him after all this." John got out of the car and went to feed the parking meter.

When they got to the corner and turned onto Illinois Street, Kate hurried ahead. "There's Ryan's car."

He wasn't in it. Abby scanned the block. There were lots of buildings crammed together, and there was no way of telling which one he had gone into.

"There. I'll bet you ten dollars." John pointed and then started toward the corner.

"That's got to be it," Kate said. When the light turned, she charged into the street, John right behind her.

"Wait, you guys," Abby said, hurrying to keep up. "Don't let him see you or he'll bolt. With the laptop."

"I'll be subtle. For example, I won't rush up and punch him," John said.

The three-story brick building was old with architectural details of an earlier time, but it had been renovated for an upscale business image. The door was of contemporary bronzed glass. Above it, a brass sign said Farwell Technology Group, Established 1871.

"It doesn't look like the sort of place for shady deals," Abby said.

"What kind of technology did they have in 1871 anyway?" Merri asked.

John looked in the glass door. "I see a reception room. I see a woman at a desk. But I do not see Ryno. How are we going to play this?"

"How about you pretend you're detectives looking for a crook?" Merri said. "Then tell them you need to search the building, room by room. I saw that on TV."

"Great idea, Merri Christmas," John said. "Except they frown on civilians impersonating officers of the court."

"I've got an idea. And it does not involve lying," Abby said. "What time is it?"

"John looked at his watch. "Exactly one o'clock."

"Perfect," she said, opening the door. "Follow my lead."

CHAPTER 27

Abby put an expression on her face that she hoped looked like one a bold entrepreneur might wear and marched as confidently as she knew how straight to the reception desk.

The receptionist looked up and smiled in a friendly manner that belied the Chicago reputation for being rude. "May I help you?"

Abby smiled back in relief. "Actually, we're here to help you. Our…colleague…Ryan Turner is here for a one o'clock appointment with Mr.…"

"Mr. Farwell."

"Yes. With Mr. Farwell. But unfortunately, Mr. Turner forgot an essential document that he'll need for his presentation. We'd like to drop it by if we may."

The receptionist looked puzzled.

Kate dug into her purse and pulled out an important-looking letter and waved it about. The receptionist was too far away to see that the return address said Ambassador College, but no doubt the gold-embossed logo looked impressive from where she sat. Kate didn't mention that the letter was from Elizabeth Withers, Dean of Students, reminding her to sign up for her senior service project.

"Oh, well, then," the receptionist said, "Mr. Farwell's office is on the third floor, on the right as you come out of the elevator. I'll call and let him know you're coming."

"If you don't mind, we'd like to surprise Ryan." Kate smiled warmly. "He's probably realized his mistake about now."

"He'll be so happy to see us," John said.

The receptionist smiled conspiratorially. "All right. You go on up then," she said kindly.

John knocked on Mr. Farwell's door and a deep voice told them to come in. John's laptop sat on the desk in front of a white-haired man who looked up from it to stare at them. Unlike his receptionist, he didn't smile. But Ryan, who sat on a chair in front of the desk, smiled widely—although a little desperately—and bolted out of his chair to meet them. He didn't seem to notice his fiancée, but went straight to John and took his arm.

"Roberts, I'm glad you're here. Tell Mr. Farwell that it's all right. Tell him the laptop belongs to you."

Kate poked Ryan in the stomach and he finally turned his eyes to her. She glared at him so hard he should have incinerated on the spot. But he only turned imploring eyes back to John.

"I've just been explaining to Mr. Turner that my great, great grandfather built his business on a foundation of integrity." Mr. Farwell's lips turned up a bit in what was probably supposed to be a smile. "And why shouldn't he? This building itself was constructed on the foundation of a church."

"What happened to it?" Merri asked. "The church?"

"It burned down during the Chicago Fire. But that's

beside the point. I won't tolerate dishonesty."

Ryan looked frantically from John to Abby as if to say, go along with me and I'll make this up to you.

"Which is why I'm a little concerned that this program Mr. Turner's been telling me about—which doesn't seem to be working at the moment, by the way—is on a laptop that obviously doesn't belong to Mr. Turner."

"Obviously," John said, glancing at Ryan. "Seeing as how my name is written in magic marker on the bottom. And the log-in avatar is a photo of me." He held out his phone. "And I've got this app to trace it if it ever got stolen. Which it did."

Mr. Farwell stood and walked out from behind his desk. He handed the laptop to John and then turned to face Ryan, arms crossed on his chest. "Mr. Turner, I'll let these people decide what they want to do about you. But as for me, I think you've wasted enough of my time." He went to the door and held it open for them as they filed out of his office.

"Don't worry, John," Ryan said as they walked down the hall. "I have a backup plan." He stopped and took out his phone. "I know someone else interested in buying the program."

Kate's eyes went huge, and she couldn't seem to come up with what she wanted to say. Merri stood shaking her head.

John lunged toward Ryan, but Abby latched onto his arm and hung onto him like a crazed monkey. It was all well and good to fantasize about beating Ryan to a pulp, but she didn't actually want John to commit a felony.

Ryan backed up a step. "All right. You're angry. I get that. I'm sorry, already. But just because you hate me...well, don't let that cause you to miss out on a lot of money."

"Turner. Get this. You are never, ever, going to cash in

on *Beautiful Houses*."

When Abby was sure John had his anger under control, she released her stranglehold and took his hand into hers. Just in case.

Ryan turned at last to Kate. "Kathryn, please. Talk some sense into them."

"I'll talk all right. You say you're sorry, Ryan? Well, I'm sorry too. Sorry that I let you make me into someone I'm not. I'm sorry I let you tell me how to dress and how to drive my car. And F.Y.I.? My name is Kate, not Kathryn. I've always hated that name, haven't I, Abby?"

"Yes. You have."

"I'm sorry. I had no idea." Ryan smiled kindly. "Okay. Kate, it is. From now on." He looked at John and his smile turned into to the man-to-man type that Abby had seen her brothers wear when they thought she was being a pesky little sister. "She must be having her time of the month," he said.

Kate and Abby sputtered in unison. John only shook his head sadly. "Ryno, Ryno, you shouldn't have said that." He crossed his arms over his chest and stood back as if he knew he could leave the task of beating up Ryan to Abby and Kate.

"You, you, you…" Kate was nearly incoherent.

"Jackass?" Merri supplied.

"Right. Thanks," Kate said. "Now, where was I? Oh, yeah. I'm sorry I let you give me this ostentatious rock." She pulled the diamond ring off her finger and shoved it at Ryan's chest.

He took the ring and blinked at her. "You're breaking up with me because I called you Kathryn?"

"And I'm sorry I gave you so many stars on your chart, because you're a sorry excuse for a man. And I'm really sorry that I was too blind to see it." She sobbed and Abby drew her into a hug.

"I said I'd call you Kate," Ryan said in bewilderment.

John looked a little confused himself. He was probably wondering about the star chart. He gulped as if he didn't know whether to laugh or growl. Then he turned to Ryan and his face went dangerously hard again. "It's not that, you moron."

John took three steps until he was in Ryan's face. Abby mentally prepared herself in case she'd need to push Kate to the side and launch herself at John again.

"Kate's breaking up with you because you're a raging racist. 'Kinky-haired throwbacks' my—"

"I'd go if I were you, Ryno," Merri said. "Because I happen to know that John really, really wants to punch you."

Ryan glared at them and then turned and stalked off to the elevator.

Kate took a step down the hall after him. "And most of all," she called, "I'm sorry that I gave you my…my…" She darted a look at Merri. "My tamper-proof seal. Now I won't have it for the man I marry."

Ryan punched the button and the elevator door opened. Holding it from closing, he said, "Once you're over being emotional, Kathryn, and you can think rationally, you'll see that I'm right." Then the door closed and he was gone.

Kate let out a huff and then sniffed. John handed her his handkerchief, and she scrubbed at her eyes.

"Are you all right?" Abby asked. "Do you want to sit down?"

"I'm fine," Kate said. "Or at least, I will be. Good riddance and all that. Now," she said exhaling loudly, "let's go find Ned Greenfield. What do we do first?"

"Well, first we find Moody's church," Abby said.

"What was the address?"

"I don't remember," John said. "The paper's in the car."

"Duh," Merri said. "Illinois Street Church was on Illinois Street. Obviously."

John grinned at her. "Obviously."

"Please," Kate said, groaning. "I don't want to hear that word again for a very long time."

"Anyway, that website last night said it was on the corner of Illinois and Wells," Merri said. "And we happen to be standing on the corner of Illinois and Wells."

Abby gasped. "In a building that was built over a church."

Merri tugged on Abby's arm. "Now do you believe me about this program? It led us here."

"God did, Merri," Kate said. "I know that now."

They found a janitor's closet across from the elevator and closed themselves inside. None of them was surprised that the first person they saw was Ned Greenfield.

Illinois Street was empty and dark except for the faint light coming from the White Swan's front window. Ned looked up at the shabby old building. It didn't look much like a church, at least not like Liberty Baptist, although that memory had faded so much it seemed like something he'd dreamed long ago. But the wooden sign creaking in the wind overhead had a faded white swan on it, just as Miz Charlotte had told him.

He opened the door a bit and peeked inside. A little fire burned in a cast iron stove in the corner. The room was mostly empty and dimly lit by a few cheap tallow candles that sat on overturned barrels. By one barrel, a man—a white man—held a little Negro boy on his lap. The man was reading from a big book that had a black leather cover, just like Miz Charlotte's Bible.

Ned shivered and longed to go in and stand by the fire. But if he went in, the man would surely stop reading, and he found that he wanted to hear the story more than he wanted to be warm. The man read:

A certain man had two sons. And the younger of them said to his father, 'Father, give me the portion of goods that falleth to me.' And he divided unto them his living. And not many days after, the younger son gathered all together, and took his journey into a far country, and there wasted his substance with riotous living.

And when he had spent all, there arose a mighty famine in that land; and he began to be in want. And he went and joined himself to a citizen of that country; and he sent him into his fields to feed swine. And he would fain have filled his belly with the husks that the swine did eat. And no man gave unto him.

And when he came to himself, he said, 'How many hired servants of my father's have bread enough and to spare, and I perish with hunger! I will arise and go to my father, and will say unto him, Father, I have sinned against heaven, and before thee, and am no more worthy to be called thy son. Make me as one of thy hired servants.'

And he arose, and came to his father. But when he was yet a great way off, his father saw him, and had compassion, and ran, and fell on his neck, and kissed him. And the son said unto him, 'Father, I have sinned against heaven, and in thy sight, and am no more worthy to be called thy son.'

But the father said to his servants, 'Bring forth the best robe, and put it on him; and put a ring on his hand, and shoes on his feet. And bring hither the fatted calf, and kill it; and let us eat, and be merry, for this my son was dead, and is alive again; he was lost, and is found.' And they began to be merry.

A noise behind him startled Ned and he drew back from the door. A little ragamuffin even filthier than he was rushed past him and flung the door open. "Mr. Moody, I'm wearing my new shoes."

"Come in, Absalom, and bring our visitor in where it's warm."

The little boy grabbed Ned by the hand. "Come on then. We're to have a story."

Ned stood inside the door. Other children came in, and within minutes the room was loud with their boisterous shouts and laughter.

"Come on, friend, don't be shy," Mr. Moody said. "Come warm yourself by the fire. After the Bible story we'll have food."

Silently, Ned went to the stove in the corner and stood watching the antics of the children. They were of all sizes and colors, all clothed in rags. All wearing new shoes. He looked down at his own bare and bloody feet.

"It's time for Sunday School," Mr. Moody called out. "So sit your selves down and listen, you little hoodlums."

Kate grabbed Abby's arm and she came back to the present. "He made it, Abby."

"I can't believe it."

"I can't believe how far he traveled," John said. "It must have taken forever on foot."

Abby sniffed and wiped away a tear. "Barefoot."

"In winter," Merri added.

"Hurry, John. I can't wait to find out once and for all," Kate said.

John set it to fast-forward. "Okay, let's go." He clicked on the settings again and then frowned. "It's doing it again. For some reason it keeps flipping to the same date—November 11, 1869."

"Maybe there's something there we're supposed to see," Merri said.

"Then let's see it," Kate said.

Ned took the key from his pocket and opened the front door of Illinois Street Church. He took off his hat as he went through the door, then his overcoat, and hung them on a peg in the cloakroom. It was a cool but bright morning and the sanctuary felt fine. There would be no need for him to build a fire in the stove. He picked up some leaves and twigs that had blown in from outside and then made sure there were hymnbooks in every pew. He liked to get to church early to check on such things so that everything would be nice when his ragamuffins got there.

He heard the front door open and smiled. It was Theodore. He liked to get there early too. Wearing a big smile, new shoes, and little else, he came running down the aisle toward him. Ned smiled fondly. Mr. Moody liked to take the children to his store to be fitted for new shoes, but he sometimes forgot they needed clothes too. Maybe he could find the boy a shirt from the donation box.

"Mornin,' Mr. Greenfield. Can I sit by you?"

"You surely can, Theodore. And you can be the first to see my new book."

Ned sat down on the front row pew and took the book from his coat pocket to show him. Theodore crowded up next to his knees, managing to step on his shoes in his eagerness to see the book.

"See, Theodore, each page is a different color."

"But where are the words, Mr. Greenfield? How you goin' read it?"

Ned smiled. "It tells a story without words. The first page is black."

"Like us, huh, Mr. Greenfield?"

"No, no, Theodore. He realized he was frowning and let his face relax. "It's black like sin. Like everyone's sin, black folk or white folk. The Bible says we are all sinners, everyone. The next page is red to remind us that Jesus died on the cross for our sins. Shed his blood for us. This page is white, like snow. Pure and clean, like when Jesus washes our sins away. Theodore—you remember this now—there ain't any sin too big for Jesus to forgive. And look at this page."

Theodore ran a grubby finger over the shiny gold foil of the last page and then looked up at Ned in wonder. "It's bootiful."

Ned squeezed the boy's thin shoulders. "That's to remind us of Heaven, son. All God's children that's had their sins forgiven will be there someday." Ned sent up a quick prayer that all his own children would be there.

A noise came from the front and they turned to look. The other children were starting to arrive. "Come on in to God's house," Ned called. "Don't be shy. Jesus said, 'suffer the little ones to come.'"

They hopped, skipped, and ran down the aisle and sat in a squirming mass on the floor in front of Ned. "We're missing some children," he said and grinned. "I guess Garrison and Abraham didn't come to Sunday School this week."

He heard giggles and pretended not to see the little boys peeking from behind their mother as she pulled off their hats and coats.

The door of the church opened again and Mr. Moody

came in, bringing the cool autumn breeze—and another batch of stray leaves. He waved at Ned and said something to the woman that made her laugh..

Finished with the children's coats, Cora looked up and smiled a tender smile that was just for Ned. The sight nearly took his breath away, and he whispered a prayer of thanks.

The children came out from behind her and hurried down the aisle toward him laughing delightedly. "Me and Garrison came to Sunday School, Papa. We're right here."

Ned's laugh boomed through the church.

"Oh, oh!" Kate said. "Garrison Greenfield. That's the name Mom and I found online. I can't remember exactly where he goes on the family tree, but—"

"So he is your Ned Greenfield?" Merri asked

"He has to be," Kate said.

"It would be a huge coincidence if he's not, but…if you want to be totally sure…"

"I agree, Abby," John said. "It wouldn't hold up in a court of law. We need to keep going to prove it."

The low battery message popped onto the screen. "Or not," John said.

"If he was going to steal your laptop, you'd think he'd at least charge it," Kate said. "Now what do we do?"

Abby hadn't thought before how closely they were crowded into the janitor's closet, and it suddenly seemed really small. She grinned at each of her fellow adventurers. "The Bible says to go into our closets to pray. We're in a closet. Let's pray."

The smile John gave her was sweet. Then he closed his eyes and said, "Dear Lord, thank you that Ned escaped and made it safely to Chicago. And thank you for saving him from his sins. And us too."

"And thanks for showing it to us, God," Merri said.

"And thanks…" Kate's voice cracked and she cleared her throat. "Thanks that no sin is too big for you to forgive. And help me to forgive Ryan."

"And," Abby prayed, "help us to find out about Ned."

"And even if you don't," Kate added, "thank you for letting us meet him and Brother Greenfield."

"Amen. Let's get out of here." John stood and helped Abby up.

"We can stay at my grandparents' house for the night and try again tomorrow after your battery's charged."

"If you're sure they won't mind?" Abby said.

"Of course not. They have plenty of room."

"Okay," John said. "I'll slip out of here and let you know when the coast is clear."

CHAPTER 28

"Get the dominoes, honey, and I'll clear off the game table."

Abby smiled to herself. Kate had obviously inherited her energy and love of life from her Grandfather Donald Greenfield.

Donald gathered up the newspapers and mail that cluttered the game table in the Greenfield family room and stacked them on top of other papers piled high on a desk in the corner of the room.

Kate's grandmother Margaret brought a tin box of dominoes and set them on the table. "Katie got this deluxe set for us last Christmas."

"Merri, how about if you team up with me?" Donald said.

"I don't know how to play."

"That's all right. I'll teach you."

"Will you team up with me, Grams?"

"You bet, Katie. We'll wipe the floor with them. You

get started. I'm going to make popcorn."

"We'll wait for you, honey. Or when Merri and I win, you'll say we took unfair advantage."

"We can't have that, can we?" John said.

"I'm so glad you brought your friends, Katie," Donald said. "It'll make dominoes even more exciting. Too bad Ryan couldn't come, although he's not very good at dominoes, is he?"

"No, he's not. Not much good for anything." Kate turned her face away and mumbled the last part.

"After this we'll look at slides. I imagine you've never seen pictures of Katie when she was little. Such a cute baby."

Abby grinned slyly at Kate who was rolling her eyes behind her grandfather's back. "That will be so much fun," Abby said.

John looked as if he were trying not to laugh. "This is a beautiful game table."

"It's hard rock maple. So solid you could dance a jig on it if you wanted to. The inlaid checkerboard is ebony and oak."

"He's being modest, John. He made it himself, didn't you, Gramps?"

"The year you were born, Katydid. It will be yours one day. You can play dominoes on it with your grandchildren."

"Kate must get her artistic talent from you, Mr. Greenfield," Abby said.

"Well, no matter my artistic talent," Kate said, "unfortunately the family tree mural will be grossly lopsided."

"Oh, oh!" Donald slapped the side of his head. "I almost forgot." He pushed himself up from his chair and shuffled over to the desk. "How could I forget, Katie? I meant to tell you soon as you got here but with all the excitement, it slipped my mind. It's here some place."

He sorted through the stacks of mail, newspapers, and flyers that covered nearly every inch of his desk. "If I don't find it, your grandmother will never stop nagging me about cleaning off my desk. Hurry before she gets back. See if you can find it, Katie. Your eyes are sharper than mine."

"What are we looking for, Gramps?"

"Here, hold this." Donald placed a stack of Popular Science Magazines into John's arms. He put a pile of Health Bulletins into Merri's arms and one of Oak Park Gazettes into Abby's.

"It's here some place, unless your grandmother got it into her head to mess with my stuff. Margaret!" he called. "Have you seen—?"

"Don't get your shorts in a twist, Donald." Margaret stood in the doorway holding a tray with bowls of popcorn. "I promise. I did not touch your things."

John hurriedly deposited his stack of magazines on the floor beside the desk and went to take the tray from her.

"I was going through some old letters," Donald said.

"He saves every one, you know."

"Yeah, well. You never know, do you, when you might need—"

"What did you find, Gramps?"

"It was in with some of Mother's stuff." He turned to the Abby and John. "She passed away last year and I've been going through her things."

"You may have noticed the car's parked in front," Margaret said. "The garage is completely packed with boxes."

"Here it is," Donald said. "I remember now. I put it with the bills to pay so I wouldn't forget to tell you."

He held out a small brown box. On the lid, in fine script, was a name and address: Virgil Greenfield, 2341

Hillcrest Street, Chicago, Illinois. He removed the lid and pulled out a necklace. A copper coin about the size of a half-dollar hung on a brown leather cord.

Kate's eyes went huge and she grabbed it from him and held it out for them to see. "Oh. My. Look, you guys. It's Lady Liberty."

Abby, John, and Merri crowded in close to see it. Abby studied Kate's face. All she could see there was joy.

"That's it then," Kate said.

"And there's this letter," Donald said. He handed a thin, pale blue envelope to Kate. She handed the necklace to John and carefully removed one sheet of nearly transparent matching blue paper. She read aloud:

October 23, 1909
Dear Virgil,

Please don't be angry that I wrote. I promise this is the last time. But I just had to thank you for the money you sent. You're a generous, kind boy to share with us.

You'll destroy this letter and all will be well with you. I imagine that you're feeling all torn up inside right about now. But I want you to rest easy that I at least understand your choice to pass. And I'm happy for you. You'll have opportunities for advancement that none of us will ever have.

With your parents gone now, there aren't many of us Greenfields left. But one day, dear Virgil, you'll be reunited with them and the rest of the family (most of them, anyway) when we stand in Glory. Don't ever forget that. And although we won't see you until that day, we'll be thinking of you and hoping you'll think of us, too.

This necklace was your great grandmother Greenfield's. I don't know anything about it, but I thought you might be encouraged when you look at Lady Liberty. I always was. I dream of the day when everyone is truly free and no one has to hide who he is just to hold a job.

Your loving cousin,
Jessamine

Kate went to the game table and slid bonelessly into her chair.

"What does it mean," Merri asked, "passed."

"I didn't get that part, either, Merri," Donald said. "But I thought the names in there might be of some help for your mural, Katie."

Kate's smile for her grandfather was watery. "I already had those names, Gramps. Mom and I traced us back to this Virgil's grandfather Ned Greenfield. But this necklace proves...." She looked up at Abby. "Well, we won't have to go back to the Illinois Street Church tomorrow after all, will we?"

"We thought you'd get a kick out of the necklace, Katie. Isn't it neat?"

"It is, Grams. If only I could show you how neat it is. I was going to wait until I had more, but now...."

"Then you must have it, Katie."

"Really?"

John handed it back to her, and after another close look, she slipped the leather cord over her head. "We come from courageous ancestors, Gramps," she said, patting the necklace at her throat. "Come over and sit down and I'll tell you what we found out about the Greenfield family."

Margaret sat down in the chair next to Kate's and took her hand. "Are you feeling all right, honey? You look a little pale."

Kate chuckled and shot a look at Abby. "I am a little

pale, Grams, but I'm feeling fine."

Kate explained about their search in Equality and told her grandparents about Hickory Hill, Miss Granger, and what they found on the third floor. She described Brother Greenfield and Uncle Henry and their connection to Ned.

"We thought they were the wrong Greenfields, because, you see, they're black. Ned and his parents were slaves."

"Oh dear," Donald said.

"Oh my," Margaret said.

"Gramps, the cousin who wrote this letter to Virgil was referring to passing from the African-American culture into the white culture. Somewhere along the line, some of Ned's descendants married white people. This Virgil was obviously light enough to pass for white."

"It sounds like he was forced to in order to get a job," John said.

"My word," Donald said, looking from Kate to his wife.

"Are you all right with that, Gramps?"

Donald blinked and turned back to her. "Of course I am, honey." He chuckled. "It's just that all this time I assumed Greenfield was a Jewish name."

"Just think of how difficult it must have been to give up your own heritage, everything you knew, everyone you knew," Margaret said.

Kate smiled, obviously pleased by their reaction to the news. "We learned Ned's parents' names—only their first names—in the slave registry. We may never be able to trace back beyond them. But I want to go down to the courthouse again someday and take another look."

"Would you like some company?" Gramps asked.

Kate threw her arms around his neck and kissed his cheek. "That would be wonderful."

"Well, we have to meet Brother Greenfield and Uncle Henry, don't we? After all, they're my cousins."

"Oh, Gramps! You and Grams are going to love them. I'll get my sketch book and show you."

CHAPTER 29

Kate bought their tickets online, insisting on using her own credit card to pay for them in gratitude for them "going above and beyond the call of duty." She drove them to the Amtrak station early the next morning, which was nice, except as was usual for Kate, she waited until the last possible minute to leave, causing Abby to sweat bullets about getting there in time.

There was no time for lengthy goodbyes, so they said them while hurrying up the sidewalk to the door of the station.

"Sorry," Kate said. "I promise to turn over a new leaf and be early for everything this fall."

"We'll be fine." They stopped at the station door and Abby pulled her into a bear hug. "But what about you, roomie?"

"I'll be all right. I'll spend a little more time with Gramps and Grams and then head on back home to Springfield this afternoon. I'll start on the mural the minute Mom and Dad leave on their trip."

"I'm sure it will be awesome. But don't get carried away on the mural and forget to come back to college."

Kate squeezed Abby back. "Right. 205b Whitaker Hall. Two weeks from now."

John and Merri said quick goodbyes, and they left Kate and went into the station. In less than three minutes the train arrived and they boarded, Abby and John settling into a seat facing Merri. The train pulled out of the station, and they were on their way to Alton.

"There's Kate," Merri said, waving furiously out the window.

"Do you think she'll really be all right?" John asked.

"Kate's strong. I know she'll survive. You wouldn't happen to know any good guys we could introduce her to, do you?"

"As a matter of fact, I was thinking about a friend who might suit her. I'll bring him when I come to visit you at your college."

"You will?"

John pulled her head against his shoulder. "Of course, girlie," he said, kissing her temple. "We'll only be about forty-five minutes away from each other."

Merri cleared her throat. "Uh. Just a reminder that I'm here, in case you plan on starting in on the kissy-face stuff."

"We'll restrain ourselves, kiddo," Abby said.

John pulled his laptop out of his backpack. When he clicked the on button the computer made its usual whirring sound. The monitor even flickered encouragingly. But then it lit up with what Timmy Tech called the blue screen of death. Windows wouldn't even load.

"That stinks," Abby said. "Try rebooting."

John tried three times, and three times got the same beautiful but deadly screen.

"Timmy can fix it, right?" Merri said.

"Sure. He'll reformat the hard drive and reinstall Windows. Which will wipe out any files I had on this thing. Or he'll tell me not to waste my time with all that and to get a new laptop. And then he can put *Beautiful Houses* back on it. From your computer, like he did before."

"Actually, I don't know if that's a good idea," Abby said. "We almost lost the laptop, after all. If Mr. Carwell hadn't been such an honest man, or if we had been just a little later reaching Ryan....Well, who knows what would have happened to the program."

"So that's the end of it then?" John said. "No more time-surfing?"

"You can always come and time-surf at my house," Merri said. "That is, if it lets us."

John yawned and slouched into his seat farther.

"We are still the three Musketeers, right?"

He kicked playfully at Merri's sneaker. "You bet. One for all and all for one."

Merri smiled contentedly and then looked out the window.

Abby looked too and saw that they had left the city behind. The grays and tans of tall buildings had given way to the greens of corn and soybeans. She realized that she would miss the country, and Patty Ann and her hills too, when she went back to college. And Brother Greenfield for sure. Maybe she'd go back with Kate and her grandparents.

Abby smiled at Merri. "We've gone from one end of the state to the other, Merri. Which one do you prefer?"

"I hated it when Mom took me away from Chicago." She closed her eyes and settled down into her seat with a tiny smile on her lips. "But if you must know, I'm kind of anxious to get back to Miles Station."

After only a minute or two, Merri began snoring softly. The rocking motion of the train made Abby sleepy too. She hadn't slept well at Kate's grandparents. That, together with the excitement of the past few days, left her feeling groggy and muddle-headed.

John bent down, untied his sneakers, and began removing the laces. Abby started to ask him what on earth he was doing, but after pointing to Merri, he put his finger to his lips in the universal shush sign. "Let her sleep," he whispered.

He didn't say anything more, just began weaving and knotting the two shoelaces together. She watched his hands work surely and gracefully to make an intricate pattern that looked a little like the macramé plant hangers that held her aunt's potted ferns.

Seeing her interest, he grinned and whispered, "I learned it at Bible camp when I was twelve."

"But what is it?" she whispered.

"Just be patient." After he had formed a plaited cord about six inches long, he dug into his pocket and took out something, which he kept hidden in his hand.

"Turn away for a minute, Abby."

She looked out the window again but didn't notice the scenery. All she could see was the sparkle in John's eyes and his lips turned up in a grin.

After a while he whispered, "Okay, you can look."

When she turned back, he took her hand in his and wrapped the plaited cord around her wrist. He tied the remaining ends into a bow and then turned the makeshift bracelet a bit so she could see that he had, somehow, woven a slot that held a penny. She lifted her wrist to study his handiwork closer.

"It's not a Lady Liberty penny," he said. "Just a plain old Lincoln Head. But it's my lucky penny. I've been carrying that in my pocket since my dad gave it to me when I was in second grade. Did you notice the date?"

Abby looked closer and saw that the penny had been minted the year John was born. How perfect, she thought. So adorable. So thoughtful. She smiled and reached up to kiss his cheek, but he pulled away before she could plant one there.

"I just realized this could be taken the wrong way," John said, his face gone serious.

Abby had thought he meant it like the promise rings some guys gave their girlfriends. She felt her heart drop. Maybe she had been reading him all wrong. Maybe he meant it like the friendship bracelets middle school girls gave each other.

"Uh…well." She found she couldn't think of a single thing to say that wouldn't come out sounding pathetic.

"I mean I'm not giving it to you the way John Granger did to Ned's mother."

"You're not?" Abby said, holding back a grin.

"I wouldn't want you to ever think that I thought of you as my chattel or anything."

Abby laughed in relief and reached again to kiss him on the cheek.

Not satisfied with that, he held her face to his and kissed her lips. Thoroughly. Expertly. Then pulling away, he looked into her eyes as if willing her to see into his heart. "I love you, Abby Thomas. And I'd like you to meet my parents. Will you let me take you to them tonight?"

She smiled and kissed him again. "I love you back, John Roberts, and I'd love to meet them." Still smiling, she settled her head into the perfect curve of his shoulder and let the motion of the moving train lull her to sleep.

The End

A Note from the Author

It was really painful to research for *Every Hill and Mountain*. I learned more about slavery in the free state of Illinois than I ever wanted to know. "Ned" is based on a real man, and Hickory Hill really exists. The stories told in Charlotte's attic are based on true slave accounts. These suffering people deserve to be heard. And we need to listen, no matter how painful, lest we forget what humankind is capable of.

I was born not far from the setting of ***Every Hill and Mountain*** but grew up "just down the road" from the setting of ***Time and Again*** and ***Unclaimed Legacy***. Today I live with my husband in Monroe County, Illinois, quite near the setting of ***Once Again***. I enjoy reading, gardening, and learning about regional history. I have three grown children, five grandchildren, and two canine buddies Digger and Scout, a.k.a. Dr. Bob in ***Unclaimed Legacy***.

Let's Keep in Touch

I'd love to hear what you think of ***Every Hill and Mountain***. If you enjoyed it, please write a review for it and post it wherever you can or as a comment on my website. (Authors need lots of reviews!)

And sign up to get V.I.P. Perks. You'll get updates on my latest books and insider information about contests, giveaways, and when my books are scheduled to be free or reduced. The sign up form is in the right sidebar of my website.

I'd really appreciate it if you'd "like," "follow," or otherwise connect with me. Thanks for supporting independent authors.

www.DeborahHeal.com

www.facebook.com/DeborahHeal

www.twitter.com/DeborahHeal

www.goodreads.com/deborahheal

The History Behind the Story

As always, I tried to weave as much real history into *Every Hill and Mountain* as I could. Can you separate the facts from the fiction? Take the **Every Hill and Mountain Quiz** to find out how good you are at unraveling the threads.

The Every Hill and Mountain Quiz

WARNING: Plot Spoilers! Don't take the quiz until after you finish reading *Every Hill and Mountain*.

Which of the following are true, false, or... maybe?

Mr. Granger, the owner of the Hickory Hill mansion, kept slaves on the third floor.
He used a man named Ned to breed more slaves.
A diary telling of events at Hickory Hill written by a daughter was discovered.
Descendants of the family scooped up the diary before its contents could be made public.
The owner of Hickory Hill kidnapped and sold free black families in a reverse Underground Railroad.
Slavery has always been illegal in Illinois.
Outright slavery was practiced in the free state of Illinois.
Actually, only indentured servants worked in the free state of Illinois.
The owner of the Half Moon salt mine secretly used slave labor to make salt.
Chains and a whipping post are still in place on the third floor of the Hickory Hill Mansion.
Liberty Baptist Church, Friends of Humanity was a real church in Equality.

Slaves from Hickory Hill were members of it.
Thomas Jefferson wanted to secure the rights to Half Moon Salt Mine at any cost.
Salt was the most important export from Illinois for many years.
Shawneetown bankers turned down representatives from the fledgling town of Chicago who came asking for a loan.
The original Red Onion was a disreputable speak-easy.
Coal companies actually do blow the tops off mountains as the worried man explained at his booth.
Rev. Dwight L. Moody helped runaway slaves in his Illinois Street Church.
The real Charlotte Miles harbored runaway slaves in the attic of her house.
"Ned" made it safely to Chicago.
Shawneetown has always been the seat for Gallatin County.
The area newspapers often ran ads offering rewards for the whereabouts of missing people and whole families.
Mr. Granger treated his personal slaves differently than he did the salt mine slaves.
Did Abraham Lincoln really stay at Hickory Hill?
The Old Slave House on Hickory Hill is a state historic site and open for tourists to see.

You can find the answers to these questions and other historical background by visiting my website.

www.deborahheal.com

For Further Study

Abolitionism and the Civil War in Southwestern Illinois. John J. Dunphy. 2011. ww.historypress.net

Black Like Me. John Howard Griffin. Signet: New York. 1962.

The Emancipation of Robert Sadler: The Powerful True Story of a Twentieth-Century Plantation Slave. Robert Sadler with Marie Chapian. Bethany House: Minneapolis. 1975.

Escape Betwixt Two Suns: A True Tale of the Underground Railroad in Illinois. Carol Pirtle. Southern Illinois University Press. Carbondale.

Growing Up Black. Jay David, ed. Avon Books: New York.1968.

Kingsblood Royal. Sinclair Lewis. The Modern Library: New York. 1947.

Nigger: An Autobiography. Dick Gregory with Robert Lipsyte. Pocket Books: New York. 1965.

Reckoning at Eagle Creek. Jeff Biggers. Nation Books: New York. 2010.

Slaves, Salt, Sex & Mr. Crenshaw. Jon Musgrave. Illinois History.com. Marion, IL. 2004.

Sundown Towns. James W. Loewen. The New Press: New York. 2005.

THE REWINDING TIME SERIES

ONCE AGAIN

an inspirational novel of history, mystery & romance

Book 1

From Professor Randall's Notebook...

Field Research Location:

Columbia and Waterloo, Monroe County, Illinois.

Goals:

Discover where Fort Piggot was located on the Kaskaskia Trail, while staying clear of attractive, single colleagues (ie. Brett!) so as not to commit career suicide, and keeping the "rewinding time" program secret, so Uncle Sam doesn't turn into Big Brother. Whew!

Merrideth Randall's day job is teaching history at McKendree College. But after hours she turns to her first love, historical research. And she has a tool other historians can only dream of—a computer program that rewinds time for a first-hand look at the past!

She uses it to find the location of Fort Piggot and other early settlements in the Illinois Country. Rewinding to the 1780s, she meets the courageous pioneers who withstood Indian attacks, hardship, and loneliness to farm the rich land. One settler even takes the Gospel to the very tribe that wreaked havoc on his family, but Merrideth can't decide whether he's a hero or a fool.

How can a person forgive a crime so huge?

Merrideth also meets James and Isabelle Garretson, ancestors of her handsome colleague Brett. He's a physics professor with rock-star status on campus, and amazingly enough, he seems to be pursuing her. But she has a firm policy against dating co-workers, even ones descended from heroic stock.

She'd love to tell him about her amazing program, but he's not so good at keeping secrets. It would never do to let the government get its hands on it, or privacy would be a thing of the past.

With her findings, Merrideth is able to help Brett with his family tree, but she can't tell him everything she learned—like that he inherited his black hair and green eyes from his ancestor James Garretson, or that his aunt's poetry is eerily similar to the verse Isabelle Garretson composed at her spinning wheel.

And Merrideth has secrets about herself that she'd just as soon Brett didn't find out either. Discretion is not his strong suit. But one virtue Brett does have in spades is patience, and he's quite willing to wait for Merrideth to figure things out.

An excerpt from

Once Again

Chapter 1

"We have to remember that in 1811, the Illinois Territory was the wild, wild West." Merrideth Randall realized she was leaning on her podium and straightened her spine. At five-foot-two it was difficult enough to look like a mature professional without slouching. At twenty-six, she was the youngest professor at McKendree College and only a few years older than her students, which was why she always dressed in suits and high heels. At times, she had a feeling it only made her look like a child playing dress-up.

She had started the day feeling confident in her new black gabardine suit. The label had bragged about the comfortableness of the three-season fabric. But even though it was a cool October afternoon, she was already sweating like a pig.

Furthermore, the fabric was a magnet for her blond hair. She picked two long strands from her sleeve and turned her eyes back to her students.

"And as amusing as it seems today, the governor's job description then included riding into battle, leading the soldiers at his command."

Apparently, they didn't find that historical tidbit as amusing as she did. The class continued to look apathetic. She mentally sighed. At least they were awake, to a degree. And most were even taking notes, in a desultory fashion. But the gleam of curiosity she had hoped to see in their eyes was absent. As usual.

McKendree College was small, the current enrollment only about 2,000. But it didn't aspire to be a large institution. Class sizes were intentionally kept small and intimate, and the professors and instructors were encouraged to get to know their students, to interact with them outside of class. All that had weighed heavily when Merrideth was deciding which of the three job offers she would accept. But sometimes she wondered if she should have chosen the large school in Chicago where she could remain anonymous and not be expected to remember the students' names, at which she was an epic failure. In the end she decided that a big school would be too intimidating. No, it was much better to be in a small pond where there was a better chance of becoming a big fish one day.

She had thought, naively it turned out, that after a couple of weeks at McKendree she would be nicely settled in, and her history classes would be well on the way to becoming campus favorites. Instead, after a nearly a month, her students remained aloof and only mildly interested in what she had to say. She found their nonverbal feedback incredibly dampening, to say the least. It was a vicious cycle, of course. The more she worried about being boring, the more difficult it became not to be.

Marla White, a seasoned pro from the French Department had advised her to act confident even if she didn't feel so. "And whatever you do, don't ever let 'em see you bleed, or they'll be on you like wolves."

But that was easier said than done, wasn't it? Taking a deep breath, she shuffled her notes and soldiered on.

"Tecumseh was off trying to organize a coordinated Indian resistance that November day in 1811. If he had been successful..."

A student in the third row—Allison? Alyssa?—raised her hand. She was a beautiful girl and always looked cool and collected, as if *she* weren't familiar with the human phenomenon of perspiration. And as far as Merrideth could tell *her* shades of blond had not come out of a bottle. She was one of the few students who ever asked a question or offered a comment. Unfortunately, they were usually so tinged with sarcasm that Merrideth had begun to dread what would come out of her mouth next. But now as always, hope rose that at last she was about to experience a lively interaction with her students.

Merrideth pointed to the raised hand. "Yes?"

"The proper term is *Native American*. Besides, they aren't really Indian anyway."

Merrideth was sure the smile she had drummed up looked fake, but it was the best she could do when her teaching competence was under direct attack. "I'm glad you brought that up. I recently learned that most Native Americans actually prefer to be called Indians."

The girl looked decidedly skeptical. "I was surprised myself." Merrideth glanced down and shuffled her notes again. "Anyway, if Tecumseh had been successful, who knows what the map of America would look like today? While he was gone, Harrison and a force of 1,000 soldiers defeated the Shawnee at Prophetstown.

"At the time it was considered a huge victory for Harrison. He picked up the nickname *Tippecanoe* from the river of that name near the battlefield. Twenty-nine years later in 1840, a Whig campaign song called *Tippecanoe and Tyler Too* helped Harrison win the presidency."

The girl raised her hand again. "Yes?" Merrideth said as pleasantly as she could.

"Will that be on the final exam? The nicknames and songs, things like that?"

"Maybe. Probably."

A disdainful expression flittered over the student's face, and then she lowered her eyes and resumed writing. Just as Merrideth looked back at her own notes, the girl muttered, "I registered for Illinois History, not Trivial Pursuit." It was said loudly enough that it was clearly intended for Merrideth to hear.

She stifled the urge to smack her. To reward herself for her restraint, she decided to wrap up class three minutes early. "But historians know," she said tersely, "that the victory at Prophetstown only ratcheted up the violence between the whites and Indians. Six months later when the War of 1812 began, the Indians naturally sided with the British. We'll talk more about that next time. Be sure to keep up with your readings."

The students began gathering their things with an eagerness that was a further insult to Merrideth's confidence. Then she remembered her announcement and called out, "Don't forget, if you want to be a volunteer at the Fort Piggot archaeological dig Saturday, there's still time, but you'll have to be a member of History Club. Just let me know if you need a sign-up form."

No one responded. No one even looked interested, much less stayed behind to get the details. She felt her face heating and turned away to gather her own things. Her embarrassment grew ten-fold when she realized Dr. Garrison was watching her from the door. With a mind of its own, her hand started to rise, intent on checking her hair. But she forced it back down to her side. She would not allow Brett Garrison to trigger any fluttery female instincts she might have.

The thought that the most popular professor on campus had witnessed her debacle just added icing to the cake. She had heard that gushing groupies congregated outside his classroom like he was Indiana Jones, and they were there to catch him before he cast off the trappings of academia and went off on an action-packed adventure.

But Brett dressed more stylishly than Indy had—never in tweed jackets with leather patches on the elbows, for sure. And he was much better looking than Harrison Ford. His black hair was thick, and his eyes were so green that Merrideth once asked Marla White if she thought he wore colored contacts. Marla had smiled knowingly and said, "No, ma'am! They're the real deal. It's the Irish in him."

The moment she was introduced to him at the faculty icebreaker at President Peterson's residence, he had set her nerves on edge. Sure, he was pretty to look at, but his vanity ruined it. Twice she had caught him admiring himself in Peterson's hall mirror. She had avoided him ever since.

But now she smiled and said, "Hi. Don't you math types do your thing in Voigt Hall?" It hadn't come out in the friendly manner she'd intended, and she mentally kicked herself for letting her rattled nerves show. He sure didn't need anything more to stoke his ego.

But he didn't seem to take offense, just grinned. It did not help her nerves one little bit.

"I was just taking a short cut to 1828."

"It was a very good year, from all I've heard."

The witticism was a mistake. He laughed, and her pulse skipped. It was confirmation that Brett Garrison was a man she should continue to steer clear of.

A therapist had once chided her for being a reverse snob when it came to good-looking men. She had reminded Merrideth that they couldn't help the way they looked any more than anyone else could. If she were here she'd tell her to give Brett Garrison a chance, for crying out loud.

"I meant the 1828 Cafe, not the year," he said. "I heard the last part of your lecture."

"Really?"

"It was very interesting."

"What?" she said.

"Your lecture on William Henry Harrison."

"Oh. Well, tell that to my students."

"They looked interested to me."

"Not Allison…Alyssa…what's-her-name."

"Ah, yes, Alyssa Holderman. I have her in Calculus. She has an attitude problem. You know Holderman Library is named for her great grandfather?"

"That explains a lot."

"Don't let her get to you. The other kids are cool."

"I'll try not to. Thanks."

"Would you like to join me at the cafe? The have good coffee."

The offer put her hackles up. "No thanks. I need to get home." She started down the hall, hoping to put distance between them, but he fell in beside her.

"So, Dr. Randall, what do you do when you're not lecturing about the past?"

"Prepare more lectures. It takes a while to get them polished into the scintillating gems that they are."

"Don't be hard on yourself. You'll hit your stride soon enough."

He held the door for her and she went out ahead of him

onto the quad. Brilliant orange maple leaves, carrying the scent of autumn, fluttered by against a deep blue sky. Nearby, Alyssa Holderman and four other girls, busily texting on their phones, paused and looked up with interest.

Brett doled out one of his smiles. “Hello, ladies. Nice day, isn’t it?”

The girls preened and twittered like pretty birds in designer jeans. “Yes, Dr. Garrison,” one said. “It sure is.”

The girls’ heads swiveled in unison as they watched their idol pass by. Merrideth was pretty sure she heard a sigh. Surprisingly, Brett Garrison didn’t seem to notice their worshipful adoration.

“So what about family?” he said.

“Oh, I’m all in favor of them,” Merrideth said. “How about you?”

He chuckled. “I’ll go first so you’ll know how to answer that question. I have a brother in Texas and a sister in North Carolina. My parents are deceased, but I do have an Aunt Nelda.”

She smiled. “You do not have an Aunt Nelda.”

“I do, in fact, have an Aunt Nelda. A very nice Aunt Nelda.”

“Oh, sorry. I didn’t mean to be rude.”

“And you being a history expert would like Aunt Nelda, for her old house if nothing else.”

“Really? How old?”

“Aunt Nelda or her house?”

“The house,” she said, smiling in spite of herself.

“I’m not sure of the exact date. The family has owned the property for generations.”

“I love old houses.”

“Then you should take the Haunted Lebanon tour in town. I know someone who could get you a ticket, if you’re interested.”

“No, I’m good. I did the Haunted Alton tour a couple of years ago, and once was quite enough for me. Life is scary enough as it is. Besides, I’m tied up with the dig.”

“See, you do other things besides preparing lectures. Where is it?”

“We’re looking for a fort that was once down in the

American Bottom."

He laughed uproariously. "I know I'm reverting to my junior high self, but a fort in the bottom? Really?"

Merrideth rolled her eyes. "The American Bottom is the southern Illinois floodplain of the Mississippi River. After the Revolutionary War it was the western frontier of the brand new United States, hence the name American. The French who had lived there for more than a century, migrated across the river to the French city of St. Louis, and the Americans began to arrive. The early settlers built several blockhouse forts there."

"And you think you know where one was."

"We hope so. Fort Piggot was the largest of them, but ironically, historians didn't even know of its existence until relatively recently when the so-called Piggot Papers were discovered. Just by coincidence, someone found them concealed inside a framed river pilot's license that had been hanging on a wall in the Green County Museum since forever. It's really fascinating and…I'm boring you to death. Sorry. I get carried away talking about this stuff."

"I'm not bored at all."

"Really?" And she realized that he wasn't. Either that, or he was a good actor.

"Sure. I don't even particularly enjoy history, but you've made me curious to know where this fort was."

"Near Columbia. About thirty minutes from here. James Piggot built it in—."

He laughed. "You're kidding, right?"

"I never kid about history."

"My Aunt Nelda's farm is not far from Columbia, above your famous American Bottom, well not yours, but you know what I mean. I had no idea historians had given the area such a charming name. Come have coffee and tell me more."

Inexplicably, Merrideth found herself standing at the sidewalk that led up to the 1828 Cafe. Somehow while she was yammering on about the fort, she had forgotten to make the turn that would take her to Hunter Street where her apartment was. Somehow, she had just followed where Brett Garrison led like a mindless twit. Worse, students were staring at them from the cafe's windows. Marla White had warned her that rumors spread faster than the speed of light in a small town, faster still in a small college. There was no way would she let false rumors about her and Brett Garrison prevent her from achieving her career goals.

"Sorry," she said. "I have to get home. Enjoy your coffee."

"Then I'll say goodbye. And, Merrideth? You should get *carried away* in your classroom like you did just now. Enthusiasm is contagious. Your students will sit up and take notice."

"Thanks for the advice. See you."

He made it sound so simple. As if being enthusiastic was all it took to be a successful instructor. It went counter to her own personality, and besides, her friend Abby, who was an excellent elementary teacher, had told her that the old "Don't Smile Until Christmas" guideline that worked for her fifth grade classes would work equally well for her college students, especially the freshmen. "If you're too friendly," she'd said, "they'll think you're soft and take advantage of you."

Maybe she'd ask some of the faculty friendlies, like Marla White and Jillian Bicklein, their opinion of the subject. But for now, her first line of defense was to be prepared with the best lecture in the world, tomorrow and every day thereafter. Sure, that didn't allow much time for a life, but what did that matter to an introvert anyway?

Today, as she did on most days, she had left her old Subaru parked behind her apartment and walked to work. The ghost of her obese pre-teen self still haunted her sometimes, even though mentally she recognized that she was now at a good weight for her height. But even if she didn't need the exercise, it was a glorious walk on a bright fall day.

It was ironic that she had ended up living in another small southern Illinois town, when for years she had longed to leave her mother's home in Miles Station and get back to Chicago where they had lived before her parents' divorce. But Merrideth had come to appreciate small towns.

And Lebanon was a pretty little town of just under 6,000 souls with quiet streets and beautiful old homes. Everyone at

McKendree had assured her it was virtually crime-free and safe enough for her to walk about alone. She had already explored quite a bit of the historic district.

Charles Dickens had put Lebanon on the map when he mentioned his stay at the Mermaid Inn in his 1842 travelogue *American Notes*. The inn still stood and was open to the public, although Merrideth had not yet taken the tour.

But McKendree College was Lebanon's greatest achievement. It was the oldest college in Illinois, established in 1828 by pioneer Methodists. It was rich in tradition and proud of its history. Several of the oldest buildings on campus were rumored to be haunted. There had been much talk of it as Halloween approached.

Her friends Abby and John, who loved old buildings as much as she did, had come one weekend to tour the school and town. Abby had gone a little nuts shopping in the antique stores on St. Louis Street. Their Victorian home was filled to the brim with beautiful old things, so Abby had turned her attention to getting antiques to dress up Merrideth's apartment.

Hunter Street was quiet and lined with mature trees that were slowly releasing their leaves onto the sidewalk. She lived on the second floor of a huge old house that had been subdivided into four apartments. Her landlord Mr. O'Conner looked as old as the house and wasn't able to keep up with repairs as well as she might like. But Merrideth didn't mind. The house had character, the rent was cheap, and the other tenants were quiet. It would do until she had the money for a down payment on a house of her own.

She trotted up onto the porch and checked her mailbox. There wasn't anything in it, nor had she expected there to be. The utilities weren't due yet, and the credit card company hadn't got her change of address yet. Her mother had never been a letter writer even back in the day when most people were. But when November rolled around she'd have at least one letter in her mailbox. The return address would read, Bradley Randall, #1254387, Route 53 Joliet, IL 60403. She wasn't certain he'd ever be "rehabilitated," but fifteen years of the state's hospitality had turned her father into a faithful letter writer. She'd give him that much.

She reminded herself to tread quietly on the stairs. Mr. Haskell worked nights and slept during the day. That's all she'd been able to discover about him since she'd been living above his apartment. He gave her suspicious looks whenever they met. She still hadn't decided whether it was his natural temperament or because he was sleep-deprived. In any case, the poor man had even less of a life outside work than she did.

Once inside, she laid her keys on the mantel. The fireplace was no longer operational, and the mantel was only faux marble, but she displayed some of her most valued possessions there. In the center was a framed family photo, taken during a brief moment of calm before her parents split. It was a terribly unflattering picture for all three of them, especially her. She was overweight and under-groomed, her dishwater blond hair hanging in her eyes. But everyone was smiling in the photo, so she kept it on display because it gave the appearance of a happy family.

To each side of the photo were the silver candlesticks she'd bought for herself to celebrate finishing her doctoral thesis. And then there were the treasures from Abby and John's girls Lauren and Natalie for whom she was an honorary aunt: a homemade birthday card, a "fairy house" made from a tissue box, and a garland of construction paper fall leaves. All were heavily glittered, as were nearly all the crafts she and the girls made together whenever she babysat them.

Merrideth smiled and then went to see what was in the fridge for dinner.